GHAZGHKULL
THRAKA
PROPHET OF THE WAAAGH!

GHAZGHKULL THRAKA
PROPHET OF THE WAAAGH!

NATE CROWLEY

BLACK LIBRARY

A BLACK LIBRARY PUBLICATION

First published in 2021.
This edition published in Great Britain in 2023 by
Black Library, Games Workshop Ltd., Willow Road,
Nottingham, NG7 2WS, UK.

Represented by: Games Workshop Limited – Irish branch,
Unit 3, Lower Liffey Street, Dublin 1,
D01 K199, Ireland.

10 9 8 7 6 5 4 3 2

Produced by Games Workshop in Nottingham.
Cover illustration by Alexander Mokhov.

This is a work of fiction. All the characters and events portrayed
in this book are fictional, and any resemblance to real people or
incidents is purely coincidental.

See Black Library on the internet at

blacklibrary.com

Find out more about Games Workshop
and the world of Warhammer 40,000 at

games-workshop.com

Printed and bound by CPI Group (UK) Ltd, Croydon, CR0 4YY

---

*This book is dedicated to my dad, who, despite being generally baffled by
Warhammer 40K, totally got the concept of orks. I reckon he would have
loved this story.*

For more than a hundred centuries the Emperor
has sat immobile on the Golden Throne of Earth.
He is the Master of Mankind. By the might of His
inexhaustible armies a million worlds stand
against the dark.

Yet, He is a rotting carcass, the Carrion Lord of the
Imperium held in life by marvels from the Dark
Age of Technology and the thousand souls sacrificed
each day so that His may continue to burn.

To be a man in such times is to be one amongst
untold billions. It is to live in the cruellest and
most bloody regime imaginable. It is to suffer an
eternity of carnage and slaughter. It is to have cries
of anguish and sorrow drowned by the thirsting
laughter of dark gods.

This is a dark and terrible era where you will find
little comfort or hope. Forget the power of technology
and science. Forget the promise of progress and
advancement. Forget any notion of common
humanity or compassion.

There is no peace amongst the stars, for in the grim
darkness of the far future, there is only war.

-- message-burst/Xenos-designate-433/
unknown vessel/begin --

Oi, Flax.

-- enact-protocol/link-denied//TNFalx/
Xenos-designate-433/refused --

Oi.

-- enact-protocol/link-denied//TNFalx/
Xenos-designate-433/refused --

Oi. Flax.

-- message-burst/TNFalx/Prvt-Frgt-Severissimus-Exactor/
respond --

My name is Tytonida Nebaszinar *Falx*, and I am a lord inquisitor of the Ordo Xenos. As you well know. This conversation
will not proceed until you address me appropriately.

A *lord* inquisitor now, is it? Only a *lord*, we reckon, if there's no one stronger'n you to say you ain't a lord, Flax. And we don't reckon that's the way things are. Reckon you're in the drops with your bosses, for contorting with the likes of us.

The word is 'consorting'. And yes, it would not... aid my position with the ordo if these messages were intercepted.

That's right. You told us not to call you outside... what was it again, *Lord* Flax?

'The most dire and pressing strategic necessity' was my phrasing, ork. And yet I note this link has been used twice in the last solar rotation, just to send me crude insults. This had better not be a third.

Yeah, we were gonna do just that. Suppose there was the thing about Ghazghkull too, but that don't matter really does it? Shouldn't've called. Going now.

-- message-burst/Xenos-designate-433/unknown vessel/end --

*-- enact-protocol/Immediate-reconnection//TNFalx/
Xenos-designate-433/refused --*

*-- enact-protocol/Immediate-reconnection//TNFalx/
Xenos-designate-433/refused*

*-- enact-protocol/Immediate-reconnection//TNFalx/
Xenos-designate-433/refused --*

-- enact-protocol/Immediate-reconnection//TNFalx/
Xenos-designate-433/accepted (disdain) --

Tell me. I'll pay, just tell me what you know.

He ain't dead. Chopping off his head didn't work.

This is known.

But when you dropped the big space station on him? Didn't work neither. The boss ain't even hurt. He's... stronger.

-- message-burst/Brth-Hendriksen[?]/
Prvt-Frgt-Severissimus-Exactor/INTERJECT --

Stronger? Explain yourself, xenos.

-- message-burst/Xenos-designate-433/
unknown vessel/resume --

You're rude, ain't you, bursting in like that? Bad diplomersea. Anyway, we dunno. We got out of Krongar sharpish. But on the way out, we snatched someone who *does* know what you wanna know. Someone... what's the word... *significated*. They know the big boss. Plans... weaknesses... everything. Thought you might be interested.

Who is this captive?

Ten-ten-ten-ten-ten guns and *Ten-ten-ten-ten-ten-ten-ten* bullets. *Ten-ten-ten big* guns, and big bullets to go with 'em. A map, with ten planets who ain't expecting to be raided. That's the price.

Who?

Ten-an'-*five* planets we can raid, then, if you want to know the name and all. And another *ten-ten-ten-ten* guns.

This filth wastes our time with jests. And besides, such a price is unthinkable. Even for you, inquisitor.

He's rude to you and all, ain't he? Thought you was a lord? If you are, the decision's yours, ain't it. What's it to be, Flax?

Brother Hendriksen is correct, mercenary. It is out of the question. I don't care how big a warboss you've kidnapped: their ranting is not worth Imperial lives.

We never said they was big. Nor a warboss. We said they was *significated*. Ever heard of Makari?

Surely they take us for fools, Lord Falx. Terminate the conn–

-- message-burst/TNFalx/Prvt-Frgt-Severissimus-Exactor
/INTERJECT/ --

----> append/data-trove-attach/
type:coordinates(spatial;simplified)

Deal. Rendezvous with us in the shadow of pulsar Acherontia-XII, at the location specified in the Hammerhead Deeps, with your engines silenced. I will meet your price. Just remember what you lost, last time that you tried to cheat me.

Didn't lose much. And I like my new heart better anyway. But don't worry. We won't do nothing funny.

Your double negative does not reassure me.

Alright then. We won't trick you. Deal's proper. Blood Axe promise.

'Blood Axe promise'? This is madness, inquisitor. This 'Makari' is not even real. He is a xenos myth, a butt for their crude jokes.

Makari's real enough, Greywords. And there ain't nobody knows the big boss better. Little git's seen everything, over the years.

We would see the warlord dead, alien, not learn his life story.

What's it you lot say about knowledge and power? You reckon you know Thraka, 'cos of Armygeddon? Not likely. You don't know the half of what's coming.

I know enough that–

Enough, both of you – I have agreed to the bargain. We will meet at Acherontia, where I will receive the captive. Pray to your strange gods, ork, that it proves worth the cost.

-- message-burst/TNFalx/Prvt-Frgt-Severissimus-Exactor/end --

ACT ONE

ACT ONE

INTERROGATION I

Falx could hear it breathing in the dark. Short, hissing breaths, like the exhalations of forge-bellows. Quiet, but crouched forever on the brink of a snarl. Hot, damp, and tinged with the stink of an impossible metabolism. The breath of a monster.

The Imperial Truth told her she had nothing to fear. That this monster was weak and scrawny, barely larger or more dangerous than a malnourished human child. And having immersed herself in the ever-shrinking comfort of the *Pax Imperialis* for too long, Falx could almost believe it might be so. She *wanted* to believe. But humanity could not simply wish its enemies into inferiority, any more than a shepherd could wish away the gleam of predatory eyes at the edge of a campfire's light. And as Falx saw it, the Imperium's fire had long burned down to embers. The hungry dark was closing in, and realities had to be confronted.

Most in her order sought solace in zeal, huddling ever closer to the dying flames of faith as if they might offer protection, rather than blinding them to the glint of onrushing teeth. Falx had chosen, long ago, to turn and face the dark instead. It had cost her most of whatever hope her youth had accrued. But somehow, after one hundred and thirty years keeping the night at bay, the dregs of that hope remained. Steadying herself as she had done a thousand times before, she forced her hand to the switch that would reveal her foe, and prepared to lose a little more.

The cell's overhead lamp flickered into life, casting a cold circle on steel, and all the way down the length of the brig, things stirred in a jungle of rivets, shutters and bars. As a frigate of the Ordo Xenos, the shipwrights had built the *Severissimus Exactor* with a containment deck fit to hold the menagerie of a planetary governor, and Falx had filled it with horrors. There were entities down here that had not walked free in decades: beasts without names, and nightmares that wore the skins of men. They rustled as they scurried from the sudden light, before falling into sullen silence once more. But the object of her attention did not even stir in its chains. It just stared at her, with a steady focus that suggested it had been watching her just as keenly in the dark.

It was a gretchin, as promised. An ork slave-beast, sharing the fundamentals of their biology, but without such... exuberance of form. Still, as ever with its kind, it was larger than Falx had expected it to be. It would have stood to her chin if it was upright, and there was certainly nothing childlike about it. It was thin-limbed and slender, but its hands spanned twice the width of a human's, while the long bones of its limbs were wrapped in muscle as dense and knotted as Catachan stranglevine.

Falx knew to be wary, even though the creature was restrained.

Life had taken her far away from bar fights, but she remembered her drinking days well enough to know it wasn't the big, belligerent fighters you watched out for: it was the bastards built like this. The ones who'd disappear as soon as a glass was thrown, then make themselves known later via a forearm around the throat, and the sudden collapse of a lung on a knife-tip.

And even in the frigid cell, soaked with chill from the void beyond the hull, it glowed with life. Wisps of steam rose from its shoulders, venting the waste heat from its metabolic furnace, and she swore that in the silence of the brig, she could hear the rush of blood through its gnarled veins. Falx's lip curled as she looked over its snaggled teeth, its gristly proboscis of a nose, its ragged bat-wing ears. While its face was laid out in the manner of a human's, topology was all it shared in common. Beneath that rubbery green skin, the architecture of its skull was thoroughly, repulsively alien.

As Falx examined her captive, its lips drew back into a thin, vicious smile, and its head tilted slowly to one side. It was evaluating her in turn. She wondered, what did it see? An old woman, if the distinction meant anything to the sexless creature, with a shock of brittle hair she had once dyed white, but which had saved her the effort ever since she had spent a week in hiding beneath the hrud nest on Kalimant. A face she had often heard euphemised as *striking*, built around a jaw like a cruiser's prow, and with little flesh to spare around its edges. Hatched with scars, bronzed by the glare of strange suns, and held so often in a cast of defiant scorn that it had been etched in permanence, Falx thought of it as a hard face.

But as those murky, pupilless red eyes probed her, looking for places to throttle and gouge and gnaw, it felt like scant armour. Her scalp began to prickle where it met the ceramite of her skullplate at the nape of her neck, and the spell was only broken by the thud of heavy boot steps approaching the cell door.

'It stinks,' sneered Brother Hendriksen as he ducked under the lintel, and threw his ship-coat to the floor with the mundane disgust of a man setting to the unblocking of a recalcitrant sewage duct. The old Rune Priest was not reserved in displaying his emotions. Eyebrows like the pelts of moderately sized ship rats furrowed down over his bright green eyes, while russet moustaches braided like bell ropes shifted as his nose wrinkled, exposing a grimace the width of a baseline human's hand.

'Could you not have hosed it down before we started?' Hendriksen grumbled, rolling up the sleeves of his fatigues to reveal forearms like grox shins, tattooed with spirals of indigo runes. 'This morning's meat was good enough, as ship rations go, but I've no wish to taste it again.'

Despite his griping, Hendriksen could not have been less disconcerted by the whole business. It was as if he saw their prisoner as a task, rather than a creature, and his workmanlike disdain chased away the eerie, choking unease that had filled the room before his arrival. Indeed, Falx had always found the darkness much easier to face with a quarter-ton of Adeptus Astartes psyker beside her, no matter how much the man complained. *They shall no know fear, indeed,* she thought to herself, letting the edge of a smile push at the callus of some forgotten wound.

'I'm not sure a smell like that can be washed away, Orm,' Falx answered, as she considered the evidence of her nose for the first time. Hendriksen was right. The gretchin stank. Its tattered jerkin reeked of badly cured leather, and besides the strange necklace that hung over it – a length of dried tendon threaded with rounded, irregular lumps of metal that stretched the definition of the word 'jewellery' – it wore nothing else. Every fold of its skin was caked in grease and grime, and hummed with the odour of stale, alien sweat. It was the smell of a species to whom hygiene was an unknown concept. But beneath it, somehow more overpowering despite its subtlety, was a deeper tang. Algal, like a stagnant pond, or a hive world food factory with poor ventilation, and underlaid with complex, volatile scents that brought to mind spilled promethium.

'I suppose it shall be worse when we open it up,' said Hendriksen, briefly eclipsing the cell's lamp as he stalked over to inspect the gretchin more closely. Even in his shipboard fatigues, with only the sigil of his old Chapter donned by way of armour, Hendriksen outmassed the prisoner several times over, but it seemed unbothered as his rune-inked cliff of a face loomed down to stare it out. Falx almost warned him not to get too close, but stopped her tongue. Hendriksen was Deathwatch after all, even if his current standing with the Chamber Militant was as murky as her own with the ordo. He knew the nature of the beast just as well as she did. He might not have shared her caution, but then he did not share her humanity, either.

As if to punctuate the point, the prisoner lunged forwards in its shackles, jaws splayed hideously. But before Falx had even registered the motion, Hendriksen's arm had swung out in a backhand blow that snapped the thing's nose with a pop of gristle, and sent it crashing to the floor along with the chair it was secured to. The sons of Fenris knew nothing of bar fights, Falx remembered, because any bar fight dire enough to draw in one of their number was swiftly reclassified as a massacre. She had learned this on the occasion she had first met Orm Hendriksen, ninety-six years prior, and the last day she had ever taken a drink.

'It's no coward, at least,' Hendriksen grunted, wiping mucus from his fist with a rag, and Falx nodded grimly. The prisoner was unusual, in that regard. For all their wiry strength, she had never encountered one of the subservient orkoids with anything less than a complete aversion to a straight fight, let alone the appetite to challenge an opponent five times its size while restrained in irons.

'Indeed,' she said. 'But then, if those pirates were telling the truth, I dare say this beast has seen far worse brutes than you in its time. I hear orks grow quite large, you know.'

'No matter,' replied Hendriksen, hauling the toppled chair upright again with one hand. 'I'll still find its limits soon enough, as sure as cold finds the holes in an old fur.' As the captive glowered at him past its collapsed nose, he took a step back to regard it, then crouched down to its eye level and pulled a slim knife from his belt.

'Why the rush, Orm?' came a new voice, thick and warm as engine oil, as the third member of the interrogation detail entered the chamber. 'We're at least three days out from the Mulciber yards, even if the warp's kind to us. That's time at least to *try* talking, before the knives come out.'

Hendriksen glanced round irritably, then rose to his full height again as Cassia appeared at the cell's entrance. He still had to look up, though. As Falx was a foot taller than the gretchin, and Hendriksen a foot taller than her, Cassia was taller still, her great ochre boulder of a head stooping as she squeezed her shoulders through the door. Cassia, after all, was an ogryn.

The battered canvas of her ship-coat creaked as she stood upright again, and as she moved towards the prisoner, it was like watching a storm system drifting in.

'Budge, shaman,' she rumbled, prompting a hiss of exasperation from Hendriksen, but still the Rune Priest stepped out of the way. The pair's constant antagonism had underscored countless shifts on the *Exactor*'s bridge, but any real enmity had long been buried under mutual respect, and they seemed to snipe at each other out of habit now, more than anything else.

With the calm attention of a technician, the giant sank to one knee in front of the prisoner, and moved a hand as wide as a landmine through the air before its face. The captive did not stir, this time. Either its aggression had been cowed, or it realised it might as well have been faced with the prospect of biting a rock.

'Let's have a sniff, then,' murmured Cassia, furrowing her slab of a brow. Her eyes narrowed in concentration, and as her jaw shifted with a slow ripple of muscle and fat, the air between her hand and the prisoner shimmered. Then, something *snapped*.

It was a sensation that Falx had never quite got used to: a slow build-up of tension that you wouldn't be aware of at all, until some ephemeral dam broke and it all rushed *somewhere else*, sleeting through you with a feeling like a week-long migraine condensed into a heartbeat. Then it would be gone, leaving only the faintest smell of ozone, and you wouldn't be able to remember what it had felt like at all.

Falx didn't like it. It had been an ordeal enough, over the years, to cope with Hendriksen's exercise of the art. And he, at least, had refined his methods through centuries of training. Now, with Cassia, she had *two* psykers in her retinue.

An ogryn psyker, thought Falx, and shook her head in wonder. Naturally, the Imperial Truth held that ogryns were stupid, just like it said that gretchin were weak. They were gigantic, hardy abhumans, whose bodies had grown into fortresses against the harsh worlds their ancestors had marooned them on. And as common wisdom had it, this fortitude had come at the expense of their wits. Most thought them incapable of three-syllable words, or even counting beyond their supply of bolt-shell-thick digits. And without a doubt, the Truth insisted that ogryns could never, ever muster the cerebral sophistication to manifest psychic talent. Falx was willing to concede that this last insistence at least might have been the case, until recently. But these were strange days. And while the guardians of the Imperial dogma might not have been willing to change their minds on such matters, there was no doubt that, across the countless worlds in their sway, *minds were changing nonetheless*. And thus, Cassia.

She had lived an ogryn's life. Born in a work camp, drafted to a penal regiment, and sent to the nearest front, in the hope that the spending of her life might keep the front from collapsing for a fraction of a second longer. That would have been the sum of Indentured Conscript C455-I's life, were it not for the moment where, during the fighting retreat from the Delq on Karkhemish Secundus, she had moved the burning hulk of a downed bomber to shield her unit's commissar from mortar fire, using nothing but her mind. In that moment, she had also moved herself far outside the Imperial Truth.

Her commissar's duty had been clear: to align reality with the Truth immediately. And indeed, somewhere in the mountainous strata of the Departmento Munitorum's records, a single line in a report attested to C455-I's execution on the spot for 'cowardice'. But that commissar had owed Falx a favour. And so the *Severissimus Exactor* had flown to Karkhemish, and left with an undocumented ogryn aboard.

Cassia, as she had named herself, had a lot to learn about her new capabilities. Her potential, it seemed, was immense. But that would only make it harder for her to grow into it. Ahead of her was a life spent walking an ever-narrowing path above an abyss of madness. But it would at least be a life. And she knew that for all his outward hostility to her, Hendriksen was quietly dedicated to ensuring she made the best of herself.

'It's got secrets, this one,' said Cassia, after digesting whatever she had gleaned from the grot's mind.

'I should hope it has secrets,' growled the old wolf, 'given what the inquisitor paid for it. And I was about to start extracting them, until you blundered in like a mastodon missing two legs.'

It was then, to the surprise of everyone in the cell, that the *second* xenos in the room spoke up.

'Perhaps,' it offered, raising a talon-tipped finger in a disconcertingly accurate mimicry of the human gesture, 'you might start… by asking a question?'

Every face in the room turned to regard the green figure lurking against a bulkhead, outside the circle of light cast by the cell's lamp, and Falx felt herself stiffen at the sound of its voice. It was quiet and snuffling, every word strung together from grunts like those of a beast at a trough. But despite coming from a larynx built expressly for the delivery of threats and commands, it was *polite*. That was unsettling enough. But worse yet was the fact that, despite having been in the cell the whole time – despite Falx having posted it there herself, just before she came down – she had entirely forgotten the beast's presence.

Orks were not stealthy. Not by anyone's measure of the truth, least of all their own. But then Biter – or *Bites-Face-Of-The-Face-Biter-Before-It-Can-Bite*, in its own unwieldy speech – was far from a typical ork. They were an interpreter, a so-called 'intelligents officer' for the pirate warband which had abducted the asset, and their services had been loaned to Falx for a further, extortionate sum, when it had transpired that said asset didn't understand a word of High or Low Gothic.

The warband did not call themselves a warband, of course. They called themselves a 'kompany'. For they were Blood Axes, and shared their wider clan's fascination with human military culture. Embarrassingly, then, Biter had come aboard draped in a poorly tailored facsimile of a Militarum officer's greatcoat, stitched from patchily tanned squig leather, and adorned with a sagging peaked cap. They had even awarded themself a row of 'medals' fashioned from hammered-flat scrap metal.

And yet, for all that their appearance was ridiculous, the ork had been compliant, and for lack of a better word, professional, since coming aboard. Enough so that Falx had made the mistake of ceasing to perceive them as a constant threat. But in her long and secret dealings with the Blood Axe clan, she had learned that ork allies were just enemies who hadn't seen an opportunity for betrayal yet. She would have to keep a closer eye on Biter.

'You're being paid for translation, not advice,' Falx said, eyes moving from her captive to the ork like the flicker of a sniper's targeting dot. 'But as it happens, I concur. Blade away, please, Brother Hendriksen.'

'As the greenskin wishes,' scoffed the Space Wolf, sheathing the knife with an expression of distaste. 'I'm sure this "Makari" will be more than amenable to a robust exchange of views, after all. So please, be my guest.' Hendriksen swept his arm towards the interrogation chair as if inviting Falx to her seat at a feast. She stepped forward again to stand in front of the captive, and tried to ignore the carnivorous smile sliding back across its face.

'I want to know Ghazghkull Mag Uruk Thraka,' said Falx, staring into the darkness of the prisoner's eyes, as her words were relayed through Biter in a string of grunts and soft, glottal barks. 'I want to know all you know of Thraka, from the first moment to the last, and nothing less.' Biter's translation of her words tailed off, but the prisoner just sat in silence, unblinking, with that smirk still fixed on her. She was on the brink of calling for Hendriksen's knife after all, when at last it spoke.

In contrast to the ork, its voice was wet and scratchy, squeezed out like the last words of a strangled man, and dripping with malevolence.

'Makari says... they will tell you everything,' said Biter, with an air of faint discomfort. 'But they say there is something you must understand first. Makari says that to know Ghazghkull... you must first know Makari. And to know Makari, you must know what it is to be *grot*.'

Hendriksen inhaled, ready to protest the prisoner's time-wasting, but Falx stilled him with a hand, while keeping her eyes on the prisoner.

'Tell me, then,' she said, 'what that is.'

The captive spoke for a good while, and Biter picked absently at their tusks while nodding along, before addressing Falx.

'Whatever the gods gave the orks,' the interpreter began, 'whatever battle-bliss kicks all the fear and worry out of their lives... they didn't give us. We live in their world, but we weren't built for enjoying it. We live to serve, and we suffer through every bit of it, except them moments when something weaker'n us is suffering.'

'It said all that?' asked Cassia, raising a doubting eyebrow.

'There were more... *perfanities*,' admitted Biter, showing an inch of yellowed fangs as their mouth contorted horribly. 'And I corrected some... syn-tacks. But yes, Makari said all that.' Biter's eloquence had taken Falx entirely by surprise, and she realised now the expression on the ork's face was their attempt at a smug grin.

'You must hate the orks,' Falx said to the gretchin, probing at what she hoped might be the edge of common ground, and the prisoner's eyes flickered in recognition of the words 'hate' and 'orks'.

'Gitsss,' it hissed, glaring straight at Biter, and the ork shrugged their slab shoulders – there was no need to translate that. But then the grot looked back at Falx, and spoke further.

'There's… more to it, though,' said Biter slyly, as the prisoner ranted. 'They hate us, surely. This is… no surprise to you, hmm? But it is… ahhh.' The Blood Axe paused for a moment. 'You might call it… *faith*, perhaps?'

'Give me the prisoner's words, ork, not your own,' demanded Falx, struggling with the idea.

'Orks hurt grots, grots hate orks, Makari says. It is the… axework of the gods.'

'Axework?' interjected Hendriksen, frowning in concentration, as if he half-grasped the idea.

'*Hit-things-til-the-shape-is-good*, literally. Design, might be the other way to say it,' pondered Biter, causing Hendriksen to tilt his head and lift his eyebrows in grudging acceptance.

'Øksarrbedin, we said on Fenris. It is much the same.'

'I will remember that,' said Biter, with studied neutrality, before resuming the translation.

'Ork cruelty to grots, and their loathing in return… it's good. It's the way of the Great Green. The way things were in the *eaten-now*, and the way they'll be in the *now-forever*. The Great Green is… it's like a fungus with many roots. Many parts. Orks, grots and all the rest. Orks are best, but they're all vital. Without us to serve 'em, the orks would falter. And sometimes, just sometimes, it's down to us grots to remind 'em of their own part in the whole. Yeah, we hate the orks. But still we serve 'em. 'Cos that's how the gods want it. And for all the pleasures the gods didn't let us have, they did give us…'

Biter halted, gnawing on a leathery green lip while rummaging for the word. 'An *eckstassy* for seeing their will done good.'

The cell fell into silence then, as the interrogators grappled with this revelation of gretchin ontology. Hendriksen, ever the least patient of them when it came to xenos philosophy, abandoned the effort in seconds.

'A saenyeti's two-day-old turds would speak more sense,' he snarled, as the knife returned to his hand yet again. 'Enough of these attempts to confound us with your xenos *gátur*-riddles. Lord Falx asked about Ghazghkull. So this "Makari" will tell us of Ghazghkull. *Ghazghkull!*' repeated Hendriksen directly to Makari, with slow contempt, as he waved the knife in the air.

'*Ghaz'ghk'ull,*' parroted the gretchin, emphasising the weird, gulping native pronunciation as if to correct him, then repeating it three times more, in an increasingly sly tone. '*Ghaz'ghk'ull, Ghaz'ghk'ull, Ghaz'ghk'ull…*' It tilted its head from side to side, as if trying to see the underneath of an idea, and then rattled off a decisive string of hisses and barks to Biter.

'So be it,' said the interpreter, with an open-palmed gesture. 'You want the story of Ghazghkull Mag Uruk Thraka – you shall have it, humans. It may not be the story you expect, though. It may not be a story you like, either. But I shall tell it all the same. It is a story that ends in green. But it begins… in white.'

CHAPTER ONE

THE BIRTH OF GHAZGHKULL MAG URUK THRAKA

Snow, as far as you could see. And you couldn't see far, 'cos of the blizzard. But there was miles and miles of it. And then, there was green. Just a speck of green, mind: a hand. Still soft, steaming from the sac, and torn where it had clawed its way up from its grow-hole. That hand was struggling. It groped around for something to pull the rest of itself up by, but the storm had been long and bitter, and the ground could've been iron.

The hand was in luck, though. A tundra squig, half-starved, saw it in a gap between flurries, and lumbered over to snap it up. Big mistake. 'Cos before it could even chew through the wrist, that hand wrapped round the root of its tongue, yanked back like it was starting a chain-choppa, and pulled the squig's guts right out of its gob.

Now squig guts, you see, are nice and hot. Full of juice. They softened the ground where the hand had come up, just enough to loosen it a tiny bit more, and with a grunt and a heave, an ork was born, in blood and bile and fungus.

It weren't Ghazghkull. Not yet. Weren't anybody. But it was a scrap of green that might become somebody – might become anybody – if it could make it through the next few hours. Lots don't make it through those hours, but this one did. Made it through days, in fact, even though the storm never let up. Made it many-many tusklengths through the snow, wrapped in the squig's shaggy hide and made strong with its meat, 'til it showed up at the gates of Gogduf and banged to be let in.

Gogduf was a Goff fort. Not much of a place, really – just a row of barrack-sheds, a squig pen, a brew-hut and a mekshop with a busted generator, packed inside a rusty wall. It wasn't somewhere you'd just walk up to without a good reason, 'cos Goffs don't much take to visitors. But the newcomer did just walk right up to it, for no reason other'n that they wanted to, stepping over drifts of bullet-smashed bones 'til they got to the gates.

Gogduf's chief was in the gatehouse tower that day, giving the guards a beasting over something or other, so they was the first to see the newcomer. They clearly had some nerve, the chief reckoned, and the pelt on their back was a big 'un, so they had some fight to them, too. In fact, it was the pelt that saved the newcomer. When one of the guards jumped on the tower's shoota to gun 'em down, hoping to get out of the drops with the chief, they only earned themselves another slap. 'Cos the chief coveted that fine black squigskin, see, and didn't fancy it full of holes. So they went down to the gate to get it in person.

And as soon as the gate opened, the newcomer walked up and they headbutted the chief. Of course, the chief just laughed at that, and beat the stripling to a pulp, before taking the pelt and heading back into the fort. But as the gate began to close, they came over all soft, and shouted for Gogduf's doc to have the unconscious newcomer dragged in and fed. Who knows why. Maybe the headbutt had reminded them of their own youth, and made 'em wistful. Goffs can be sentimental like that. Or maybe it was the gods speaking. Maybe the headbutt *was* the gods speaking.

The newcomer healed up quick, and made 'emself useful enough around the barracks to be taken on as a trooper. All that meant was a tin helmet, a rusty choppa, and their own head's weight in meat each day. But it was enough. They joined one of Gogduf's mobs for raid after raid on other clans' forts, and they got strong. While fighting a bunch of Bad Moons over the wreck of an old stompa, they even got themself a shoota off a dead enemy, and they learned to use that too.

And though there weren't much knowledge to be found in a place like Gogduf, the newcomer learned. They learned what it meant to be an ork, and they learned about the gods. In the fight shed, they met Gork. And at the brew-hut's dice table, over rounds and rounds of clattering snotling-knuckles, they met Mork.

The newcomer's education weren't entirely religious, though. They also learned about something called the *galaxy*, where there were millions and millions of other worlds to fight on, and that this planet – Urk, the troopers called it – was just one of 'em.

Most orks would've been satisfied at that. But the newcomer kept asking the chief about Urk and the galaxy and stuff. Usually they got a smack in return, for being weird. But one night, as all the mobs packed the brew-hut to guzzle grog stolen from an Evil Sunz convoy, the old Goff – they must've been in a good mood – decided they'd answer the newcomer.

Urk, the Goff said, was a pile of grot's turds. Baked to cinders round its middle, and frozen hard everywhere else, with barely anything to fight over, besides the scrap from fights that'd happened before. But it was *their* pile of grot's turds, and so it was a good place.

There were other people in the galaxy, the chief explained, who sometimes tried to own places that rightfully belonged to orks (which was to say all of 'em), and Urk had been trespassed on plenty over the years. Once, long ago, by skinny, weak things with pointy ears and stupid hats, and then later on by some massive lizards made out of crystal or something, and so on.

The chief had got properly into the story now, and half the brew-hut had stopped wrestling and knife-fighting to listen. All those empires had been and gone, the chief said to the newcomer, driven away by the orks. Not always on the first try, mind. But every time they got killed off, the chief explained, plucking a tuft of fungus from behind their ear for emphasis, the orks came back. They grew out of holes in the ground, just like the newcomer had done, until there were enough of 'em to get the job done proper. And once a set of interlopers had been driven off, they never came back.

Apart from the humans, that was. Because of all the creatures that had ever offended Gork and Mork with their presence in the galaxy, the humans were the thickest. They thought that if they believed something it must be true, just like orks did. Only it didn't actually *work* for humans. So even though they'd been kicked off Urk by the orks twice now, they still held on to the mad idea that the planet belonged to them.

The chief went quiet then, gazing out the window of the brew-hut towards the mountains. The newcomer followed their eyes, and saw a cluster of tiny, cold lights, like rubbish stars, on the tallest crag in the range.

'That's a human fort,' the chief said, draining their brewpot grimly and slamming it to the table, before kicking a grot for another. '*Beakies*. Big armoured gits, packed in cans. They left it here to spy on us, right under our noses, and somehow we ain't burned it down yet. What do you reckon, stripling? Have I gone soft or something?'

The newcomer thought about their options. They were keen to insult the chief, as it'd mean a good fight. But they looked at those lights, and realised they might mean *the best fight of all*. It was a weird idea, but something about it made their head tingle. So they went with Mork, and only insulted the chief a little bit.

'Nah,' they said. 'Not soft. Old, though. Had a lot of good fights, taken a lot of knocks to the head. You forget things. S'alright though. Why don't we smash it up when the sun rises?'

The chief's face folded up in confusion as they tried to work out how angry they were. But then the idea hit them, properly, and their frown fell off into roaring, spit-spraying laughter.

'Listen up,' they bellowed to the crowded hut, lurching up so fast they nearly banged their skull on the hut's rafters. 'The gods've given me a big idea,' they half-lied, tapping their scar-riven skull with one talon before stabbing it out towards the night. 'See that beakie fort, up on Rukblud Peak? I've had enough of it. Soon as the sun's up, we're gonna do it in. Full assault. Heavies at the front, and…' – they thought for a second – 'everyone else at the front and all.'

'But first,' they finished, as a crooked grin spread behind the rusted iron teeth of their fight-jaw, 'we're gonna drink this hut dry. Brew's free until it's run out, so get stuck in – if anyone's not got a headache by tomorrow, I'll be giving 'em one.'

* * *

As it happened, that fight would turn out to be the newcomer's last.

At the start, it looked like it'd all come to nothing. As the full strength of Gogduf charged the gates in the narrow pass, there was no response except the clang of their own choppas on the human metal, and a roar of disappointment went up. The humans hadn't left anyone behind to fight. But while the fort – or the *monittering outpost*, as your lot called it – might've been empty of actual humans, it weren't defenceless.

Soon as someone started prising armour off the gates for scrap, a row of squat little turrets rose out of the wall with a nasty, quiet whir. Then they found their aim, and made a big, big noise.

It was the worst kind of fight, with loads dead, and no violence more satisfying than hacking up machines. Gogduf's orks won, but the spoils didn't come close to making up for losses. Of eight-many-many orks who went up the mountain, just many-many-and-four were still standing when the last turret got wrenched off its mountings.

The newcomer wasn't among 'em.

They weren't dead, but they weren't walking home neither. And since Goffs didn't do carrying, that meant they'd been left for dead. It was fair enough. But as the last survivors limped away, the newcomer couldn't even hear their boots on the scree. 'Cos they only had one ear left, to start with. But more importantly, 'cos the bit of their brain that dealt with noises and that was three-many tusklengths away, splattered across the rock with half the insides of their skull. With one shaky, nearly numb hand, they pawed at what was left of their face; the eye they couldn't see out of was gone, along with most of the face around it, leaving just a deep, ragged crater. When one of their legs started spasming like a squig with a choppa in its spine, they decided to stop probing to see how deep it went.

They did not know where they were. They did not know how they had got there. All they could see was the sky, and they did not know what that was. If they could have seen anything else, they wouldn't have known what it was, neither. The newcomer hadn't ever been given a name, so at least they couldn't lose that. But otherwise, everything they'd learned in their short life had been ripped out their head by that bolter shell.

Everything, that is, but the knowledge of the gods.

Somehow, whatever glob of meat held the names of Gork and Mork had clung on tight to the bone as the slug had torn through everything else. And that bit of brain seemed to throb now, even as the blood that made it alive trickled away into the dirt through the hole in the back of the newcomer's head. So the newcomer thought about the gods, and *demanded* divine intervention, to get them out of this mess. When no answer came, they roared in anger, but all that came out of their gob was a weak hiss.

Gork and Mork didn't stay quiet 'cos they were offended, yeah? It's fine to boss the gods around, so long as you remember they don't have to listen. Nah. They were quiet 'cos sometimes, the gods say things best when they stay silent. They were telling the newcomer that this mess was their own to sort out, and if they could do that, *then* they might be worth listening to.

That seemed fair enough. So the dying ork did the only thing that made sense. They got up, held their brains in, and went to find someone who could fix their head.

INTERROGATION II

As Biter narrated the aftermath of the nameless ork's wounding, Falx found her attention was focused more on the words of the prisoner themselves. Although she could not understand them, the fervour in its tone was intriguing – it spoke with relish, tongue flicking over its fangs as if recalling a sumptuous meal, rather than a catastrophic head injury. While by its own admission the gretchin simply enjoyed seeing others injured, Falx felt there was more to it than that. It was as if the wound had been a turn of great fortune in the young Ghazghkull's story, rather than a monumental setback.

Unconsciously, Falx's hand went to the back of her neck, where her fingers found the place, just above the base of her skull, where stubble parted around a two-inch oval of polished ceramite. That had been the work of a krax gonochela, rather than a bullet, and the creature had left her brain intact after cutting away the skull, as food for its growing larvae. Luckily, Brother Hendriksen had carved the thing off her before too many eggs had been laid, and an unpleasant hour with a mirror and a las-scalpel had been enough to tidy up the damage. It wasn't much of a wound, really. But even so, Falx had enough familiarity with cranial trauma to know it was an odd thing to celebrate.

Then, as the prisoner's jabbering continued, she noticed it fondling that grubby necklace it wore, rubbing each lump of metal in turn with a ritualistic, almost tender precision. And on one of the pieces, worn almost smooth by years of such fidgeting, she saw what looked a lot like the edge of a stylised, winged sword.

'That's the shell that split Ghazghkull's head, isn't it?' she asked, gesturing at the vile adornment with her chin as she snatched her hand back from her head. 'Those are its shards.' Biter relayed the question, cutting across the prisoner's reminiscence, and the grot shot the interpreter an angry, crest-fallen squint, before curling its lip and muttering a few short phrases.

'Quite... the opposite, Makari insists,' said Biter, clearly omitting some more colourful comments. 'They say it is the shell that birthed Ghazghkull.'

'Checks out,' offered Cassia with a shrug. 'That necklace had a real hum to it, brainwise, that's been bothering me ever since he came aboard. Smells green, I guess, and that'd be why. I suppose this really is Makari, then.'

Hendriksen exhaled loudly then, getting up from the crate he'd been half-sitting on throughout the account, and resuming his habitual pacing.

'Don't forget, young *steinblokk*-head, I sense the warp-strangeness of the necklace just as keenly as you do – though I would scorn, as ever, your calling it a *smell*. But yes, it is surely made from the shell which passed through Ghazgh-kull – trust the sons of the Lion to make ammunition so poor it turns foot-soldiers into conquerors.' He snorted in amusement at his own joke, but his frown remained. 'Even so, it proves nothing. This runt could be any fleck of scum, netted up by opportunist brigands and given a tall tale to tell, then handed this... *trinket* to justify their price.'

'I dunno, Orm,' said Cassia, folding her tree-root arms with a creak of canvas as she leaned back against the door frame. 'This ain't your average grot. And if that tale's a Blood Axe fiction, it sounded damned convincing to me.'

'By Russ' hairy knuckles, girl, your head's big enough – *think* with it. Does it not occur to you that there's something missing from this story? Something small and green that stinks like carnyx-piss?'

'Orm makes a point,' interjected Falx, before the pair could get too entrenched in their bickering. 'This creature speaks of Thraka's life with astonishing detail, and yet it has not offered a single word to account for its own presence in the tale.'

The grot muttered again, still sullen from being interrupted in its description of a good maiming, and Biter spoke up.

'That is because they did not exist at the time,' they said cryptically.

'So this is hearsay, then,' scoffed Hendriksen. 'Threadbare legend, which we could pick up from any greenskin, and in a thousand different variations to boot.'

'Oh no,' argued the ork with uncanny delicacy. 'It is the truth. This is what Ghazghkull experienced.'

'Because Ghazghkull said so, right?' asked Cassia, as even her credulity stretched thin.

'Because Makari saw it all,' corrected Biter, in what they probably thought was a mysterious tone.

'But they just said…' began Falx, as both Cassia and Hendriksen protested the contradiction at the same time.

'It is… complicated,' Biter insisted, holding up the backs of their hands to placate them, in another of their off-key attempts at human body language. 'But it will be explained, if you will be patient.'

Hendriksen pressed his lips together to contain his outburst, and looked to Falx for guidance. As hot-tempered as he was, he did sometimes manage to remember who was in charge, after all.

'Urged to patience by a representative of the most reckless species known to humanity,' she murmured, largely to herself, as she glanced down at her boots to find her calm. *What an exciting new departure this was.* 'Very well, ork. We are not short of time, after all. But your promise of an explanation is noted – do not test my lenience too long in keeping it.'

At her nod, the prisoner's account continued. But it wasn't long before the story was interrupted again. The gretchin had claimed that the ork had walked alone across two hundred miles of badlands before reaching what passed for civilisation at a place called Rustspike. Apparently, not only had they held their ruined skull together the whole way, but they had also stopped to fight no less than three ferocious beasts en route. This was too much for Brother Hendriksen.

'Orks hold together well,' he said, stabbing a finger into his palm for emphasis. 'I will give them that. But I know a thing or two about seeing off wild beasts in the wilderness, from the winter I took the Spirit of the Wolf…'

Falx, of course, knew all about wilderness beast fights too, given how often Hendriksen found excuses to tell the story of his initiation rites. As Cassia looked over and cast a faint image over Falx's mind's eye – of a haggard tally-mark being added to a wall already scratched with hundreds – it was hard not to smirk. And sure enough, Hendriksen proceeded to boast his way through a string of animal murders, complete with oversold mimings of each death-blow, as Biter's blank red eyes looked on.

'And no feat such as *that*,' he concluded, with a summative flex of his shoulders, 'could be boasted of by a creature who undertook it with half a head.'

The prisoner grinned as a much-abbreviated version of Hendriksen's argument was relayed to it, and leaned forward to stare mockingly at the Space Marine as it answered.

'Unless you're the ork that will become Ghazghkull Mag Uruk Thraka,' Biter translated, then looked shifty, as if unsure whether to translate the rest of the prisoner's speech as well. 'Makari also made a reference to the… hmm… *durability* of Space Wolves, which I… did not fully hear.'

Hendriksen stiffened despite Biter's attempt at *diplomersea*, his eyes growing pale and hard as if seen through ice. But Cassia spoke before his rage could crystallise further.

'I heard another story. It was doing the rounds in the trenches back on Karkhemish, though I dunno where it came from. This version had it that after Ghazghkull got shot, he got dragged away by his own mob. They'd heard about some messed-up ork doctor paying good money for bad injuries, so they drove him across the badlands and sold him for a few handfuls of bullets. Sounds more believable to me.'

'Is that true?' Falx asked Biter wearily, and the ork held up a claw as they conferred with the prisoner.

'Yes,' they stated simply.

'So Makari lied, then?'

'No,' said Biter.

'No more riddles!' growled Hendriksen, his patience stretched as far as it would go. 'Is the first account true, or the second?'

The grot made a single gesture, which earned it a resentful glare from Biter, and the ork spoke through what seemed to be a cringe.

'Yes?' they answered, and Falx took a deep, steadying breath.

Nearly an hour had passed by the time the situation was resolved, and even then, it was more an expedient way out of the headache the argument was giving everyone than a true resolution. As far as it could be grasped, orkoid minds seemed capable of believing more than one objective truth at the same time. Indeed, they could hold several entirely contradictory facts in their conscious reckoning at once, and not feel the slightest bit of mental discomfort.

In the end, and with some irony, they had agreed to disagree. But, before the prisoner's account could continue, the Deathwatch veteran had found one more bone to pick.

'Ghazghkull is a *he*,' he grumbled, wagging a finger at Biter and receiving an uncertain grunt in reply. 'You keep saying *they*,' Hendriksen clarified, 'but Ghazghkull is a *he*.'

'But… they… *he* is not a man?' said Biter, their brow-ridge creased in bafflement. Falx cut in then, before another messy debate could ensue.

'We've been through this, Orm. Orks have no… reproductive anatomy, and consequently no understanding of sex or gender.'

'Some of us understand *sexangender*,' interrupted Biter, keen as ever to demonstrate their unusual expertise in humans. 'I find it all… quite funny.'

'Silence, ork,' Falx snapped, impatient to get back on track. 'From now on, Ghazghkull is a *he*, whether it makes sense or not.'

'As you wish,' the interpreter said, casually inspecting the rust-eaten buckles on the sleeve of their greatcoat, then turning to address the gretchin in their own tongue. *'Smakh-snohtt-rhunt. Miff-baahk. Lug-ug-bohss'gihtt, Ghaz'ghk'ull ogh-nahr...* "Boyz".'

At that, the gretchin broke out into frantic, snivelling yelps, which Falx would have taken for the onset of some sort of mental collapse if she hadn't known it was laughter, and which prompted a snort of amusement from Biter. But the interpreter knew they had pushed their luck with the aside, and after one look at Falx's face, urged the smaller creature on in a language they could all understand: a vicious blow to the temple.

CHAPTER TWO

GHAZGHKULL DIES, FOR A WHILE

When I first met Ghazghkull, he was dead. Of course, he wasn't quite Ghazghkull, and I wasn't quite me either. But he was definitely dead. For a while.

He'd arrived in the middle of the night, and had been on Doc Grotsnik's table until just before sunrise. That was near enough a miracle in itself, 'cos even warbosses – usually the ones who'd run out of cash, mind – rarely made it an hour on that slab without either getting fixed, or drifting into the wrong side of 'kill or cure'. In fact, word around the Rustspike brew-huts was that Grotsnik only stayed in business, and in one piece, 'cos none of the surgery's failures lived to make a complaint.

This patient *should've* died plenty of times. He just didn't fancy it. Dying wouldn't even have been a big deal, usually. But he had a strange feeling he was just getting started, and he wanted to stick around to find out what he was just getting started *with*.

Grotsnik didn't make it easy. By the peak of the operation, the patient's head had been taken apart like a faulty shoota, with all its bits laid out on a bench to have more grease slapped on 'em. He'd gotten through a whole cage of transfusion squigs, and he probably didn't have a drop of his original blood left.

He didn't have too much of his brain, either. What the turret had left him with had ended up stapled to a medley of scraps from the dingy bucket where Grotsnik kept his 'cuttings', and which were now a bit ripe, having not been 'frigerated in three days. But the bit of that original brain that mattered held on, and made quick work of bullying the rest into line.

Grotsnik, of course, was gleeful. Operations this complicated never lasted long enough to be any fun, but this was something special. So special, in fact, that the doc decided to break out a bit of kit that'd been waiting for just such a day, and which was probably worth more than everything else in that grimy medical tent put together.

It was a bit of metal. Really, really hard metal, though. If the scav who'd brought it to the doc was to be believed, it was the arse plate off of a human *termynater*, found under some distant dune in a krumped aircraft, whose cockpit time-knower had said it was nine-many-many-many years old. Grotsnik had figured that if metal was like fungus grog and got better with age, this had to be a *Gork-smacked-good bit of metal*, so the doc'd shanked the scav immediately, and ran off into the night with the mysterious plate.

Here, at last, was a patient stubborn enough to match it. And as Mork would have it, the plate turned out to be the perfect shape for holding in their new thinking-meat. So with a bit of saw work and a few rivets, on it went, leaving room for a bionic eye to boot. Better yet, the patient was still breathing when the last clamp was attached – the operation had been a success!

Unfortunately, Grotsnik was too excited to stop there, so Ghazghkull ended up going straight into a pioneering knee-replacement op the doc'd been wanting to try for ages. That worked too, with the bionic joint being slightly better than the healthy knee it had replaced.

But that bit of extra blood loss was the cannon that broke the squiggoth's back. By the time the doc had wiped the worst of the gore off his hands in the grey light of pre-dawn, the patient was stone dead. Grotsnik wouldn't have minded that much, though. It was more the… *doing* of medicine that motivated him, than the outcomes.

The patient was rolled off the table with a wet thud, and dragged to the back-flap of the tent by whatever down-on-his-luck goon Grotsnik had hired to shift corpses that week. By the time they'd been hoyed on the Failure Pile in the yard out back, the doc would've forgotten all about 'em. But when something stops being an ork's problem, it usually becomes a grot's – and by Mork's filthy lies, that weren't ever truer than at Grotsnik's.

Once bodies ended up on the Pile, it was the job of Grotsnik's lowliest orderly – an overworked grot who lived under two sheets of corrugated metal at the edge of the yard – to prise out any functioning bionics with a rusty getting-stick, put 'em back in Grotsnik's 'bitz box', and chop the rest up for the squig pens. And that's where I come into the story. 'Cos I was the grot.

I think so, anyway. Someone had to be. And since I *remember* being the grot, I suppose it was me.

I got up with a groan, grabbed my getting-stick, and got to work. It was barely light in the yard still, and the ground was bitter cold, but the doc would want this body cleared before it started drawing git-swarms, so I didn't waste any time.

Grotsnik's last two yard-grots had both died from trying to get bits off orks who weren't quite dead yet, so I gave the body a good few jabs with the getter just to be sure. Then I jumped up on its chest to start levering that shiny plate off its head. But as soon as my getter touched metal, there was a sharp *crack*, and I stumbled back, feeling like I'd jammed my hand in a charged-up zapcoil.

The body started twitching. Then it started shaking, and then it was properly thrashing around, clawing blindly at its new skullbits like it was trying to find something. It went completely rigid for a second, every muscle tensed so hard I thought something was going to snap, and then sat bolt upright, mouth wide open in what was either complete confusion, or some kind of awe. Like it'd seen something... *mega*. But before I could work out what was happening, the body grabbed me by the shoulder, and I had the same shock I'd gotten from the getter, only longer and burnier and *worse*, 'cos the body wouldn't let go. It held on 'til steam started coming off me, but I didn't have long to worry about that, 'cos that was when the body looked right at me. And in its one proper eye was a green so green, that it became the universe.

I'd had visions before. Most grots in Rustspike had; we weren't allowed in the brew-huts or the fight sheds, so on the rare times when we managed to dodge our graft, we'd gather in groups of the grots we hated least, and guzzle the skinny mushrooms that grew in the warpheadz' drops on the edge of town. They weren't much good, those visions: they were just headaches with colours, really. This, though? This was something else. This was an audience with the gods.

It was nothing, to start with. Just dark, and damp, and cold. And then, way up above, there was a voice. Voices, in fact. They was so big and so deep it was hard to tell what language they was speaking, let alone what they said. But it must've been Gork and Mork. And they were fighting, which is fine, because that's what they like doing best. I couldn't see it, but I could feel it – massive, rumbling impacts that made the dark thunder, and would've knocked me off my feet if I'd had any kind of presence.

And then, a spark. A tiny little mote of green, bright and hungry, drifting down through many-many-many tusklengths 'til it touched the floor of wherever I was. The green spread out from that tiny point, rippling in big bright circles, and pooling in spots that spread circles of their own. It spread faster and faster, until everything was covered in it, as far as I could see. Now it was lit up, I could see I was in some kind of cavern. Or rather, a big twisting mess of caverns, like the cells in a hive of sugar-gits, but *massive*.

The walls were… meaty, I reckon is the word. Damp and red and crinkly, like the folds in a brain, which I'd seen enough of in my brief life to know well enough. As the green gathered on 'em, they changed. They started sprouting fungus. Moulds and slimes at first – the sort of stuff you eat when there's a duststorm on and the orks've had all the good grub. But then murkworts and bilecaps, and huge, complicated things like nothing that grew on Urk.

And just like it is outside of holy visions, wherever the fungus grew, so did other green things. Squiglets first, the kind so small you can only see 'em as mean little specks digging into your armpits, then squigs as big as talon-tips and fists and heads. Next came snotlings – who are to grots what we are to orks – crawling and yipping and scrapping with each other in big, writhing piles. Everywhere, there was snotlings eating squigs, and squigs eating snotlings, and with every jawsnap, gnash and gnaw, the green grew brighter and more alive.

Then there were grots. *Swarms* of grots, and they got straight to work lashing together meagre little tools from squig-sinew and capwood, and bullying the snots into working too. Faster'n I could keep up with, they beat the fungal jungle back, and started building farms and drops and brew-huts and barracks. They were just in time for the first orks, who were clawing their way out of their grow-holes now, and were hungry already.

The orks kept coming, and they kept getting bigger, until even the runts among 'em were as big as the warbosses on Urk. And above it all – way up, on what might've been the cavern roof or might've been infinity – the stars were coming out. More stars than every mek on Urk could've counted in a lifetime, and every one of 'em that bright, angry, beautiful green.

I was so distracted by the stars, that I didn't see the squiggoth.

It was a brilliant thing. A horrible thing. As big as a battlewagon it was, and it made the skinny, sag-throated beasts raised by Urk's snakebite herders look pathetic. It nearly smashed me to mush with its foot. But I didn't live to three years old by not being able to roll out of the way of a stomp Mork-snikked fast, and once I was on my feet, I followed the beast. I dunno why, but it felt right. Soon, there was a whole herd of squiggoths, lumbering along at something like a gallop, and barging each other with enough force to flatten forts. I ran along with 'em through that untameable garden, and I didn't care if they stamped me flat, 'cos it felt like fear wasn't something worth feeling in this place.

Up above now, where the green stars shone, there were warriors. Huge orks, *perfect* orks, every one bigger than a clan chief, and rippling with green light. I don't know how I knew, but they was orks *as they was meant to be*. They glowed bright enough to out-shine the stars, and as they strode through the sky, I could feel the gods above 'em, grinning down in violent pride. Then clashes and booms and roars started coming from up ahead – the giants were wading into a scrap.

It was hard to see what was going on, given I was look-ing up from between the flanks of the galloping squiggoths, but it was a big, big, *big* fight. It kept getting bigger. And I think the orks won. Surely, they couldn't have lost? But then, when the noises of the fight faded away, the presence of the gods did too. It was like the whole cavern got cold and dark again, like it had been to start with. The squiggoths stopped in their tracks, and so did every other thing in the whole of the Great Green. It was like everything was lost, suddenly, looking around and wondering what to do now.

Of course, they started fighting. It was a frenzy, above and below, from the giants trading punches like comet-strikes in the sky, to the snotlings wrapping skinny claws around each other's necks down below. And with no gods to bang every-one's heads together and tell 'em to pack it in, it went on until the whole place was like a butcher's tent, and there'd been enough murders for the survivors to have some space.

It weren't peaceful, then, but it weren't a bloodbath nei-ther, 'cos all the really hard things, like the orks in the sky, were dead. It went on for ages like that. There were orks, still. But they were nothing like the colossal fighters who'd been there before. And they was all stuck down on the cavern floor. Watching 'em was a bit like watching raindrops get swiped away by a trukk's hatch-wipers: every time one got big enough to seem like it might make it up to the sky, all the others nearby ganged up and beat it into shreds, so none of 'em got as big as they should've been.

Until one did, that is. It wasn't even that big when it got attacked, but it properly *demolished* every ork that came at it, delivering headbutts like point-blank cannon strikes, and pulling any survivors into line to fight alongside it. As more and more enemies flooded in, the fighter got larger, and so did the pile of bodies in front of it. Green lightning started to strike all around it, and soon that body pile reached all the way up to the sky. Seeing this, the new giant began climbing the mountain of the dead towards the stars.

With every step, the winner grew more bulky, more… vigorous, and soon the cavern started glowing bright again. The stars swelled, and I knew that Gork and Mork was back, somehow. Or that they'd never been gone, but had just lost interest for a while, until there'd been something worth looking at again. Soon, the champion reached the top of the body pile, where the stars had grown so big there was no black left between 'em, and it stood there for a moment, like it was thinking.

Looking up at that titan, which had horns now, as well as loads of arms bearing all sorts of different guns and choppas, I was terrified. But I also knew what joy was, for the very first time.

And then the titan looked back down at me. There were spaceships flitting across the green sea of its one good eye, looking like tiny bin-gits, and as the full weight of that glare bore down on me, I thanked the gods that they'd let me die like this. But the giant didn't kill me. It curled a finger big enough to flick a moon into a planet, and it *beckoned* me. Then it turned and stepped into glorious, infinite green, leaving only flames in its boot prints.

When I came back round in the yard again, Ghazghkull Thraka was standing over me. It was *him*. He looked bigger than the body he'd been, somehow. And he looked down at me with an eye which, though it was red like a normal one, held the exact same expression that'd been turned on me at the deep end of that vision.

And as he looked at me, I wasn't sure I was me anymore. I was *me*, instead. But there wasn't time to think much. 'Cos rather than beckoning me like the giant had done, Ghazghkull was thrusting his finger towards my face, and I will never forget the first words I heard from him.

'Now listen close,' he said, **'or I'll batter you.'**

As much of an impression as that left, mind, you'll likely be more interested in what he said next. After tracing a claw along the ridge of ugly staples bordering his shiny new bonce, and scowling with satisfaction, he sank down to one knee so we were eye to eye, and spoke again.

'Some orks are clever. Some orks are strong. I'm both.'
That was it. He'd say more, in time, but at that moment, it was all he needed to say. Truth is, I've never heard anyone sum up Ghazghkull more neatly than Ghazghkull did right there in Grotsnik's yard. And as soon as he spoke, we both knew I was bound to him, as simply and as unbreakably as that plate was clamped to his skull.

I didn't know where this ork had come from, besides the Failure Pile, but I knew where it was going. Gork and Mork had such big plans for this one, that they'd spilled into my head when he touched me. This ork was going to turn the stars green. And I knew that somehow, in some way I didn't need to understand yet, I was part of the plan.

What can you do, when your whole idea of what life's about gets kicked apart in an instant? Well, I did what any good grot would do in my position: I told the prophet of Gork and Mork there was something behind him, so that he turned round to look. And then I ran like a squig with its arse on fire, before I could get dragged into something dangerous.

INTERROGATION III

'You *ran*?' asked Cassia through gritted teeth, crabbing her hands against her temples as she spoke. During the grot's description of its supposed holy vision, Falx had felt a headache coming on, but to the psykers in the cell, it had been an ordeal. Even Hendriksen, for all his celebrated mental discipline, had a queasy look as if he were trying to keep down a half-keg of used engine oil.

'Of course they ran,' said Biter, as if defending the prisoner's honour. 'They's a grot!'

'But you said you felt a... bond with Ghazghkull,' said Falx to the captive, more interested in what it had to say than Biter's editorial commentary. She received a sneer and a dismissive mutter in response.

'Yes, they say,' Biter clarified. 'But also – *they's a grot*. A grot's bond of service cannot be sincere if it is not tested repeatedly by attempts to shirk it. Constant recal... relact...'

'Recalcitrance,' offered Brother Hendriksen irritably.

'Yes. *Rencalcinence* is, you could say, a way of making sure a master has good wits.'

Falx scratched at the scarring around her cranial plate, and turned to Cassia. 'The vision pained you, Cassia. Is the grot a psyker?'

'No such thing as a grot psyker,' said the ogryn psyker, then grunted in mild annoyance as Falx raised an eyebrow at the irony. 'Or at least, there's no such thing on this ship. Like I said when I smelled 'em out before we started, there's *something* to this one... but it ain't that.'

'She's right,' Hendriksen announced, with more than a little bluster. He never liked it when Falx went to Cassia first with questions of the mental arts, after all. 'There *is* something to him. And there was something to... *that*, too. The vision. But even within the crude witch-lore of the greenskins, there are tricks. Crude resonances which can be cast on a lesser being, to impart a sense of power – or to deepen the fidelity of a forgery.'

'Not that I would... *compradict* you,' wheedled Biter, brow-ridges lifting as they raised a talon, 'but... look.'

Hendriksen swung his shaggy head towards the prisoner and harrumphed; the grot had pulled down the collar of its jerkin to reveal a great, blackened mark in the rough shape of an ork palm print, seared across its shoulder. Falx was sure it had not been there when they'd scanned the creature for explosives. But now, she could even see the lumpy ridges where the prisoner's skin had bubbled up around the burn.

'The hand of the boss,' said Biter quietly, failing to conceal a near-infrasonic growl of awe, while the prisoner's face stretched into a mean, tight-lipped smile.

'The handiwork of a Blood Axe trickster,' contested Hendriksen.

'We shall see,' said Falx.

The evidence that Makari did indeed sit before them was certainly mounting. But she had learned long ago that Hendriksen's instinct for a ruse was to be ignored at her peril. For every nine false positives, his tenth suspicion would be the one that saved them from a Devourer-cult patriarch or a Gollmaihre face-wearer, and he seemed more certain than ever that they were being deceived.

She would have to take measures. Subvocalising a command to the chamber's servo-skull, she sent it puttering off to the brig's entrance, with a message for the warden of the ship's vivarium. She would wake Xotal, and then they would have the truth. But for now, she bade the prisoner continue.

'I didn't make it many-and-five tusklengths, mind,' translated Biter. 'The second I was up off the dust, Ghazghkull kicked back with his heel – it was the leg with the new knee on it and all – and without even turning round, he punted a rock right at the back of my skull. Masterful, it was. Knocked me down flat, as absently as if he was swatting a bin-git off of his brew. And all the while, he kept looking at the flap that led back into Grotsnik's tent.'

'He was thinking,' said Falx.

'No,' said the prisoner, with sarcasm so poisonous it required no clarification from Biter in translation. 'He was scratching his arse. *'Course he was thinking.* And since his brain was busy, he told me to write down everything I'd seen in the vision so he could think about it later. That was a problem though.'

'Why?'

'Nothing to write with, gut-brains!' Biter's face froze after saying that, as the ork calculated whether they had gone too far in getting into the spirit of the gretchin's words, and the grot cackled at their predicament. But Falx had been called much worse, and made a rolling gesture with one hand to keep the account flowing.

'The doc had a can of paint for surgical markings, but it'd dried up years back when he started eyeballing his cuts, and all I owned in the world was the two sheets of metal I lived under, plus my getting-stick. So Ghazghkull told me to stab him in the leg with the getter, and use his blood to write with.' From the look on the grot's face as Biter relayed this last detail, this was a particularly treasured memory.

'I thought your kind had no written language beside crude hieroglyphs?' queried Falx.

'Writing, drawing... same word, for us,' said Biter. 'Same word as "fighting", but you say it quieter, with less... how do you say...?' At that, the ork's eyes flared, and they let out a vicious, abrupt growl that made every muscle in Falx's back stiffen at once, and had Hendriksen's knife out of its sheath in a heartbeat. The ferocity was gone at once, but it was as if a vile sun had briefly glimmered through clouds: for all of their bizarre affectations, and their fascination with *diplomersea*, she reminded herself, this was just another beast that happened to wear a most unusual mask.

'Quite,' she said, with a smile as thin and precise as a duellist's blade, as Biter grinned back at her.

'Anyway,' the translator continued, clearing their throat with a sound like a shovel stuck in a bilge pump, and taking on their 'Makari voice' again, 'I grabbed the metal sheet that was half of my house, and started to write down the vision. Only the most important bit, though – that massive, perfect ork, with the horns and all the arms holding guns, standing on a big pile of bodies with spaceships going round its head. I had to get fresh paint a couple of times, and I waggled the getter in the hole a bit more than I had to when I did, but

Ghazghkull didn't even flinch. He just kept staring at the tent. Like he was getting ready for something.

'It was to Ghazghkull's liking, at least – he only kicked me lightly after I gave it to him, and after turning it a little to see how it caught the light, he worked his thumb into one of the gaps between his head-stitches, and… *annoyted* the image with the gore of his holy wound. He tore the strapping from an old boot lying in the dust, used it to lash the metal sheet to my getting-stick, and *then* it was a banner.'

'What then?' asked Falx.

'Then he gave it to me, and he gave me a name. And then, just like that, I existed.'

CHAPTER THREE

GHAZGHKULL'S BIG FIGHT

'**Makari**,' said Ghazghkull, after looking at me for a few seconds. Wasn't a name I'd heard before. I'm still not totally sure he weren't just clearing his throat. Didn't matter though. I might've lost two of my three possessions to make the banner, but I'd gained a *name*, and that was treasure. Like most grots, I'd never had one beyond 'git' or 'you', for the same reason you wouldn't bother naming a bit of wood, or a polishing rag, or a bullet. Grots are there to be used up. But if an ork names something, he means to keep it.

I had a new job and all.

'**You'll hold that. Where I go, you go, and you'll hold it high,**' said the boss, '**so they know who's coming.**'

'What if they don't know what it means?' I asked, risking a beasting for talking back, but Ghazghkull just snorted.

'**Then I'll teach 'em,**' he said, cracking his knuckles with a noise like a butcher pulling a leg off a squig. Then he gave a shiny, adamantium-plated nod to the tent flap. **'Best get started.'**

Ghazghkull walked right past Grotsnik's goons, into the main bit of the tent which served as Grotsnik's operating theatre. The doc himself was there, with his earlier failure already forgotten, and his arms up to the elbows in the belly of Rustspike's smelter boss.

The doc hissed with frustration, and turned around with his eyes smouldering like furnace-slag in their baggy sockets. He was ready to cut whoever had dared walk in on his procedure. But when he saw the intruder was his patient, back from the dead, it was like he'd stood on a sand-git with no boots on. Those nasty eyes went wide with alarm, 'cos he knew he was about to get a pasting, but then they went even wider in excitement, 'cos he saw that his surgery had worked after all. The doc was so thrilled, in fact, he stood bolt upright with half the smelter boss' guts still in his hands. That didn't make the smelter boss very happy, but his griping stopped soon enough when he clapped eyes on Ghazghkull. Just like Grotsnik, he could smell the danger in the room.

I was really looking forward to seeing the doc get hammered into the ground, after all the beatings he'd given me over the years. But Ghazghkull steamed straight through the operating room, ignoring the doc altogether, and headed for the tent's entrance flap. *Where I go, you go*, he'd said, so what could I do but follow? If the doc was bothered to see me saunter out of the tent behind the living corpse, he didn't let on. Perhaps he realised I wasn't the same grot anymore. Perhaps he didn't want to push his luck. Either way, he said nothing as Ghazghkull ducked under the rolled-up hide door and walked out into the light of morning in Rustspike.

This place wasn't a fort, you understand. Wasn't a city, neither, though it might as well've been – six-many-many-many-many Deathskull orks lived there, with more arriving every day. But they still called Rustspike a camp.

It had been, once. It'd just been a single tent, actually, at the start. A few sheets of squighide draped over a prospector's trukk, right where its engine had failed, next to a big rusty spike of metal in the badlands. But Mork had fancied a laugh that day, and when the prospector had gotten to digging for gubbins, he'd found the spike was the tip of a tower. There was a whole human city down there, it had turned out, covered in dust and rocks and never looted once. Well, it got looted plenty after that. And Rustspike had got fat off the loot.

The sun was just climbing up over the jumble of the camp's skyline, throwing long shadows down the street, so a great black giant slid ahead of Ghazghkull as he walked. It was like the ork who'd climbed the sky in the vision was half-there, its shadow leading him down the street. We were lucky it was early, too, as the knee-deep slurry of junk and squig turds that covered the trukkway was still half-frozen from the night. It'd be a river by noon, but for now it crackled under Ghazghkull's boots, and held my weight so I didn't have to wade.

It was quiet. A lone grinder was throwing up sparks in the cave-like wagon garages of the mekshop across the way, and there were only a couple of brawls underway deep in the big brew-hut next to Grotsnik's, as the last revellers settled their tabs before heading back to work.

Given the state he'd arrived in at the doc's tent during the night, this would've been Ghazghkull's first look at proper civilisation. He didn't seem impressed.

He just stood there, looking it all over, for a long while. And I stood a few steps behind him, holding his banner for nobody to see, and feeling like a right fool. But I knew better than to ask what we was waiting for, and I was right to keep my trap shut. 'Cos that morning, I learned that when Ghazghkull expects something, it doesn't take long for it to happen.

A racket started up down the far end of the trukkway, where it turned a corner round the bullet-mill and snaked out to the camp's main gate. I couldn't see what was causing it, 'cos of the bullet-mill, but I reckoned it was either a fight or a celebration, and I turned out to be half-right twice: it was a celebration of a fight. And its source was only bloody Dregmek, the warlord of all the Deathskulls on Urk, with his entire retinue walking along with him.

Dregmek was a big, big ork: easily five times Ghazghkull's weight, and taller than the two of us would've been if we were stacked up. And that weren't even counting his armour. Dregmek's rig was a one-off, hammered together from alien bones out of the eastern desert, then plated with an extra layer of lead sheet 'cos the warlord didn't reckon it was heavy enough. Hydraulics hissed as he plodded towards us, and as he bragged to his cronies, his huge, blue-striped fight-jaw bobbed up and down in time with his real one.

Just from the mimed punches he swung at the air as he swaggered along, I could tell he was boasting to his mates about a fight. They'd all have been there too, of course, but none of 'em wanted a krumping, so they roared with laughter and surprise as their boss recounted every blow.

Like any grot, the only thought that crossed my mind when faced with an approaching boss-mob drunk on a big win was the impulse to run and hide in a very small place. But Ghazghkull had told me to hold the banner, so I stayed and held the banner. If Dregmek's lot came at Ghazghkull, I figured, I could always revise my options.

It didn't come to that, though. 'Cos Ghazghkull came for

them. Just walked right towards Dregmek, chin thrust out like a trukk's ram, with nothing to fight with but his hands. I would've run then, if I'm honest, but I was too shocked.

'You're an offence to the gods,' said Ghazghkull. It weren't even a challenge. Just a *statement*. A fact, bland as a fungus-biscuit, like he'd pointed out that Dregmek was wearing blue armour. And though he didn't even shout, it carried all the way down the street, echoing off the buildings, and stopped the chant in mid-flow. Dregmek looked at Ghazghkull, with his brows crunched up in confusion. Then he looked round at his mates, and they looked back, and they all laughed at once, as loud as a row of krumptrukks opening fire.

'You what, runt?' rumbled Dregmek, after he'd had enough of laughing, and beckoned for the gang of grots who carried his gun to lift the eight-barrelled cannon into his hand.

'You heard,' said Ghazghkull.

As he began winding the crank on the weapon's dakka gauge to get all its bits charged, Dregmek squinted at the smaller ork over the jagged teeth of his fight-jaw. Back in the camp's early days he'd got a bionic eye off of Grotsnik, and his testimonial of 'suppose it's an eye' was still daubed proudly over the door of the doc's tent. But that was about the best you could say of the prosthetic. With Ghazghkull standing many-many tusklengths away on the trukkway, and the sun rising behind him, Dregmek was having a hard time seeing his accuser.

But then he clocked the checkmarks on Ghazghkull's leather armour – the same armour he'd worn to Gogduf's assault on the human outpost – and his good eye shifted from a squint to a crinkle of violent excitement.

'Now hang on, lads,' said Dregmek to his crew, with relish. 'Am I seeing this right? Is this a *Goff* runt, walking about in *my town*?' He squinted again. 'No, wait. It's even better'n that.

It's a Goff runt *left over from the lot we just battered*, and he's been put together again by Grotsnik so we can finish the job!'

Looking back at the tent then, as I tried to work out my odds of legging it back inside and swearing blind I'd never left, I saw Grotsnik himself was standing at the door, rubbing the giblets off a pair of forceps. Other faces were peering from the shadows of doorways, balconies and looking-holes all along the street, hoping to see a bit of blood.

'What's it you're after then, runt?' bellowed Dregmek cordially.

'I told you,' said Ghazghkull, like there wasn't some massive git wearing half a tank pointing an artillery piece at him. **'You're an offence to the gods. You fight other orks, squabbling over human scrap like a snotling. You're no sort of ork, and Gork and Mork know it.'**

When he'd finished, Dregmek laughed again, but not as many of his cronies laughed with him this time. It wasn't the fact that Ghazghkull wasn't afraid that unnerved 'em. Orks *can't* be afraid, the lucky gits. It was the fact he was talking like he'd already won the fight, and Dregmek didn't know it yet. It was weird.

'I'll wait for Gork and Mork to tell me that themselves, thanks,' said the warlord, less cheerful now, and levelled the sights of his weapon at Ghazghkull. 'For now, you give 'em my regards, after I pull this trigger and you're waiting in the Great Green to get belched into a new body. Now, do us a favour and tell us yer name first, so I can have it painted on this gun.'

'I am the warlord of warlords, and the prophet of Gork and Mork. They speak through my tusks, and my fists, and my head. I am Ghazghkull, and I will bring great slaughter.'

There was a long silence then, as every ork watching found another ork to look confused at. Dregmek peered at Ghazghkull, looking confused himself, and then shook his head.

'Yeah, that's not gonna fit,' he said, and pulled the trigger.

ACT TWO

INTERROGATION IV

'How does this great tale play out, I wonder,' said Hendriksen, pausing to tear a strip from the block of dried meat he had somehow produced during Makari's story. 'Did every bullet bounce off Ghazghkull's incredible new skull? Did he defeat every one of Dregmek's house-guards in a big, jolly brawl. Is that right, xenos?'

'No, it is not,' said Biter, with a sly expression that Falx couldn't parse, until she recognised it as simple jealously at the fact the Rune Priest had food. 'You would not have thought that fight... jolly at all. Our *rukkh-razzha* – our... battle-bliss, maybe? – is not joy as you would recognise it, human.'

'You might be surprised,' said Hendriksen quietly, words limned with the eerie lilt of his native accent. He smiled without warmth, flashing teeth as long as fingers. 'And you would be wrong to call me human, ork.'

Falx shivered, despite herself. She had worked with Hendriksen for so long that she had begun to forget. Outside of his armour, it was all too easy to see the Fenrisian as nothing but a very large, very capable man. Like many of his former Chapter-brothers, there was a certain *vivacity* to him; a sense of deep-rooted heartiness that was as likeable as it was irritating at times, and which could easily be mistaken for humanity. But as convincing as it was, it concealed something *other*.

Whenever she was reminded of what lay beneath the old wolf's eccentric affectations, it was like looking over the side of a small boat, and seeing something dark and vast beneath. Brother Orm Hendriksen was not of her kind.

Indeed, for all the near-incomprehensible things Falx had seen in the shadows between the stars, there were ways in which the Astartes were still the most alien of all creatures to her understanding, and their veneer of familiarity only served to make them more uncanny. There was a bleak humour to be found, she thought, in the ordo ostracising her for treating with alien cultures, when the last hands sheltering mankind's guttering candle were themselves anything but human.

Biter, meanwhile, was untroubled by Hendriksen's statement, and seemed more bothered with their desire for the rank piece of meat in the Rune Priest's hands.

'As you wish, *Space Marine*,' the translator said, trying not quite hard enough to keep the words from sounding mocking, and Falx took this as her cue to lift the conversation out of harm's way.

'So come on, ork,' she said. 'Enlighten us as to how Ghazghkull survived eight barrels worth of *dakka*.' Her lip curled at the ugly feeling of the xenos word in the mouth.

'Very easily,' Biter responded, funnelling their lips for an abrupt hoot of mirth, 'because nothing hit him! He walked right up to Dregmek – he did not even run, Makari says. And while the street was… *umbliterated* around him, and many, many onlookers were shot, Ghazghkull was untouched.'

'And you're telling us none of Dregmek's hangers-on stepped in to help?' asked Cassia, whose upbringing had left her perennially inclined to examine conflict from the perspective of bodyguards and henchmen.

'And tell Dregmek they had no confidence in his ability to kill an unarmed stripling? I don't think so,' scoffed Biter.

'And when Ghazghkull reached Dregmek?' Cassia continued. But before Biter answered, they turned to Makari, and asked a series of brief, purposeful questions. There was a lot of quick, violent miming, and a lot of hissing from Makari as Biter's gestures were corrected. Falx knew that to orks, fights were the most important parts of any stories, and that gesticulation was critical to their telling.

'So it started like *this*,' announced Biter at last, punctuating the end of the sentence by lurching out of the shadows in an explosion of sudden speed. The ork was fast enough to cross the cell before Falx even registered them moving, and since she had always resisted neural augmentation beyond basic data-vis implants, if the ork had intended to kill her, only Hendriksen's reflexes would have stood in their way. But the old shaman was still. Clearly, he had assessed the threat and discounted it, before Falx's eyes had even managed to tell her brain she was about to die. Biter was, of course, just mimicking the first punch Dregmek had thrown at Ghazghkull. But Falx could not shake the certainty that it had also been a testing of her guard.

The fight, as the *Exactor*'s crew proceeded to learn through Biter's re-enactment of every blow, had been extremely long, and extremely one-sided. Ghazghkull had not gone untouched, but

Dregmek's colossal armour had hindered him, and the speed imbalance had whittled his constant onslaught of blows down to a scattering of clips and scrapes. Ghazghkull, meanwhile, had been methodical, patiently waiting for opportunities to prise away armour, and then going to work on the flesh beneath.

The wounds, when they came, had been grievous. Orks were so abominably durable, after all, that clean kills were precluded by anything but ordnance and heavy-calibre fire-arms, and in hand-to-hand combat they had to be dismantled piece by piece. It was a slow, grisly business, and the story of Ghazghkull's fight with Dregmek was a bleak case study in just how hard an ork could fight despite an increasing short-fall of anatomy.

By the time the fight had turned into what could only honestly be described as a beating, Dregmek was barely recognisable. Eyeless, earless and fingerless, he could not even bite at Ghazghkull, given his jaw was hanging by a scrap of sinew. The remaining bulk of his extraordinary armour was nothing but a hindrance to the maimed warlord, and his assailant did not relent for a moment.

If she had not understood Biter's words, though, she would have thought they were recounting a comedy. All their usual strange reserve had evaporated in the thrill of the telling, and they kept having to pause for fits of wild, huffing laughter, grinning at Falx all the while, as if she would suddenly get the joke. Makari was cackling too, but she noticed that while Biter tended to be most excited by punches being thrown, the gretchin seemed to take more relish in their landing.

They laughed and barked and roared, and the translator's mimed blows became fiercer and fiercer, pounding against bulkheads and bars with a speed and force that was chilling to watch. And of course, Dregmek's retinue, standing in a circle around the mauling, would have been overcome by the very same rapture. They had cheered for Ghazghkull, as Biter told it, and had even started walloping each other, when they could no longer contain their excitement. It had not been disloyalty to Dregmek, so much as loyalty to the greater cause of a good fight, that had driven them.

Orks can't resist the appeal of an overdog. That's what Lord Inquisitor Kryptman had told her, back when she had been his acolyte, and the concept had never made more sense than it did now.

This was no time for pondering, though. Biter's racket had set the brig's other monsters off by now, so the shadows clamoured with hoots, screeches and rattling bars. That brought a sudden jolt of anger, as she felt her sovereignty over the ship was being tested. Falx suppressed the feeling out of habit, but after weighing up the situation, she decided it would be expedient to make her emotions known. So she drew her pistol and fired, permitting herself the smallest flicker of catharsis as the weapon bucked in her hand.

'Enough,' she said, in the sudden quiet after the shot, and slid the weapon neatly back into its hip holster. Biter looked down at the hole that had appeared in their leg, and then back up at Falx. She could see several different potential responses wrestling to take hold of the ork's body, and she kept her hand on the weapon's grip, ready to draw again. But Biter, it seemed, was a true diplomat.

'Good shot,' they muttered, straightening themselves again, and Falx nodded. It had been.

'So, Dregmek was finished,' she concluded for the ork.

'Coulda endured all that damage easy,' countered Biter, their Gothic rougher and more halting after their performance. 'Ghazghkull couldn't... let him though. It was... what'sa thing you say... *nothing personal*. Had a job to do.'

Keeping their movements tighter now, and only partially because of the bullet wound, Biter mimed the final blows of the fight. They concluded by removing their embarrassment of a commissar's cap, and cracking their neck with the flat of their palm to loosen it.

'I am guessing from your preparations,' murmured Hendriksen joylessly, gesturing at Biter's hat, 'that this great *holmgang*, this noble duel of heroes, finished with a headbutt?'

'A *very powerful* headbutt,' Biter clarified, with what could have been called an air of dignity. Then Makari spoke again, and it became clear just how powerful a headbutt it had been.

CHAPTER FOUR

GHAZGHKULL LOOKS TO THE STARS

Dregmek weren't much more than a pile of meat at that point, lying in the street with his guts all churned up in the thawing filth. Ghazghkull was stood over him like a squiggoth over a fresh kill, blood running from his knuckles. He should've been bellowing in triumph. But instead, he looked hacked off. Like he wasn't done yet.

'**Get up,**' he said, and let me tell you now, *it weren't a request.* I dunno how Dregmek even had the blood left in his body to breathe at that point. But somehow, he found the strength to stagger to a knee, and then to his feet. The whole street'd gone dead quiet now, so the only noise was Dregmek's breath, coming gurgling and ragged from his wrecked face. The warlord's cronies had stopped cheering, 'cos the fight was done. It was something else now. A demonstration, maybe. Or an execution.

Ghazghkull looked across at the biggest of the retinue – an

ork who was maybe a head taller'n Dregmek, but weirdly lean, without even a bit of a gut on him. It was like the gods had packed all his meat into the top of him, and he was tattooed all over with glyphs, inked in lucky blue, to represent all the stuff he'd looted. Bit like the human over there with all the hair on his face, actually. Only, y'know, *proper*. He was holding a big chain-choppa with a blue haft, and it was revving away quietly, but he looked wary, like he didn't know what to do with it.

'**You watching?**' said the boss, but not like it was a threat.

'I'm watching,' said the lanky Deathskull, just as neutral. The whole camp was watching. And the gods were, too. Ghazghkull looked around him, breathing slow, taking in all the crowds who'd showed up over the course of the fight. He grunted in faint surprise, like he'd forgotten there was an audience.

'**That's done now,**' he told the orks of Rustspike, tilting his head to the ruined Dregmek. Then he fixed his eye on me, and extended an arm to point at the sheet of scrap I held in the air, with my drawing on it. So many orks looked at me then that I nearly scarpered, just on instinct. But they was all looking at the banner, and it was like I was just part of the stick that held it up.

'**That,**' said the Prophet of Gork and Mork. '**That's the now-forever.**' Guess you'd say *future*, though orks don't have a word for that. Don't have a word for *past* either. They call it the *eaten-now*. That's what Ghazghkull dealt with then.

And yeah, it was a headbutt. But what a headbutt! Dregmek's brains went up in the air like a cannon shell had hit him, but that weren't even what was so special about it. That was the lightning.

It struck the spike the camp was named after, sticking up from the ground just a few hundred tusklengths from where the fight had taken place. The bolt touched the old metal at the exact moment Dregmek's skull caved in, so it was like Ghazghkull's blow had made the sound of thunder. And unlike normal lightning,

It was green.

Every ork in the camp looked up at the spike, so that nobody even saw the splinters of Dregmek's head rain down onto the street. Angry little loops of electric stuff were crawling all over the rusty spar, like it couldn't all get into the ground at once, and there was a stink in the air like someone'd just turned on some massive machine.

I wasn't looking up. I was looking at Grotsnik, and it turned out he wasn't looking either. 'Cos he was looking at Ghazghkull. And Ghazghkull was looking down at Dregmek – or at least that's where his head was pointing, while he looked at stuff nobody else could see.

Grotsnik, though... well. His face weren't blank anymore. I can tell you that. I couldn't tell you exactly what he was thinking. But I wouldn't have survived working for him as long as I did, without knowing the look the doc had when he was planning something nasty. And that was the look, as strong on his face then as I ever saw it.

Grotsnik wanted to look Ghazghkull over once the fight was done. And the doc, as you can probably guess, was the type to look with his hands. Already had a scalpel in his talons as he slunk towards the boss, in fact, and his making-things-bigger-goggles on. But Ghazghkull just stared at Grotsnik's hand as it reached out to him, and it was like his eye was a traktor beam, lowering the doc's arm to his side again. Ghazghkull could say a lot with a look, and what he said there was dead clear: he might've been Grotsnik's work, but if the doc ever mistook him for his pet, he'd be mince in seconds.

Besides, there was no time for *doctoring*. Running Rustspike was going to be a lot of work, and Ghazghkull needed to find someone to do it while he planned his next move. He didn't need to look far. Dregmek's former second – the big, thin ork who the Prophet had spoken to right before doing in the Deathskull warlord – was now the de facto boss of his whole clan, and was standing right there, looking down at his mashed-up predecessor. Bullets, he was called – or *Finds-Bullets-He-Has-Not-Lost*, on account of his luck. And that's fitting, I s'pose, as he'd just been handed the keys to Rustspike.

'Course, Ghazghkull offered him a fight first. That's just what you do when you kill someone's boss. Manners, right? And Bullets thought about it hard. But for all the work Gork'd put into his shoulders, it seemed Mork'd put a good head on him, too.

'I want to,' he said, looking like his face was wrestling itself. You could tell he weren't lying. 'I *really* want to. But… I reckon… there's gonna be bigger fights, if I serve you. Yeah?'

'Yeah,' said Ghazghkull.

Bullets' face knotted up again, as he thought about that, and then he nodded. Turning and revving his chain-choppa until smoke came out of it, he bellowed for all the street to hear that Ghazghkull ruled Rustspike, and the Deathskull clan with it – and that if anyone had a problem with that, they could go through him.

About a third of the street rushed him then, some 'cos they wanted a shot at the big job, and some 'cos they were just so pumped up from Dregmek getting krumped. But Bullets had a mob of great big gits by his side, and Ghazghkull walked away, confident the chain of command would hold. And I swear, when he walked away from that fight, he was whole tusklengths taller than he had been when he'd come out of Grotsnik's.

In the days to come, Bullets got busy with all the stuff Ghazghkull wanted doing with Rustspike, and the Prophet got busy thinking. He stood out on the third-storey balcony of his boss-fort – a knackered old starship that had been gutted and turned into a slaughterhouse, and which he'd claimed 'cos it still had a lot of its armour – and he looked down over the camp's main trukkway, and he *thought*.

Sometimes he'd get a headache, wincing a bit, then knocking on the side of his skullplate to clear it out. But he only ever thought harder afterwards. And me? I stood by him for six whole days as the camp was transformed, and I said nothing. I just held that banner up, like I'd been told to do.

Ghazghkull had said on day one, that there was to be no more fighting from the looter gangs in the tunnels below. He'd said they was all one gang now, and that he wanted the old human city emptied of anything useful by winter. He hadn't said why. But the orks that worked the undercity had set about the task like hauling-squigs all the same, 'cos they'd known Ghazghkull spoke for the gods. And with the gangs all hacking at the ruins instead of each other, the camp got rich.

Every day, more orks came. On the second day it was just the usual flow of Deathskull prospectors, plus a few mobs from small forts in the badlands, curious about this new git who'd apparently given Dregmek such a pasting. But on day three, Ghazghkull had Bullets announce the Big Rule – that orks from *any* clan could come into Rustspike and not get killed, so long as they accepted Ghazghkull as the boss. And then things went mental. All sorts of mobs started showing up. And since the different clans was still allowed to *fight*, so long as no one was too dead to work afterwards, they had the time of their lives.

That street below Ghazghkull's balcony turned into a riot of different coloured armour. And when I say riot, I'm not doing one of those *metorphors*. It was an actual riot. A massive, joyous street fight between the clans. And it never stopped, as unconscious fighters were always being dragged out, and replaced by fresh fists coming off shift in the tunnels and the foundries. The fighters looked up to Ghazghkull on his balcony, bellowing his name when they won. *And* when they lost. Sometimes they got a nod, or even a side of squig ribs chucked to 'em, in return. Ghazghkull looked down on them all, and on everything else he was making, and he saw that it weren't bad at all.

And then, on the morning of the seventh day, after he'd spent the whole night staring down at the brawl, Ghazghkull turned to me and said that he had a plan.

'I've got a plan,' said Ghazghkull. 'This can't last. The camp's getting full. Soon, these boys'll want more fighting than the Big Rule lets them do. I have to make of Urk what I've made of this camp. Means the other warlords need to go.'

'Just like Dregmek,' I said, with the wickedest grin I could fit on my face.

'Not like Dregmek,' said Ghazghkull, raising a claw to warn me against trying to do any thinking for him. 'That was messy after. Wasteful. And it could've gone worse, and all.'

That was a funny old thing to say, I remember thinking, 'cos it wasn't usual for orks to reckon that anything they'd done had gone anything other than perfectly. It was almost like… well, like *grot-think*. Not that I said that to Ghazghkull, mind. Or anything more at all, for that matter. I just listened.

'**This thing I do next, needs to be *better*. I'm going to beat all the clan bosses at what they do best. Challenge them,**' he said, with the rumbling promise of thunder far away. '**Tests, with Gork and Mork as witness, with terms so they can't argue when I win. Got it?**'

I got it. And so after the boss told me the details, telling me he'd hurl me off the balcony if I forgot any of 'em, he had me fetch grots to send to the clan strongholds as *envoys*. Messengers. Diplomersea-ers, if you want, like the weird git talking to you now. The warlords killed the first lot that went out, of course. And the three sets after that too, 'cos they'd not heard of messengers and thought they were some kind of trick. But in the end they all got the idea. All except Ugrak, the chief of Urk's Goffs, who just sent back the grot's head. But even that was progress. Ghazghkull expected nothing less of him.

And then the Prophet of the Great Green left Rustspike. He told Bullets to look after the camp for a bit, then went to his balcony and bellowed down for all of the ever-spreading fight to hear.

'**I'm off for a bit,**' he said, '**but I'll bring back a planet.**' Then he pissed off out of the camp's gates, with me in tow. And that was that.

Shazfrag was first. The grand speedboss of the Evil Sunz he was, whose full name means *Arrives-At-The-Fight-Before-It's-A-Fight*, and there was no better driver on Urk. Ghazghkull challenged him to a race round the walls of *Where-The-Trukks-Live*, his citadel out in the eastern desert, and brought only a rusty old trike with a knackered squig-gas engine to ride for himself.

That trike shouldn't've left the starting line. It wasn't even painted red. But when Ghazghkull kicked open its throttle, it leapt forward like a chaser-squig after a sand-git, and kept pace with Shazfrag. I was clinging on to the back, pressed fast to the trike's frame and holding on as tight as I could, so I didn't see much of the race. But then I glanced across and saw the boss was dead level with Shazfrag – and that the Evil Sunz boss was reaching out with a shoota aimed at our fuel tank.

I think I did what I did next before I'd actually thought of it, 'cos suddenly my hand had a bolt in it, from the hopper of spare parts behind the trike's saddle, and then it was throwing the bolt right at Shazfrag's face as he leered down the sights of his weapon. Dunno if you've ever thrown a bolt between two vehicles going half as fast as bullets, but it's not something you'd expect to work. And yet that bolt landed right in the barrel of Shazfrag's shoota right as it fired, and the barrel burst like a rotten sporeglobe fungus.

It only set the ork a little off balance, but it was enough. That tiny wobble from the gun blowing up sent Shazfrag through a patch of rough rocks, which turned the little wobble into a big wobble. Then there was a rush of red rock, which I saw was a canyon we were headed into, and a great jagged outcrop sticking out from its wall. And then – 'cos an Evil Sunz git never dies slow – we were riding down that canyon on the wings of a plasma motor explosion. I lost the skin on my back, but Ghazghkull said I'd done good, and that felt better'n having skin, in the end. Everyone thought it'd been Ghazghkull who'd done for Shazfrag, 'cos nobody had seen that it'd been me. And 'cos they thought it'd been Ghazghkull, that meant it *had* been Ghazghkull. Which is how it should be.

Even Shazfrag thought it had been Ghazghkull. Turns out he'd leapt from his bike right before it'd hit the outcrop and exploded. And though he'd leapt straight into a rock, breaking just about every bone he had, he was in good spirits. Shazfrag thought Ghazghkull's trick with the rock had been brilliant, and while he said there'd be no hard feelings if the boss wanted to finish him off, he also said he'd rather follow Ghazghkull and see what happened next. So the boss let him live.

Once the grand speedboss was back on his feet after a couple of days' kip, he loaded his whole horde onto crimson, smoke-belching trukks, and followed Ghazghkull out onto the great western steppe. This was the land of the Bad Moon warlord Snazdakka, who ruled over the steppe like a pirate king with his armada of fort-sized battlewagons, and who called himself the Mega Admiral–

INTERROGATION V

'Stop,' huffed Hendriksen, raising a palm wearily. 'There were six ork clans on Urk, yes? And the conquering of the Death-skulls and the Evil Sunz left four?'

'Yes?' replied Biter, sounding affronted by the interruption.

'So can we just assume that Ghazghkull enjoyed four *astonishing* further victories, and move on from there?'

'If you want that,' said Biter with a shrug, as if Hendriksen had just asked for a handful of turds. The ork had clearly been getting quite into the tale of Ghazghkull's trials, and Falx was ashamed to realise that she had been, as well. But if there was one thing she knew about Hendriksen's tastes in entertainment, it was that he hated the retelling of his enemies' glorious feats almost as much as he enjoyed the retelling of his own.

'Shouldn't we at least get the basics?' protested Cassia, eyes wide in exasperation.

'Agreed,' ruled Falx, before the Rune Priest could argue. 'Give us the whos and the hows of it, xenos, and move on.'

As Biter relayed the change in plan to the prisoner, the grot's lip curled in disgust at the poor taste of its captors. A few terse sentences were spoken, and then presented to them by a surly-looking Biter.

'Snazdakka, the Mega Admiral, Ghazghkull beat in a sea battle. It was on a bone-dry plain. But the Bad Moon thought it was a sea battle, so that was what it was. Ghazghkull wrecked his whole fleet, but he let Snazdakka live. In exchange, the boss got his mighty power klaw... but that's a story for another time. Then it was on to Grudbolg, chieftain of the Snakebites.'

'Hmm,' mused Hendriksen. 'Snakebites... the beastmasters, no? Let me guess, ork – Ghazghkull won Grudbolg's loyalty through some sort of contrived arena battle against monsters.'

'No,' said Biter, with a little grunt of satisfaction. 'Knife fight in a swamp, actually. Grudbolg still refused Ghazghkull after being beheaded. So Ghazghkull held Grudbolg's head against his neck 'til his spine grew back, and gave him another try. He said no again, Makari says.'

'So he cut off his head again?' asked Cassia, squinting in disbelief as Biter nodded.

'And stuck it back a second time. And then Grudbolg said yes.'

'What about Ghazghkull's old clan, the Goffs?' asked Falx.

'They were next, yes,' said the translator. 'Ugrak, their warlord was called. He'd refused Ghazghkull's original challenge in disgust, but as clan after clan fell in line, he came to Ghazghkull in the end, marching to the walls of Rustspike with a whole host of orks behind him. They were just for show, of course – Ugrak wanted to settle things personally, in the Goff way.'

'What sort of fight was it?' asked Cassia.

'Headbutts.'

Cassia winced. 'Really chose the wrong game, didn't he?' she said, and Biter's look was grave as they nodded back at her.

'Yes. Yes, he did. But don't be mistaken, humans – Ugrak was no weakling. As most reckoned, he was the biggest ork on the planet. Or at least, he had been. But when Ghazghkull went down to face him, with all of Rustspike watching from the camp's walls, and all the Goffs watching from the other side, it was like watching a seasoned trooper standing over a stripling, fresh from the grow-hole.'

The grot behind Biter muttered something, and the interpreter nodded to acknowledge it.

'Makari says the boss grew taller even as he walked out towards Ugrak. He grew with each step, like he was climbing into the sky.'

'I'm sure he did,' said Falx drily. 'And did Ugrak survive the headbutting?'

'Just about,' said Biter, wincing hard enough to show a full row of tusks. 'His eyes never lined up right afterwards, and he had trouble speaking, but he lived. Kept his hold on the Goffs, too – his retinue even battered their own skulls in out of solidarity, so they'd look like him. Ugrak's Uglies, they called themselves. Anyway, there you have it. The subjugation of Urk.'

'Not quite,' argued Hendriksen, wagging a sly finger. 'Unlike your sort, I do not struggle to count to four, and you have only recounted three further victories. What of your own clan, the Blood Axes?'

'Oh, yes,' replied the interpreter, as if they'd somehow forgotten. 'That matter was not settled in the open. We are, as you might know, unusual among orks. We don't mind avoiding a fight, if there's something to be gained. And so, on the night after Ugrak's defeat, Genrul Straturgum – he was the warlord of the Blood Axes on Urk, and an *asponnishing* mind – came to Ghazghkull's balcony personally. Got to within stabbing distance, actually, to prove a point. And then offered his clan up on the spot.'

'Sounds cowardly,' sneered Hendriksen.

'Or efficient,' countered Biter, taking off their cap and pressing it to their chest in an incredibly awkward, yet sincere, parody of human respect. 'Straturgum always knew which way the wind was blowing. He was a genius. One of the very best.'

Falx looked over at Hendriksen, and then at Cassia, and found two mirrors of her own perplexion in their faces. Biter's sudden eulogy was... unusual.

'That's... useful,' she concluded, unsure of what else to say. Luckily, Hendriksen filled the silence.

'I have a question, about all of this,' he said, with a glint of fang in his smile as he crossed his arms across the inhuman breadth of his chest.

'I had thought you wanted it kept short,' protested Biter. 'But... yes?'

'Where is the burn scar?'

'Hmm?' asked Biter, not quite following.

'Well, ork. If "Makari" lost the skin on its back during that incredible bike race against Shazfrag,' explained the Rune Priest reasonably, 'it must have a scar that could tell the story for itself! So. Show it to us.'

Of course, thought Falx, as the translator conferred with the captive. While she had put all questions of authenticity aside until Xotal finally emerged from the vivarium deck, Brother Hendriksen might have just found the thread that unravelled the entire credibility of their asset. And yet, while the wily psyker seemed delighted at the trap he had sprung, Falx was surprised to find herself dismayed. Because for all she was dedicated to the attempt to bolster humanity's defences against the ork prophet, somewhere during the grot's narrative, she had begun to... root for him. She *wanted* his story to be true, for all the unholy power it conferred to its subject.

'There is no scar,' said Biter, wrinkling the leathery arches of their nostrils in what Falx had learned was an ork expression of bafflement. But they didn't seem concerned, even when Hendriksen unsheathed his bolt pistol and chambered a hollowpoint shell.

'Then this is not Makari, I'm afraid,' said Hendriksen, gesturing at Ghazghkull's supposed banner-waver with the weapon. 'And we have wasted our time.'

'But of course it is Makari,' replied the ork, as if the old wolf's reasoning made no sense.

'What, Grotsnik had a special balm, did he?' asked Cassia, waving her hands mockingly. 'Or was it Ghazghkull's magic?'

'It was neither,' said Biter, 'but if you listen–'

'Enough,' snarled Hendriksen, his brief satisfaction turning to anger now. 'I have endured enough waste-speak.'

He levelled the weapon, and Falx felt a bizarre flash of regret so strong that it opened her mouth and said '*No!*' before she had time to back the statement up. For all she had done to chain down her impulses over the years, they still took the wheel sometimes, and when she least expected it.

'No,' she repeated, as Hendriksen shot her a hard look of warning, followed by his words in her mind.

+This would not be the first time your fascination with a specimen has led to undue mercy, lord inquisitor. And to great danger.+

But she shot him an even harder look in return, and visualised the words in the manner he had taught her, so he could hear them without invading her thoughts.

True, she said. *But it wouldn't be the first time that said danger had led to a greater reward upon its overcoming, either. Besides, I am your lord.*

+And it is my honour, if not always my pleasure, to protect you. But if you would rather I leave you victim to your own whims, so be it… lord. Indulge these xenos troll-riddles. But never let it be said you make my duty too easy.+

I would never claim that, Brother Hendriksen. But be patient, and trust that I have things in hand. I have just had word from the vivarium, in fact – Xotal is awoken.

+The Cupbearer? By the Throne, Falx! Every day, another league sailed into the dark. I'd hoped you would keep that thing locked up in its vat for good, after last time.+

You wanted the truth, old wolf. And you know Xotal shall find it.

+Forgive me, Lord Falx, if I am less than reassured. But proceed as you will.+

'We shall hear the prisoner out,' said Falx, after the silent conversation was concluded. 'But if it has any desire to live, it should probably explain the miraculous disappearance of this fabled burn scar.' She looked grimly at the xenos' now blank shoulder. 'Not to mention the intermittent appearances of Ghazghkull's supposed handprint, in due course.'

'And remember,' added Hendriksen. 'There is a shell ready in this weapon for the prisoner, should it fail to do so. And as for you, ork? I will take pleasure in inflicting justice with nothing but my hands.'

'I would very much like to kill you, too,' replied Biter, with the strange, mistaken warmth of a returned compliment. 'But *alas*, it will not be so, as Makari will soon explain. If… we may continue?' The beast turned its heavy head imploringly to Falx, and as Cassia let out a low huff of disbelief, she nodded for the translated account to continue. Even if it was all false, she thought – in a place where she was sure the wily old psyker could not overhear – Falx couldn't help it: she wanted to hear more.

CHAPTER FIVE

GHAZGHKULL'S DILEMMA

Unifying Urk, in itself, weren't that impressive. Plenty of orks had done it before, in fact, and there were all sorts of chants about the warlords who'd called that mean little world their own at some point. But then any old bruiser can swallow a borer squig whole. The *real* feat is in keeping one down. Or at least keeping it from making its own, messy way out.

Ghazghkull wanted the stars. But to get 'em, he needed all those tribes he'd just bunched together to play nice, and work together. The idea he wanted to get in their heads was *smekhn-unh-snikhek-nukh*. It's a grot word: means 'hide now, stab 'em tomorrow'. Like, if you want something of someone else's, but you're going to get hurt nicking it, you hide and make weapons and that, until you see a chance to hurt the other person *and* take the thing.

The reason it's a grot word, though, is 'cos it makes no

sense to orks, except maybe Blood Axes. Look at *Bites-Face-Of-The-Face-Biter* here; he hates your guts, but he knows if he's nice to you, he'll get richer and have more stuff to kill you with next time. Biter's weird.

But most orks ain't Biter. If an ork sees something he wants, he'll go at it 'til he's got it, or 'til he dies in the fight. And since what an ork wants is usually just a fight anyway, they can't see the point in waiting. So the Prophet had his work cut out for him.

For a while, he found other fights to distract 'em. There were outliers, and rebels, and orks claiming to have invented their own, rubbish, clans. And then when they ran out, there was space. Urk had a meagre belt of orbital stuff – mostly old human space stations, but long since overrun by orks, who'd lived their own strange lives up there for ages, unreachable from the surface. Until now. Snazdakka, it turned out, had been building massive, explosive-carrying rockets, as he'd always fancied an atomic war. But with their warheads replaced with big metal crates with chairs in, they proved to be decent assault carriers, and soon, Urk's orbit was Ghazghkull's too.

Even Urk's twin moons fell under his hand after that, along with the strange, skinny, clanless orks that lived on 'em. Ships, too – nothing that could get out of the system, but some chunky warships nonetheless, that'd been drifting empty for many-many years. The fleet made Ghazghkull hopeful he could draw his space war out a little longer, by launching an invasion of the system's outer worlds. But then the outer worlds came to Ghazghkull.

There were hundreds of ships. So many that their plasma jets doubled the stars in Urk's sky when they started getting close. And Snazdakka's rockets were just being turned back into bombs again to turn 'em into ash, when word came from a Blood Axe spy station out past the moons: the ships were flying *Ghazghkull's banner*. When I saw the pictures from the making-things-bigger machines, projected on the wall of the throne room, it was like my blood glowed green: there was the picture *I'd drawn*, in the Prophet's own blood, painted half a mile high on the ram-jaws of warships.

The outer worlds were small, and cold, and even more rubbish than Urk. But between 'em they held swarms of orks, and after they started hearing the electric-talking signals coming from Urk during Ghazghkull's conquest, they wanted a piece of it. So they came, in numbers I couldn't believe, heralded by a single question: *'Who we killing, then?'*

And that was when the Prophet ran out of ways to dodge his problem: he'd run out of war. Which meant that soon enough, unless he could convince 'em of that grotly idea of smekhn-unh-snikhek-nukh – of hiding now and stabbing tomorrow – his legions would make war of their own. It was the hardest scrap he'd faced yet.

'Gork's not given me the tools for this,' the Prophet said to me one night on the stormy edge of winter. He was pacing about like a caged squiggoth in the room next to the boss-hall's balcony, which was where he went when he wanted to think, and where nobody else but me was allowed to follow him.

Outside, Rustspike's perpetual inter-clan street fight was still raging. But that night, the racket of roars, gun barks and blade-clashes coming from the fight had an *edge* to it. It had sounded less happy and more angry every day since the unification. And even though Ghazghkull had reinforced the Big Rule with a few beatings of his own, it was getting tested every day.

Tonight, it felt like the brawl was a pool of liquid squig-gas waiting for a flame. And the boss knew that if he was to wade in with his fists, it could be the spark that set it all off; a fire that spread as quick as ork rage, and burned his fledgling empire to the ground. So he was right; Gork's gifts weren't going to solve this.

There was an obvious answer to that, of course, but I didn't fancy getting kicked through a wall, so I kept my mouth shut and lurked in a corner, like I was meant to. That was how me and Ghazghkull talked, for the most part – with me lurking, and saying nothing – and it worked.

'I know, I know,' snarled the boss, stabbing a talon angrily at me, as if I had spoken. **'Mork'll have the answer. And I'll find it. I just need to thi… thi… thnnnnnNNNNGHHHH…'**

It was like something had swooped down onto him. Or right *into* him, by way of his skull. Ghazghkull's enormous body flexed into a crooked, rigid arc, as enough muscles to lift a trukk contracted violently against each other all at once, and his good eye bulged. Then he started to shake.

'Gnnnnnnnn,' said the Prophet, trying to roar through a jaw clenched tighter'n steel. And then, with a splintering crack, one of his fangs shattered in a spray of yellow shards.

The headaches were definitely getting worse. He'd started getting them when he'd been plotting the conquest of the planet. But what had been brief twitches back then were now seizures that could grip him for minutes at a time. They were a laugh to watch, for sure, but I didn't like 'em beyond that. Seeing Ghazghkull weak wasn't right. It was like seeing the sun go out, or seeing a grot help another grot. It was… unholy. And while I knew that fits like this could happen sometimes, when your brain had been minced and grown back, I was convinced that Grotsnik had a hand in it.

Or a scalpel in it, more like.

As Ghazghkull had got bigger, his adamantium plate hadn't

grown with him, nor any of the other new bits in his head. And since Grotsnik was the only one who knew how all the stuff inside the boss' skull fit together, Ghazghkull kept going back to the doc to have his skull reassembled. Rich from his sudden fame, Grotsnik had abandoned his old tent and taken over the towering brew-hut next to Ghazghkull's boss-fort. He had a mob of minders at the door downstairs, and dozens of grots to do his dirty jobs.

But it was the same old Grotsnik. He could've had Gork himself under his knife, and he still wouldn't have cared for anything but his own nasty fancies. He did work keeping Ghazghkull's head together, I won't deny it. But I watched him. I watched him close. I watched him sprinkle stinging-gits on the Prophet's exposed brain. I watched him poke bits of it with a dirty talon, just to see which bits of the Prophet twitched. I watched him leave a spanner inside the Prophet's skull before sealing it closed again, and laughing to himself after. Which was fair, 'cos it was *classic*. But it weren't right.

He watched me watching and all, and he didn't care. Why should he have cared, though? I might've been the boss' grot. But that just meant I could make the run to fetch the boss' morning squig livers without suffering worse than a light kicking. At the end of it all I was still a grot, and if I'd told Ghazghkull not to trust Grotsnik, I'd have been stamped just as flat as any fungus-tender who tried the same thing.

So as Ghazghkull writhed and thrashed, it wasn't even as if I could say I'd told him so. All I could do was watch the show, as he stared blindly through the ceiling and ground his tusks to splinters.

At last it was done, though. Ghazghkull straightened up, cracked his neck with a sound like the suspension coming off a warbike, and vomited angrily for ages. Then he vomited some more, before spitting out a chunk of bitten-off tongue, and using his klaw to lever out the stub of his broken tusk.

'**A beating-of-the-mind,**' he said at last, through a shuddering breath. '**That's what I'll give 'em.**' He said it like he'd just had a quick think, rather than a massive seizure. But that was the thing about Ghazghkull's headaches. Because they stopped his body moving, he couldn't just kick furniture to chase nagging problems away. He had to *think* about 'em. And when his eye couldn't see the real world, I fancied it was seeing the Great Green instead. Down there, in that shell-wrecked, gods-touched cavern of a mind, that was where he was closest to the divine.

'**Hmm,**' he continued, before peering over his shoulder like he'd just spotted me. '**It will be like… What is that thing, where you… shout, to make your mobs kill harder?**'

I just carried on lurking, but the Prophet growled at me, and gestured angrily with his klaw.

'**Come on! My brain hurts. Find the word for me.**'

'A speech?' I snivelled, like I was treading out onto thin ice over a slurry ditch.

'**A speech,**' he rumbled, turning now to face the balcony overlooking the fight. '**Only… like a sort of reverse speech. One that makes your mobs want to kill… less.**'

Answering the boss again would have been testing my luck, so this time I just sneered, but in a sort of admiring way.

'**Fetch Bullets,**' commanded the Prophet. '**Have him round up the other bosses. Then go to the very-cold-hole, with all the grots you can bully up, and get all the meat from it. I'm about to wake the thing we once were, and it'll be hungry.**'

Orks don't record history, for the same reason they don't make tombs. 'Cos the past is dead. And just like dead orks, they reckon it's best left to rot away, rather'n having rocks piled up on it and clogging the place up. Time is cramped for orks, see. *Now* might last forever, but it comes in tiny slices, and there's no point filling 'em with what's been done, when they could be *doing* instead. And besides, just like the dead rot away into stuff that grows into new orks, the past rots into stories, which only get more true over time.

Grots are different, mind. We want to know what those who came before us hated, in case they were things we hadn't thought to hate. And it gives us some small pleasure to insult our masters in a way we'd never be battered for, 'cos they'd never think to try and understand it. So we scratch our woes in secret places: in the tunnels under the drops, the soles of boots we're meant to be mending, and the underneath of trukks. I've cowered under battlewagons that were like your *libories* – axles, drive trains and fuel pumps etched all over with the spite of centuries.

But all there was to know about Urk's history could have been scored on the back end of a bullet. Orks fought each other over rubbish. Sometimes people invaded, and got beaten, and left new rubbish to fight over. Empires grew and collapsed. Orks fought each other over rubbish. You get the idea.

But that night, on the balcony of the boss-fort, something different happened for the first time.

'So you want a fight, do you?'

It was that voice he'd used when he'd called out Dregmek. Not a bellow, or a roar, or a shout, but loud in the same way as a Bad Moon carrier-zepp cruising overhead, travelling through the inside of everything and making loose screws rattle. Even through the din of their brawl, the orks heard it, and a forest of torch-lit tusks turned towards its source. As the last punches landed, with meaty thuds that tapered off like the last drops of a rainstorm, the crowd looked confused, and then angry. *What sort of a question was that?* But Ghazghkull gave 'em no time to answer.

'Do you want the biggest fight there is?' he asked, pointing his klaw down at them all in challenge. **'Would you kill so many the gods lose count, and drown cities in the blood of your boot prints? Would you run in a mob so big it turns worlds green?**

'Would you?' he taunted, in the first silence that'd fallen on Rustspike since that prospector pitched his tent.

The answer was like an explosion, given half in howling, and half in punches to neighbours. Ghazghkull leant right over the balcony and swept the street with a glower, drinking in the pent-up fury of the mobs. Then he replied – and this time he roared.

'Well you won't get that here!'

It doesn't take much to start a riot, when you're talking to orks. The echo of the Prophet's voice was still crashing across the city when the front ranks of the crowd started scaling the boss-fort, but Ghazghkull was ready. The other bosses, who'd been lined up behind him, came forward with iron cudgels, and began smashing every green finger that appeared on the balcony's railing. Every time an ork did manage to start hauling itself over the edge, a sharp *krump* would sound from the grog-vat on top of Grotsnik's premises, where Genrul Straturgum had set himself up with a far-away-shoota, and a body would tumble back into the surge.

Ghazghkull let them come. And after a while, he spoke again.

'You won't get that *here*,' he said, voice flattening the crowd's rage like the pressure wave from a passing fighta-bommer, **''cos it's up *there!'*** He thrust his klaw up at the underlit smog-clouds above the city, and the street's fury faltered a bit, staggering briefly back into confusion.

'We can't fight clouds,' shouted a voice in the press, after a short lull. But even as the barks of agreement began to stack up, the wind picked up, and the clouds began to move. 'See,' came the voice again, as the wider mood swung back towards murder. 'Big wet gits are running already.'

'Look further,' commanded the Prophet. And as he spoke, a patch of smog peeled away on the wind, and showed the stars beneath. **'You've been fighting clouds your whole rotten lives! Throwing yourselves away in battles that change nothing. Battles that bore the gods. But up there, where the stars are, there are battles bigger than your most brutal dreams. There are...** *wars*.**'** He said the word like it was syrup from a git-hive. **'Or there could be, if you only had the hunger to fight 'em.'**

'So get the spaceships,' called out a Bad Moon in armour festooned with glowing, neon-yellow skulls and bones – one of the arrivals from the outer system, I figured – to roars of approval. 'Let's leave tonight!'

'With what fuel?' snarled Ghazghkull. **'And what engines? You think you know space, do you?** *I* **know space. The gods showed it me. It's massive. Your fleets couldn't get an eighth of us an eighth of the way to a decent scrap. And what then – will you get out and push?'**

'Yeah,' said the gaudily armoured pirate, but his heart wasn't in it.

'I can get you there. The gods have told me how. And *when* **we get there, I promise you this – there'll be more to kill than you can even know, now. You'll feel nothing but rukkh-razzha, the most pure battle-bliss, for the rest of your lives. Then, when you die, Gork and Mork will send you back stronger, for more.**

'But there's a thing about fights.' Ghazghkull paused then, looking up at that exposed scatter of stars with his good eye narrowed, and not a single voice stirred under the silence he'd put down. **'The bigger they are, the more they hurt. The more pain you give, the more you get. But then, what do orks think of pain?'** The boss looked down on the sea of faces then, with a glare of challenge, and a look of brutal pride half-formed in the set of his maw.

'Nothing!' came the answer, from many-many-many-many throats at once, and the boss' face split into a triumphant, crack-tusked leer.

'Nothing!' he bellowed back, slamming his klaw through the balcony rail for emphasis. **'And all that's new about the pain of this fight – this *war!* – is that some'll come before it. It'll be the pain of not-fighting. The pain of *waiting*. Are you scared of that pain, orks? Are you too weak to bear it?'**

The crowd thought about that. They thought hard. And as they turned it over in their heads, and the wind rattled the loose scrap plates on the towering slaughterhouse before them, they looked at the warlords who headed their clans, lined up with bloodied cudgels beside Ghazghkull.

'I can take it!' snarled a proper hill of a Goff, from the ground where he'd fallen after getting shot in the heart by Straturgum.

'I'll take it *twice*,' boasted a Deathskull standing next to him, not wanting to be outdone by one of his clan's despised rivals.

'Easy!' cackled a wizened old Evil Sun, waving a red hammer welded together from old bike parts. Then the whole crowd started up, with every ork looking to outdo the ork next to them in their derision of the task. And nobody punched anyone.

'So take the pain,' boomed Ghazghkull, good eye blazing

with hunger for the future that was opening up on the street before him. **'Let it make fire in your blood. Let it starve you, so your tusks are all the more sharp for the feast to come.'**

That was my signal. With a hiss to the other grots lined up along the balcony, I heaved my side of squig-meat up onto the rail and tipped it over, and they all did the same.

'I will give work to your axe-arms until then,' promised the boss, as the hunks of flesh began raining into the crowd with a volley of soggy thumps. **'There are mountains to be smashed, and lakes of oil to drink up in the deep rock. There are forges to be fed. Blades to be made sharp. War machines that need dragging from the nightmares of our enemies. Under my hand, which has the strength of the gods, you will build yourselves into a host that will turn the stars green.'**

Then he threw his huge, plated head back and howled the most ancient of all war cries, which every ork makes with the first breath in their lives, and usually the last, too. Every ork from every clan howled back, until the sound joined together into one great voice.

WAAAGH!

It was like a giant had climbed from its grow-hole beneath the city, and for a moment, with that earth-shaking yell surrounding me, it was like I was back in the Great Green.

I even found *myself* joining in, which shocked me, 'cos that's not what grots do. But when I started, so did every other grot on the balcony. And when they started, so did every grot in the city, until there was a second howl – higher pitched and nastier – skulking into the sky behind that of the orks. All I can say is, in that moment, I wasn't a grot. I was just one bit of something vast and green and terrible, poured into a grot-shaped body.

Maybe Ghazghkull didn't grow much more than usual that night. But every ork in Rustspike, I swear, was half a head taller when that howl was done. And when they were out of its grip, they saw that the clouds above had been whipped away altogether – like they really had been scared of getting beaten up – leaving nothing but stars, behind the crackling green light of Urk's northern aurora.

The aurora was a sign, of course. But not the one I, or any other creature in Rustspike, thought it was. While us grots grinned and cackled at this omen of victory, and the orks barked triumphantly through mouthfuls of gifted meat, Ghazghkull just snarled, and stalked back into his fort. 'Cos he knew the truth – that the green light wasn't just a symbol of the destiny waiting for him up in space. It was a warning from Gork and Mork, telling him not to waste any time in seizing it.

The gods had got bored, you see. And now, at last, something had their attention again, and they were hungry for Ghazghkull to carry out their will. You remember what I said about orks? That if one sees something he wants, he'll go at it 'til he's got it, or 'til he dies in the fight. Well, the ork gods are the same. Only they get other things to do the dying. And in this case, it was Urk.

INTERROGATION VI

As engrossed as she was in Makari's tale, Falx heard the quiet huff of Hendriksen's breath – the one which always preceded a furious interruption – just in time to shoot him an icy look across what she had, concerningly, begun to think of as 'their' side of the cell.

+This grows more preposterous than a drunkard's tale before dawn,+ he thought at her. +Where is that rotten beast Xotal?+

Being prepared for transit. Its current form is… impractical. But it will come. Until then, we let them proceed.

The old shaman deigned only to bare his teeth in reply, but he let Biter continue.

She knew what Hendriksen's problem would be, of course: the complete lack of explanation for Makari's missing burn scar, despite the assurances of an imminent explanation. Admittedly, she was a little surprised herself it had not come up yet, considering the grot was ostensibly speaking for its life. But she was far less bothered about the fact than her Deathwatch companion. If she was completely honest with herself, in fact, Falx was increasingly unsure how much the issue of Makari's authenticity mattered to her at all.

Hendriksen dealt in absolutes. He was Astartes, after all. More than human. And Fenrisian, to boot. In his world, it was great, decisive confrontations between mighty heroes that shaped the fate of the galaxy, and little else mattered. If Makari was not the genuine article, therefore, then it was less than worthless to the Rune Priest. Even if it *was* the genuine article, its entire account would hold little value to Hendriksen if it did not provide some game-changing nugget of strategic information; some vital, pulsating point of data that could be used to set up some dramatic, pivotal confrontation.

But Falx was human, and so was her understanding of the Imperium's struggle for survival. Their miserable, never-ending war was doubtless punctuated by the actions of heroes. And yes, it was true that such deeds could save whole worlds. But what worth was the saving of a world? In the immensity of the galaxy's strife, even the greatest application of individual prowess could only amount to a tiny peak, barely protruding from a sluggish ocean of attrition. Behind the tiny, gleaming spear point of the Adeptus Astartes, the human war machine was a thing of pure *mass*; its quality was defined almost entirely by quantity, and its most infinitesimal changes of fortune were measured in millions of lives. Sometimes lives saved, but more usually lives lost.

Because in the glacial madness of its collapse, the Imperium had willingly blinded itself to any understanding of its foes. Even her own order – the order dedicated to defence against non-human threats at the very highest level, she reminded herself bitterly – had made a taboo of anything beyond the most basic comprehension of adversaries. They thought *hate* would be enough to keep them safe.

'You implied Urk was dying,' said Falx abruptly, in the middle of a story about a teleporter accident that had fused an ork with an entire pack of snotlings.

'Its *star* was dying,' corrected Biter smugly. 'But according to Makari, nobody but Ghazghkull realised this. Most orks just thought it was a really long winter, until it entered its second year.'

Unbeknownst to the translator, Falx knew all about Urk's star. She had subvocalised for the ship's archivist to access all information held on the world once called Urokleas at the start of the interrogation, for the sake of fact-checking.

As Ghazghkull had risen to power, the star had been at the very terminus of its decline, burned down to a dense, radioactive cinder of heavy metals. The green aurora Makari had described had been its death rattle: a brief, final cough of radiation before the core winked out entirely, and exploded in a catastrophic nova.

It had been the handiwork of brute physics, not any so-called gods. And there was certainly no way Ghazghkull could have been aware of what was coming. And yet, as was frequently and maddeningly the case with orks of a certain prominence, *he had acted exactly as if he had been aware*.

'Have Makari tell us of the final days on Urk, and how Ghazghkull filled his time. And then,' Falx added, as Hendriksen threw out his arms like he was protesting an unfair ruling on a wrestling bout, 'you will remind it to explain the matter of the missing burn scars.'

CHAPTER SIX

GHAZGHKULL LOSES SOMETHING

Ghazghkull's peace held, but the mood didn't. By the second cycle of Urk's final, permanent winter, the days were only a couple of hours long, and the street slush in Rustspike barely ever thawed. It weren't just the ice that was new. The camp had changed a lot since the day the Prophet had delivered his beating-of-the-mind, three years before. It was the only city on the planet now – a sprawling mess of factories and foundries that held more orks'n you could imagine. The horizon glowed deep furnace red in all directions, and between the skinny stripes of smoke rising from the burners, the stars were hard and bright, 'cos the clouds had frozen ages ago.

Ghazghkull led his *counsill* of clan-bosses to the boss-fort's balcony one night (it was always night, but you get the idea). And though he didn't say why, one look at the street below made it clear. The orks were a river flowing by torchlight, carrying sacks of scrap for the fires, and pulling wagons full of brand-new shells. But they were *knackered*. Their washed-out, soot-dark faces looked glumly up at their Prophet, and as I looked along with the clan-bosses, I realised what a state they was in.

The burns were new. Radiation's quite nice for orks, which is lucky, given how most meks reckon that shielding reactors is boring. But there are limits. And when there was no space left to put up hammocks round the warmth of the forges, the work mobs had started sleeping in great stinking drifts next to the atomic cores of the giant new tanks. They had growths and blisters and that, but they figured it beat freezing solid.

And where it weren't burnt, the skin of those orks was stretched tight over their cheek-ridges. They was thin as grots, some of 'em. The last of the fungus crops'd been harvested months ago when even the undercity caves had frozen over, and the last of the food-squigs had been minced soon after that. The butchers had turned to snotlings next. And now, as I noticed how few grots there were in the street, I reckoned the snotlings had run out too. But that was fine. It was the way things should be, whether we liked it or not. The gods made us to keep orks alive, even if that means from inside their bellies. We'd be back again soon enough, when things improved.

And that was the last thing I noticed in that sea of filthy, burned, skinny faces: *faith*, that things would still, somehow, get better. Orks always know when a leader ain't worth following any more, and that hadn't happened with Ghazghkull.

Not yet.

But it wouldn't be long, under these conditions, and the boss knew it. Even though he spoke for the gods, he knew he weren't a god himself. The orks of Rustspike were close to giving up, and if he wanted 'em to carry on, he knew he had to earn it. Just as I was starting to wonder how he'd pull that off, the first of his shoulder plates hit the balcony with a clang.

Ghazghkull took off all his armour without saying a thing, each piece dropping to the steel like a boulder, as the camp watched on. He tore off his furs, and let 'em fall to the frozen street. And then, when he had nothing but his skin to keep out the cold, he stepped right to the edge, and spoke in that voice I've told you about before. The one that's big as space, without being a shout at all.

'One week,' he said. **'One more week, and the gods will build our bridge to the stars. The sun's death is just the gods, telling us we're nearly done. But we're not done. And until we are, you work. You work twice as hard. Burn all that is left. Smelt every scrap. Store every drop of fuel. And the flying machines I ordered? The rockets? Make them ready. We will need them. One week.'** The prophet held up a single talon for a long stretch. Then he leant forward and bowed his head.

'Until the gods reward us for the work, I will stand on this spot. Won't eat. Won't drink. Won't _breathe_, when I don't need to, until the gods speak. And if I can take it, you can take it. Got it?'

His last speech had been good. But this one... This one was something else. The crowd made a noise that didn't seem possible from such a bunch of worn-out gits, and it spread and spread, rippling out through the camp until it came from every horizon. Soon, there'd be orks tens of thousands of tusk-lengths away, roaring their lungs out for no reason they knew, except for that the ork next to 'em had started first. Then the work would start.

But for now there was just faith. Faith and shouting. And when the shouting got as loud as it could get, there was another _mirikle_.

Weren't lightning, this time, nor shiny lights in the sky. But it was still green. The thinnest, weakest beam of green light you can imagine, shining right on Ghazghkull. You could barely see it, but I'd swear on everything I ever nicked it was there – proof the gods were watching the boss just as closely as we were.

Ghazghkull didn't move, even when the cheering died off, and the orks threw 'emselves back into their work with new, impossible energy. After a while, the clan-bosses started looking at each other awkwardly. They weren't sure what to do. Bullets even looked down at me, and he got as far as opening his gob to ask, before realising that'd be a shameful thing, and grunting in irritation at himself. He did good. But he still needed answers for the council, so he took an uncertain step towards the boss.

'You all heard me,' said Ghazghkull in a dangerous voice, before the Deathskull's boot even hit the floor. **'There's work to do. Means you lot, too. So sod off. Be useful.'** The doc had appeared on the balcony now too, but the boss had clearly heard him readying his tools, 'cos he carried on in the same breath. **'You too, Grotsnik. I told them I would stand just as I am. So that's what I'll do. There's plenty of burns need patching – go and patch.'**

As the doc stalked off with a black look, I couldn't resist having a little caper on the spot. But I didn't gloat too hard, 'cos I knew I'd be next to be sent away. But as I made to slink off (in a different direction from the doc, of course), the Prophet stopped me.

'The banner stays, Makari. And you with it, so long as you can stand it.'

'Cos there were no days now the sun had died, it was hard to track time. But the foundry towers still sounded their klaxons for shift changes, and I swear Ghazghkull went a whole day without shifting position. I weren't as committed. I writhed about like a soil-git, trying to find some way to stand that didn't make it feel like my arse was going to drop off and shatter, and I had to wrap my nose and my ears to stop 'em getting frost-chewed. At least holding the banner was easy, 'cos my hand was frozen to it.

But the Prophet didn't even look bothered. His whole body was speckled with tiny bits of frost. But that tiny, pale shaft of green light was still shining right onto the top of his head, just as still as he was, even while the city bustled through its mad, final burst of work around him. It was insane. You could hear the hammers smashing like they'd never smashed before, everywhere at once. But there was Ghazghkull standing dead still in the middle of it all, like he was some kind of battery keeping it all running.

Halfway through what would've probably been the third day, the furnaces started going out across the camp. Some had run out of coal. Some had run out of things to melt. But as they stopped churning out fresh steel, the factories started going quiet too. By the time the sun would've been rising on the fifth day, every last wheel had been bolted to every last axle, and the city had stopped.

Ghazghkull's people had, somehow, finished ahead of time. And now, all they had left to do was find whatever shelter they could, and wait for the gods to reward 'em.

The river of orks on the street below dwindled into a stream, and then into a trickle, hurrying 'cos the cold was biting down twice as hard now the fires were out. But even the last few stragglers stopped in front of the balcony before they staggered off to find shelter. And when they did, they took a last look at Ghazghkull, still standing with his head bowed, and barked their allegiance to him.

By the end of the fifth day, I'd been on so many sneaky excursions inside to scavenge furs that I was almost too bundled up to move. I couldn't think about anything except how zogging cold I was. I couldn't even hold the banner any more without losing a hand, so I just huddled in a ball on the left of the boss, and leant it against my side.

But I stayed out there, for all I hated it, 'cos that's what the gods wanted me to do. At one point, the Prophet's chest stopped moving for ages, and I even thought about going to Grotsnik for help. But if Ghazghkull was frozen solid, what good could the doc do? I felt happy then, figuring that if the boss was dead at last, it meant I was free. But then I remembered it probably also meant the gods had abandoned us, and the world was about to end. So I thought I'd at least check on Ghazghkull, before I found somewhere quiet to die.

'You still there, boss?' I said, and my voice was the only sound in all the big, silent camp. There was no answer. But for all that I was a creature made for slinking away from duty, I found I just couldn't leave.

'Yeah,' Ghazghkull said at last, with a cough as his chest shuddered into movement again. **'Just forgot to breathe for a bit. Gods are coming. Not long now.'**

Nobody was in the factories to work the klaxons by then, so there was no way to tell how much time was passing. And I kept losing big chunks of time. I'd get groggy after a big bout of shivering, then wake up without realising I'd even been asleep, with no idea how long I'd been out. I might've been dying, now I think of it.

I woke up once and saw snow was falling. Which was weird, 'cos there were no clouds in the sky. I found out later, it was the heavy bits in the air, turning solid and falling to the ground. That was bad news. The next time I came round it was totally black everywhere, as the last torches in the street had all guttered out. But that green light was still shining – the only light, probably, on the whole of Urk – and it still shone right on the frozen white shape of Ghazghkull. I took a breath to ask if he was dead yet, but then I blacked out myself.

But one time I woke, and there was light. Not daylight, and not the green light either. Weird, coloured light in the dark, like a squig-tallow candle flaring. I wondered if the camp was on fire. But the light was coming from *space*. Blinking, I raised my head and peered up through the breathing-hole I'd left in my furs, to look at the top of the sky. And there was a great big hole there. It had this ring of light all round it, like you see when a warphead's about to get a burst skull from too much dodgy-thinking. A big hole. In space. And something was coming out of it. I was so cold I think my brain had half-stopped. But then it all came together. *The gods!*

I looked to Ghazghkull, but he might as well've been a statue. Icicles and everything. *Oh no you don't*, I thought. *I am not zogging well outliving you, you big sod.* And I will never know where I found this energy. But before I knew it, I was on my feet, tingling with proper anger at the idea that the Prophet could have died right on the brink of leading us all to glory.

'Boss,' I croaked. '*Boss!*' But he didn't budge, even after loads of tries. So I poked him with the banner.

'Hmm?' said Ghazghkull, very, very quietly, like he was waking from some dream that was realer than the world.

'The gods are here,' I said, as the light fell bright and strange over the drifts of air-snow that covered the camp.

The ice on the Prophet's body cracked, and then it started to fall away in thin sheets. Beneath it, his skin steamed like he was being born all over again, and muscles were twitching for the first time in days. With a crack like a cannon barrel breaking after a botched shot, that mountain of a body straightened out at last, and Ghazghkull shook his head to clear the worst of the frost. Then he squinted up at the weird, quiet dawn, and nodded slowly, like he knew what he was looking at.

I didn't, mind. But when the thing was almost all the way out of the hole, it was obvious. It was a massive, massive spaceship. Loads of spaceships, in fact, but all smashed together at weird angles. So still a sort of spaceship. Whatever it was, it was big enough to hold every ork on the planet, and then some, plus every gun, bullet, tank, bike and dread they'd spent the last three years building. Ghazghkull had delivered on his promise, and so had the gods.

'I TOLD YOU GITS!' bellowed the Prophet across the crispy silence of the camp, in a voice loud enough to shake the snow off roofs across the street. He'd never been louder, but he weren't angry. He was the opposite. In fact, even though I've seen him feel a lot of things over the years, I think that was the only time I ever saw Ghazghkull feel pure triumph, at least without a load of frustration running under it over how he should've triumphed harder.

'I TOLD YOU!' he roared again, voice raw with exhilaration. 'NOW STOP HIDING LIKE A BUNCH OF GROTS, AND GET YOUR BOOTS ON. IT'S TIME FOR WAR.'

You wouldn't have believed that just minutes ago, Rust-spike had seemed dead and empty. Ghazghkull's summons weren't even done echoing when the camp exploded into life. Under the nasty, flickering, orange-purple light of that hole in space, orks poured from doorways, from the under-city shafts, and even from burrows they'd dug to escape the worst of the freeze. At the launch pads that'd been built all over the sprawl of Rustspike, cans piled up at the bottom of gangways, as orks downed the last half-heated tins of grot meat, and charged aboard their assault transports.

There were a lot of piles of cans, 'cos there were a lot of transports. When the ships had come from the outer system, carrying all the orks who'd heard about Ghazghkull's growing legend, the boss had ordered them all sawn up, 'cos he'd known they'd be no use for what he'd need to do next. He'd had the bits dropped to the surface, and rebuilt into short-range transports, ready for this moment. These things had been made to burn fast and hard, like those nasty long-leg squigs you use for hunting fast stuff, but which drop dead after a few sprints.

They'd need all the speed they could get, though. The gods don't like to make things easy, after all, and even as the first transports were climbing into the sky on fat plumes of smoke and fire, a knackered-looking mek came running out onto the balcony with bad news.

'The hulk ain't stopping!' he barked, with the type of anger that's the nearest an ork gets to panic. It was drifting right past Urk, he said, by which he meant 'whipping past like a comet', since apparently stuff moves really fast in space.

Somehow, though, Ghazghkull was ready for that too. As well as all the transports, it turns out the boss had set his pet meks to work on some *even faster* machines. Ramships, they were, and they made the troop carriers look like shell-gits. Before any of the transports had even climbed higher'n the top of the spike, they came screaming out of their silos on fusion drives so fierce they would've mashed a normal pilot, and pissed off into space. And their pilots weren't even mashed. 'Cos the ramship pilots were brains.

Shazfrag's best-worst racers, they were. The kind who love going so fast that you *know* they're gonna get blown to bits in crashes. So Grotsnik had been given orders that when any of 'em ended up in his klinik for repairs, they'd be offered a deal: if the Evil Sunz gave up their bodies, they'd be given the fastest, most killy deaths ever. Well, it weren't really a deal, as Grotsnik was told to just put their brains in the rockets anyway, but all of 'em said yes anyway.

They did Shazfrag proud that day. As the transport swarm started climbing into orbit, Ghazghkull looked up at the hulk flying past Urk, and counted down under his breath. Right as he reached two-and-a-bit, and nearly all at the same time, the ramships smashed into the big derelict, leaving angry little holes all down one flank.

'You zoggin' did it, boys,' said Shazfrag, who'd come out onto the balcony to watch by now, and he sounded like he was having some emotions. 'You'll always be the real brain-boyz to me,' he whispered, doing something with his arm and his face that might've been a salute.

I didn't know what the ramship pilots had done. I'm not sure Shazfrag did either. But there was no time to ask. 'Cos the balcony was shaking, and so much smoke was pouring up around us that I thought an assault transport was taking off right underneath us. I was nearly right.

'**Hold on to something,**' Ghazghkull commanded me, and strode back into the boss-fort with a brutal grin on his face. '**This might be rough.**' As I hurried inside after him, a big metal shutter slammed down across the door behind me, sealing off the outside world. There was a few seconds of dark, before a load of flickering red lights came on, and at last I realised why Ghazghkull had got me to round up grots to paint the whole building red a few months back. And why all those meks had been down in the basement for ages, working on big weird machines.

Clocked it yet? Well, remember how I said the boss-fort had been a starship, once? Yeah, well. Turns out Ghazghkull had got it working as a starship again. And now it was launching into orbit.

It was a short, scary trip. Well, scary don't do it justice, really. I spent it face down, clinging to a pipe to stop from sliding across the boss-hall, and pretending I was in a nice, safe hole.

I did look up in the end, as Ghazghkull had his meks show us the view from outside on a big screen, and I found out what the ramships had been about after all. They was anchors! Every one of 'em had been linked to a gigantic traktor cannon on Urk's fatter moon. And with a whole row of 'em lodged in the middle of the target, it was tethered like a marsh-squiggoth full of harpoons. The harpoons hadn't stopped the hulk, which we later called *Wurld Killa*, but they'd slowed it enough that the assault swarm could catch up and smash into it.

We smashed into it.

The boss-fort went in first, through one of the holes the rams had punched. The boss had his meks switch on some special electric bubble thing that'd let us breathe, even with the big hole we'd just flown through being open to space. Then the balcony shutters came down, and out we rushed: the boss and me, as well as the six clan-bosses of the counsill, all their hardest orks, and Grotsnik.

I'd hoped that we'd find the ship empty. But Gork likes nothing better than kicking a grot right in the hope. So of course, the big metal cavern we'd set down in turned out to be full of horrible, slavering... *fings*. You know, the ones you find lurking about in the warp. Daemons, I think you call 'em. But I didn't know that at the time, having never seen a living thing that weren't either orkoid, or one of Urk's native git types, so they were just *fings*. And they was all staring right at the balcony with mad, glowy eyes.

I was terrified. But Ghazghkull? Time of his life, I swear. he knew those nasty, squiggly, tentacly, leathery-wingy fings'd be the first enemies he'd ever killed that weren't orks, and that was a bit of a special moment for him. He looked round at the six bosses, who'd tooled up in their best gear during the trip, and at all the scar-covered, snarling orks pouring out onto the balcony behind them, and saw they felt exactly the same. It was a proud moment for him, this first conquest of what was technically big enough to be a new world, and he scrunched up his face for a second as he thought of some words to mark the occasion.

'Do 'em in,' he said. And then, 'cos there was none of that *gravity* up here, at least in this bit of the ship-mess, he simply jumped, and sailed into the daemons like a brick thrown by the arm of Gork himself. Bullets was next, chain-choppa raised, and then Shazfrag, whooping with the thrill of being able to fly. Then Ugrak with his wonky face, and Grudbolg with his club bigger'n I was, and Snazdakka in a floating cloud of unmoored trinkets, and Straturgum with the nastiest pair of knives I ever saw. And where the Prophet went, his banner had to go too. So off I jumped an' all.

Those seven orks and their mobs had saved up three years' worth of wanting to kill stuff for this moment, and they carved into the daemons like a fusion torch through squig tallow. Not even Ghazghkull, the best counter I ever met, could've kept up with the tally of monsters they cut to pieces. They killed so hard, and so fast, that the air filled up with blood, and we had to swim for a bit.

'Course, they made it through, caked all over in the grim, icky pulp of the daemons. And as a fresh wave of screeching, racing shadows started pouring into the cavern through three different tunnels at once, they realised this had only been their first taste of the feast of violence that awaited them here. That big lump of stuck-together ships was *infested*, so it was, and being as big as a runty moon, it was quickly obvious that nobody was gonna get bored for ages.

Not that a grot's opinion counts for much on these things, but I'd even have argued there were *too many* daemons on that ship-thing. And as mighty as they were, even Ghazghkull and his boss-mob might've been overwhelmed in that cavern, if they'd been left on their own to fight the tide. But it was like Ugrak always said: orks are strong, but they're even stronger when there's loads of 'em.

And soon there were loads of 'em in that cavern. Transport after transport swooped through the mek's field with a snapping, crackly pop, and depending on the enthusiasm of the pilots, either set down somewhere near the boss-fort, or just smashed through one of the cavern's walls to get deeper into this new world. Mobs came leaping off ramps to join the fray, and then eventually bikes, dreads and heavier stuff, as the bigger ships started arriving. At one point in the fight, some Bad Moon lads even managed to get a full-on *battle-wagon* out, and you should've seen the joy on the faces of its turret gunners as it drifted through the air, spinning clumsily on its long axis, with a flock of fiery-winged nasties doing their best to peck through its armour.

It weren't long before the warriors of Urk outnumbered the warp-fings on their own turf, and even before the cavern was all mopped up, ecstatic mobs had started to push into the unmapped depths of the ship. Those ships what were intact enough to make a second trip, lumbered back down to Urk for more fuel and more orks, and Ghazghkull's war was on at last.

I weren't so scared, now that I'd seen those horrors crumple up like bags of fried squig gizzards on the boss' fists. And by the time we'd reached a bit of the ship where there was gravity again, and we could run instead of pushing ourselves off the walls, I had a wicked grin plastered all over my nasty little face. When humans run, they get tired, especially when they're running into wave after wave of abommynations from the warp. But the more clumps of fings the boss-mob ran through, the faster they went, and the louder they shouted.

There was a moment, running right behind Ghazghkull down a huge corridor in the depths of the ship, when we heard a proper racket coming from up ahead. It was a shrieking, roaring din of such a size that I had a moment of panic, thinking maybe we was about to meet our match. But it was just more orks, as it turned out – a load of rowdy Death-skulls, mostly, who'd come in through another hole further down the ship. Oh, how the two mobs laughed as they nearly smashed into each other. The Prophet even let 'em have a bit of a punch-up, just for the joy of it, so good was his mood that day.

That day bled into what must've been another, and another, and what I guess might've been a whole week, until we'd been fighting for as long as we'd spent waiting on that balcony before the gods sent the ship. And in all that time, I doubt half an hour went by without something with loads of teeth getting busted up by a fist or a shoota just a few tusklengths away from me.

Orks sleep sometimes, when there's nothing better to do. But they don't *need* it. Grots do, mind. And we can't keep up a run for more'n a couple of hours, let alone a week, especially when we're half-starved and weakened from cold like I was after the last days of Urk. But it was as if the gods had let me opt out of being a grot for a while, and be Makari instead, so long as Ghazghkull was pressing forward and needed his banner beside him. The other orks in the boss-mob were well impressed. 'He's still goin'!' they'd exclaim, as I barrelled along on my skinny little legs, and they'd even slap me on the back, but in an *approving* way, rather than to try and break my spine.

In time the boss-mob split up, as each of the clan-bosses ran into enough of their respective lots to put together big mobs of their own and strike out in a new direction. Even Grotsnik managed to scare up a mob, made up of all the orks he came across who'd had parts of 'em replaced with other things.

Of course, there was no plan for how to cover the whole of the enormous botch-job of a spaceship, and there certainly weren't no map. But it was like someone had tipped a sack of angry stripe-gits into a locked-shut brew-hut (which I'd seen happen several times on Urk, as it was a popular joke), and eventually, Ghazghkull's counsill bosses reported back from all over, and it seemed we'd pretty much reached the end of the ship in every direction.

There'd still be pockets of fings hiding out here and there, but we had *control*, more or less. Or so we thought. There weren't an obvious centre to the ship, but one day the boss' meks found the button they were absolutely certain should make the whole thing sod off into the warp and fly off towards its destiny. So that was the bridge, then. But although they'd checked the electric pipes and everything, the button didn't do anything. Then one of 'em managed to get some of the cracked old screens on the bridge working, and after fiddling about looking at different empty rooms, they found a feed from the city-sized chamber where the warp engines were. Or where they were meant to be. But there was something else in there instead. Warp stuff. *Nasty* warp stuff. I don't understand all that business, so the explanation the meks gave washed right over me. I think Ghazghkull could've understood it, if he'd wanted to. But he didn't see the point, when he could just go and solve the problem by kicking the guts out of it.

The Prophet started walking at what you'd call a leisurely pace down the crooked spine of the ancient derelict. And as word got round that Ghazghkull was headed for a showdown with something *proper big*, orks started flocking to the middle of the ship to follow behind him. When we reached the place where the engines'd been, there were enough orks behind my banner to have filled the old, pre-Ghazghkull Rustspike, and they was all chanting what'd become a sort of unofficial holy song for the prophet.

'Here we go, here we go, here we go,' it went.

Went on like that for ages, usually, before changing to the word 'orks' said over and over again to finish with. I reckon it'll probably lose something in translation, but I'm sure Biter'll make a go of it.

Anyway, as the song reached its peak, Ghazghkull stepped out into the enormity of the engine chamber. And even though the room was so huge it had clouds and that at the top of it, that chant of 'orks, orks, orks' was big enough to fill the whole space in an instant. Just like that, the place felt like it was *ours.*

We'd still have to fight for it, though. Suspended in its centre was a big, ring-shaped platform, with tech all over it, connected to the chamber's entrance with a long, skinny bridge. And below the bridge and the ring, filling the whole of where the floor should've been, there was a chasm with stars at the bottom. Space, I reckoned. But since we could breathe and all, there must've been some sort of force field on the way down.

And in the middle of the ring was the problem. It was, as far as I could tell, a great big hole punched in reality, and it glowed with the same sickly, orangey-purply light that the ship itself had emerged through, in the sky over Urk. That was what needed shutting, apparently, before we could get the engines on and head off towards our destiny. So, needless to say, every ork present who'd brought a shoota started firing right at it. That just seemed to make it bigger if anything. But it wasn't worth giving up on the plan, so Ghazghkull had a couple of mek-built artillery pieces hauled up, and pounded away at it for an hour or so. That didn't work either, but I'd be lying if I said the boss looked disappointed.

'**Looks like I'll have to do this myself,**' he announced, to a deafening cheer, and started walking up that long, steep bridge towards the ring.

It would've been a bit of an anticlimax if he'd just... got there, of course. But the gods was kind: as Ghazghkull got a quarter of the way up, the glowy hole flashed red a few times, and out climbed a *proper brute*. It was a fing, but it was the fing version of a Ghazghkull, if you know what I mean. A Big Daemon, I think you call 'em. And you know how warp-fings come in different sorts of... themes, based on different ideas that humans reckon are bad, like disease, or enjoying yourself, or change? Well, this was one of the ones where the theme was 'anger', with horns and big wings and a magic whip and all that.

Ghazghkull actually rubbed his hands in glee as he saw it come out. I have to say I was less excited, but it wasn't like he'd given me the day off banner-waving, so I put one knobbly foot in front of the other and carried on following behind him.

'**Nah,**' said Ghazghkull though, after I'd made it about fifteen steps, and held out his hand in front of me like a wall. '**It'll wreck you. It's alright. Wave the banner from here.**'

It probably won't surprise you that I didn't argue. I stayed at the foot of the bridge, at the very front of that massive crowd of orks, and none of them so much as jostled me for a better view, 'cos I had the banner.

Ghazghkull couldn't keep the swagger out of his step, he was that excited. He'd been happy enough to fight the hordes of nasties in the cavern when we landed. But this, at last, was a real challenge. The Big Angry Daemon was bigger'n Dregmek and Ugrak stacked together, and I thought it might actually have been bigger'n him, or at least taller. But best of all, it was something mega to kill that wasn't an ork.

Personally, I wasn't fully confident. I mean, I didn't *doubt* Ghazghkull, as such. But then the grot in me had a Gork-smacked good instinct for when to run from a fight, and its scarper-sense was tingling hard now. This scrap looked like it was gonna go down the same way as Ghazghkull's fight with Dregmek, but in reverse. That Big Daemon was taller'n Ghazghkull, like I said, and it might've been lighter, but it was all lean, ropy muscle and long reach, plus that magic whip to boot. It looked like it was going to dismantle him at a distance, and it had the high ground and all.

Sure enough, as he waded up towards it, the fing twisted about and weaved to and fro, striking down at Ghazghkull with that horrible purple lash to put him off balance. Would've put him off balance, too, if he'd tried to avoid it. But Ghazghkull was way too hard for that. He just let it hit him right in the chest, carving a big bit of his armour off along with some of the meat beneath, and then in his left hand, where it sent his thumb spinning off into the dark below. But that'd been the moment he was waiting for. The lash snagged for a moment on his wrist armour, and he grabbed it with his good hand, before yanking it out of the fing's grasp, and chucking it into space with a sneer. His hands were smoking from gripping it, and he was down a thumb, but they'd still work. And more than that, the boss had an army of orks watching the fight, who all knew for sure he'd win.

'Lost yer whip,' said Ghazghkull, nodding down at the distant flicker of the falling weapon, and I think it was the nearest thing to a joke he ever made.

The big fing did a big hissy roar, and spread its claws wide – posturing, basically. But Ghazghkull was having none of that. He just sprinted right at it, faster'n you'd believe something that big could move, and uphill too. Everyone knows you can't go fast in armour – it's either one thing or the other, right? A trade-off. But Ghazghkull didn't do trade-offs. Some orks are clever, and some are strong, he'd said to me when we met, and he was both. 'Cos whenever Ghazghkull had a choice between two things that he wanted, his answer would always be to take both of 'em. Ghazghkull believed you could go fast in armour, so he went fast in armour.

As he ran, he arched the whole of his mountainous bulk backwards, rearing for an almighty punch. And you know, don't you, that when the snarling daemon had got itself good and ready for that, he chucked out a leg fast as lightning, and kicked it right in its stupid, warp-spawned guts. Every ork's got a favourite god out of the two, and when all those who favoured Mork saw such a perfectly done bit of gittery, they lost the plot. The cheer was so forceful it was like weather, and the most incredible thing happened – at the very peak of the ork roar, the hole the fing had come out of sputtered and went dim for a second.

The monster was staggered by the gut-kick. Only for a heart-beat, but that was all the boss needed. He charged in so fast I'm surprised he didn't overtake his own foot, and just smashed into the daemon with all the elegance of a scrap-train hitting a cliff. He barrelled the horror to the ground, pinning it there under his enormous weight, and that made all the Gorkers in the crowd erupt. The hole in the world crackled and went dark again, and for longer this time.

The fight was over then, in truth. All the agility in the warp ain't no use when there's a massive warboss sitting on top of you. And it wasn't like Ghazghkull was gonna give his enemy time to think of a way out. Even before his foe's back hit the steel, the Prophet's forearm was coming down, and it hit like a boulder. That arm thudded down again and again and again, while the boss held the daemon's horn with his wounded left hand. They weren't *punches*; he was using his whole arm like it was a club, for its raw weight, smashing it down in such quick succession you'd swear it never came back up again after each strike. And all the while that stupid monster just scrabbled at him hopelessly with its claws. The crowd began chanting in time with the blows, barking the word 'orks' fiercer and fiercer with each hit, and the warp-hole started pulsing on and off, so the whole chamber was strobing to the rhythm of the Prophet's rage.

Ghazghkull kept hammering down long after the daemon stopped fighting back. I don't *think* those things can die, so I couldn't say he killed it. But it was busted up so bad it couldn't move, and when he'd got bored of battering it, Ghazghkull picked up the body and chucked it back through the hole in the world. And then with nothing else to fight, the boss squared up to the guttering portal itself with a grimace of pure hate.

'**Is that it?**' he bellowed into the warp, voice soaring with the contempt of the gods themselves. '**That was *pathetic!*** ' he roared, and I swear if it was possible for an unknowable rent in the fabric of space to cower, that's what I saw happen then. **'Send something bigger!'** demanded the Prophet.

But nothing came out. There was just the hole in the world, standing between Ghazghkull and the galaxy he'd claimed. I'll admit we still had one big problem, which was that we were still stuck drifting around Urk's dead sun, until there was a way of getting that hole closed. But of course, Ghazghkull had something in mind.

Dunno if this will surprise you, but he headbutted it. Or at least, that's what I heard he did. And you might scoff, humans, but to an ork, a headbutt is something… spiritual. To smash a problem with your head is to solve a problem with the gifts of Gork *and* the gifts of Mork: hitting something with the thing that you think with. It's the opposite of giving a speech, but it's also the same thing, because speech is just another way of hitting people with your brain. Beatings-of-the-mind, right?

Now, I can see the big hairy human's face fur start to flap, 'cos I said I'd only heard about that headbutt. I suppose, then, that I'd better explain where I was, or he'll only stop me again for more stupid questions.

The truth is, for all the weird, special status I had as Ghazghkull's banner-waver, I couldn't opt out of being a grot. The same rules as ever still applied. And I'd been cheering Ghazghkull on so hard while he smashed in that daemon, waving that banner about with all my strength, that I'd forgotten the first rule of surviving as a grot: *always look behind you*.

So as Ghazghkull walked towards the portal over the carcass of his enemy, I felt a set of gnarled talons settle on my shoulder, and smelled the stink of rotten fangs from right behind my neck. Grotsnik. And with all the orks around me totally consumed with the action up on the bridge, nobody was in a position to give two teeth about me, even if they'd been inclined to.

'Hello, Makari,' he said, in that sneaky way where you sound really friendly but you're clearly intending murder. 'What an amazing day, eh? You must be dead proud of the boss.'

'What you here for?' I said, baring my fangs as I turned round to scowl right into Grotsnik's long, greedy face.

'I've come to commiserate you,' he said, with slimy mockery on his miserable face. 'On the terrible accident you had, tripping and falling right at the moment of the Prophet's victory. Such a shame,' he said, and kicked me off the edge of the deck into space.

I could hear the cheering as I fell, and the light of the chamber flickering more and more intensely as it vanished into the sky. And then I could hear nothing, 'cos I was through the force field, and out in space. Already, my eyes was freezing over, and everything was getting misty, but I could just see the belly of the great ship, sliding past silently overhead. And then something green, which confused me, until I saw the dirty talon on it, and realised it was Ghazghkull's thumb. I grabbed it before my arm froze stiff, so at least I wouldn't be completely cut off from the Prophet as I died.

But it was so cold, it made being back on the balcony with the boss during his long, cold wait seem like it'd been a summer day. And that cold had been fine, 'cos I'd had Ghazghkull nearby. Now it was just me. And his thumb, I suppose.

That, I reckon, is when Ghazghkull must have sealed the rift. 'Cos there was a pulse of green light from the direction the ship had slid off in, as if Gork had clapped his hands around space. It spread out in a ring, speedy as light, and rippling across space with all the energy of every ork crowded in that chamber on the ship. There was a second, brighter flash then, which must've been the engines igniting at last, but it weren't the nasty bruise-colour of warp light. It was as green as green could get.

The light got wider and wider in a huge, crackling, silent sphere, and dying as I was, I was happy just to be able to look at something so powerful. Then it shrank back into a tiny point of light, and winked out. The Prophet was on his way at last, and I was – to my knowing, anyway – the last green creature left in the whole of the system.

My vision started fading then, and my body had frozen stiff. But I was turning slowly in the black, and as I drifted, my eyes followed the ring of green still spreading from that first pulse. It was like that first sight I'd seen in that vision of the Great Green, I realised, where that little mote of light had spread across the whole of that dark cave and made it good and holy.

Just as I realised that, the green ring touched something small and hard and angry in the dark. Urk's star. That green light poured into the wrathful little ember, and made it quake. Cracks of light shot across its dark surface, and it looked – as much as anything ever did – like something that was about to explode. It exploded, and as a wall of emerald light slammed towards me, I figured it wasn't a bad way at all to go, for a grot.

And since there was nothing after that, I suppose that's when I died. Which explains why I don't have a burn scar any more.

ACT THREE

INTERROGATION VII

'That's when you died,' repeated Falx, rotating the statement in her head to see if she was missing something.

'That is what happens, when you fall into space,' explained Biter helpfully, as Makari's scratchy voice piped up again. 'They say they're not bitter about it. Nine years, they lived. That's ancient for a grot, you know.'

Cassia was next, leaning forward with a groan of canvas and wrinkling her nose in confusion.

'But you're here, right now. In the room.' She turned her head ponderously towards the translator, giving them a profoundly weary expression. 'Biter, is this a sodding *ghost story*?'

'Do not be silly,' reprimanded the Blood Axe. 'Ghosts are not real.'

'But you died,' said Hendriksen quietly, as if confirming the most trivial detail. 'Is that right? You died, did you?' He had been standing motionless since Makari had said it, and now he only moved to fix the prisoner with the coldest, glassiest blue stare. He was calm as Makari nodded: dead still, with all the usual restless bluster drained from his stance, and Falx knew all too well what that meant. The darkness was stirring beneath the ice.

Cassia shifted in her seat as she felt the Rune Priest's silent rage ripple through the room, and reached out towards the Space Marine with an uncertain hand. Falx didn't need a psyker's gifts to know where Hendriksen's mind was at, but she did not reach out to him. She had decided to let it happen.

It would not have been her choice. She wasn't even certain she *had* a choice. But as engrossing as Makari's tale was, this latest stretch of credibility was… ridiculous. It demanded testing. And besides, she had been growing increasingly uncomfortable, for some time now, with the feeling that the interrogators were being played. The balance of power needed redressing, and Hendriksen was an expert leveller of playing fields. What use was a wolf if you never let it run off the leash?

'Go on,' she said quietly, without even looking in the Rune Priest's direction, and violence happened.

He moved like wind-stirred snow, still one moment, then whipping over the ground, as if carried by some unstoppable force. And when her eyes caught up with him, he had Makari by the throat, held nine feet in the air with chair, chains and all swinging beneath them. And Hendriksen's bolt pistol, still loaded with its hollowpoint shell, was in his free hand.

The grot's limbs were stretched taut by the weight of the steel, tendons looking close to popping from the strain, and the creature's eyes bulged from the clammy skin of its face. Hendriksen's rune-inscribed fist closed around its scrawny neck, looking as if the smallest clench might pulverise the grot's spine to jelly. But still his face was calm. Falx had underestimated the old wolf – he had not lost his temper at all.

'So what would happen,' enquired Hendriksen, gesturing with the gun, 'if I were to kill you now?'

Makari squeezed out a rattling croak.

'They say they would die,' said Biter, who had been leaning, untroubled, against a bulkhead throughout the encounter.

'And then?'

'And then, I should imagine you would have to clean up.'

Hendriksen hurled the prisoner to the floor, chair and all, like a fresh-emptied ale horn, and bones snapped in the tangle of steel and green flesh. Then he rounded on Biter.

'You like to play games, do you not, ork?' said Hendriksen, moving across the cell until he towered over the mercenary in their shabby leather coat. But Biter continued leaning, with an expression of replete ease, even as the Rune Priest's face loomed down to within a few inches of their own.

'You think your safety is guaranteed here, I suppose? *A guest in our hall.*'

'Not at all,' said Biter. 'But that is not a concern. You know, after all, that *my* kind believe in… *re-imcantation*. But you would be a fool to kill me, when I have not told you a lie yet.'

'Is that so?' said Hendriksen, still icy quiet, as he gestured to the shape on the floor, hissing in pain behind him. 'Yet you would have us believe the tale of a prisoner who speaks of events they were not present for, and then recounts *their own death*? You think yourselves clever, I know, *intelligents officer*. But this deception has been poorly clad. It reveals your wit as that of a beast.'

'I do not see what is so hard to understand,' protested Biter, seeming genuinely baffled. 'The grot with the burn scar died, Makari lives. And they have much tale left to tell.'

'So what about the other mark?' asked Cassia, with studied calm, and Biter looked even more confused. 'The burn, in the shape of Ghazghkull's hand.'

'Ah,' replied the ork. 'That one… comes and goes. Like… what is the thing, where your *saints* begin to bleed sometimes, for no reason?'

'Stigmata?' guessed Cassia.

'Yes. The burn scar belonged to the grot who died. The hand mark belongs to Makari. It's special.'

'Right…' murmured Cassia, unsure of where to go from there.

At that moment, however, an alert message pulsed gently over Falx's vision. It was the brig's guards, reporting that the shipment from the vivarium had arrived at last. After muttering a barely sincere prayer of thanks to the Throne, Falx suppressed a shiver at the thought of the shipment's contents, and cleared her throat to speak.

'Luckily for us all, we can settle this matter without recourse to further… debate, as the Cupbearer, Xotal, has arrived.'

There was a muted rumble of wheels in the darkness down the brig corridor, and then a dull light, moving towards them past the reinforced cages that lined the passageway. The light was the headlamp of a haulage servitor, trudging along behind a low, heavy cart. As the vehicle approached, nightmare faces loomed briefly to either side of it in the dim glow of the lamp. Long, predatory fingers probed out between the bars of cages, then fell into the darkness as the cart passed. Something hissed in cruel anticipation. Many of the horrors down here had seen Xotal's visits before, and they knew what was to come.

The door to Makari's cell rose with a rattle, and the servitor pushed the cart inside. It was around nine feet long and chest high, rounded at the front and tapering at its rear end, like a casket built for a giant. It was covered with an ornate leather drape, and a console protruded from a mount on one side, bearing a flickering green oscilloscope and a dusty speaker grille.

The servitor had some difficulty bending in order to clamp the cart's wheels, and the sight of the thing spasming, with a look of abject incomprehension on its face as it turned one way and then the other, was utterly wretched.

'For pity's sake,' snarled Hendriksen beneath his breath, and began moving over to assist the servitor. But Biter, to Falx's surprise, was already there, bending to lock the clamps with speed that was at once liquid and graceless, and then smoothly – *gently*, even – turning the servitor back around to its original bearing.

As the cart settled, there was a quiet noise of sloshing liquid from beneath the drape, and something like a muted, sloppy gasp. This time, Falx could not hold back a bone-deep shudder.

She did not like the Cupbearer. In fact, she *hated* its present form. But its utility had been indisputable during its long stay aboard the *Exactor*. And for all she loathed it, it was not a prisoner, but a guest. So she set her jaw and rotated her shoulders to relieve some tension – wincing at the hollow click that came as always from the right-hand socket – and pulled away the drape.

Inside was a heavy armaglass tank, filled nearly to the brim with murky, tannin-stained water. And in the water, surrounded by drifting fragments of decaying vegetation, was a shape. It was a mottled, greyish beige in colour, bulbous at the front, and with a long, ragged-finned paddle tail wafting listlessly behind it. The shape moved forward with a lazy beat of its tail, stirring up a cloud of muck from the tank's floor, until it was resting at the end of the aquarium facing the prisoner.

As the speaker console crackled to life, emitting the muddy, distorted sound of moving water, the Cupbearer rolled in the murk, and turned its head sideways to press one pale, lidless eye against the glass. Beneath the eye, the crook of a long, snaggle-toothed jaw turned upwards in a sly smile. And after taking in the sight of the prisoner on the floor, and then Biter, the creature spoke.

Gifts!

Xotal's voice was vile. Falx had no idea how the creature approximated human speech, given its lipless, ambush-predator's mouth, but from the grinding, creaking sounds picked up by the tank's hydrophone, she guessed it had something to do with the rasping of internal teeth.

What dish is this

most presumed-delicious

Lady Falx?

'That is precisely what I have summoned you to ascertain, Cupbearer.'

It seems orklike

Have you not something more...

exotic?

'It might not be a new meat, Xotal, but its pedigree is astounding. Or so it claims. You are to determine the truth of this.'

A taste test, then.

Unknown meats. These are good.

Nourish me.

The Cupbearer rolled slowly in delight, and on its loose, sallow belly, Falx saw the stubs of quills. It was hard to believe, but Xotal had been a kroot once. A master shaper, no less, that had consumed its way into a living nightmare.

Kroot culture *was* eating, and the creature's longing for new foods was nothing untoward in itself. But Xotal's appetite had been too curious, too prodigious, even for a society where cannibalism was daily custom. It had sought novel opponents with obsessive fervour, making its body a treasure-hoard of stolen genetics as it consumed species after species.

Inevitably, Xotal had become fixated on a desire for the one meat forbidden to it: the flesh of its species' masters, the t'au. And at last, concealed by the smoke of a battle's aftermath, it had given in to temptation. The master shaper had torn a sliver from the body of a fallen warrior, and had crossed a horizon from which there could be no return.

After that, Xotal had gone rogue, rampaging through space in an orgy of consumption, with all caution eclipsed by ecstasy. Eating its masters had changed it, in a way that made instant sense of the taboo long instilled in the kroot. Xotal had learned to make drastic alterations to its own form, achieving in months the sort of change that would have taken other shapers generations. But more chilling still, it had learned to change its *mind*, and its brain had become a thing of horrible power.

Falx had wondered, many times now, why she continued to offer the thing refuge. With the contents of Falx's brig to feed on, it had galloped through morphologies, with its body barely recognisable from one decade to the next – and it had become quite insane. One day she would have to put an end to it. But for now, the Cupbearer was a formidable asset.

'Well, you heard the Cupbearer,' said Hendriksen to Biter and the supposed Makari, unsheathing his combat knife with a flourish. 'It's hungry, so let's get it a prime cut.' The old wolf never seemed unnerved at all by Xotal, and even seemed to be finding some relish in its presence. But his satisfaction soured, when he realised that neither of the two orkoids seemed any more bothered by the ex-shaper than he himself was.

The supposed Makari sneered up from the floor as Hendriksen advanced with the knife. But as he reached out to make the cut, the Rune Priest paused and stroked his beard thoughtfully.

'Actually, ork, I think I shall give *you* this honour,' he said, and tossed the knife to the translator with a cruel smile. On many ships of the Ordo Xenos, it would be considered poor practice – to say the least – to throw a weapon into the hands of an unrestrained ork captive. But this was not, Falx supposed, a typical ship of the Ordo Xenos.

'If you like,' said Biter, keeping eye contact with the old wolf as they caught the knife by the blade with one hand.

'Take the flesh where the hand mark appeared,' commanded Hendriksen, 'and don't be gentle about it.'

'I hadn't planned otherwise,' said Biter, cool as the blade in their hand, and advanced on Makari. 'Going to cut you now,' the ork told the grot, and the grot just shrugged.

The prisoner did scream bloody murder as the Blood Axe hacked away in a rough circle around the mark of Ghazghkull's hand. But it didn't struggle, or try to writhe away from the blade. This was, Falx realised, just an ork hurting a grot: a confirmation of the natural order that the prisoner seemed to find so spiritually fulfilling.

When the carving was done, Biter placed the blemish-free flesh unceremoniously in Hendriksen's palm with a damp slap, and handed him back the knife. Nodding once, the psyker tossed the scrap into Xotal's tank with a look of disdain, and wiped his hands on the thighs of his ship-clothes as the water erupted in eager splashing.

'There, vile thing. Enjoy your meal.'

The kroot prodigy snapped messily at the scrap of skin and meat, working its jaws to align with the fragment, and then gulping it down with an ecstatic roll of its eyes.

A plain morsel

but such rich undertones!

Unusual…

The interrogators were more than content to ignore the thing as it deliberated on the meat, and an awkward silence thickened in the cell while Xotal smacked its lipless jaws in the water. Hendriksen began to pace, as was his habit when there was nothing else to do.

If the now absent scar proved truly to be the mark of Ghazghkull – and the Cupbearer would know it, if it was – there would be many possible implications. All of them were unsettling. Falx was used to the unknown, of course, as it was the business of her life. But she preferred the unknown when it was a question of tentacles and claws. When it was *physical*. As strange and vile as alien life could be, flesh was inevitably comprehensible, in the end.

But whenever her duty took her into questions of the spiritual, she felt profoundly unsettled. It was still fundamentally against her belief to shy away from truth, and if the mark transpired to be genuine, she would continue regardless. But she would proceed with caution; the creature currently digesting its meal in the tank behind her was a fine reminder, after all, of where unbridled curiosity could take a person.

The creature which Biter was now inclining their head towards, ever so casually, with their brow-ridges raised in intrigue.

'Your fish,' Biter said. 'It does not look very well.'

Mind alight with paranoia, Falx half-expected a trick. But when Hendriksen looked up from frowning at his own feet, and she saw the shock light up in his pale blue eyes, she spun round to face the tank.

The water was entirely choked with a mass of twisted, green-tinged fungus. From the look of the thicket, it had all sprouted from a mass in the centre of the tank, and had filled the container to its edges almost instantly. The few scraps of beige flesh visible amidst the profusion explained the rest of the story. Xotal had died an agonising, silent death, and Biter and the battered prisoner had been watching the whole time, waiting until it was done to let them know.

Falx felt a quiet horror seize her at the base of the neck, and her ceramite implant seemed to grow cold with it. The small part of her mind that took satisfaction in solving problems noted that at least the ever-nagging dilemma of what to do with the renegade kroot was solved, but the rest of her, which had always been better at creating problems, was unmoved. Because now, in the proof of the prisoner's authenticity, she had what she had wanted since that first message-burst from Biter's warband. And she wanted nothing more than to be rid of it.

'So we have Makari on our hands after all,' said Hendriksen gravely, in a tone which audaciously suggested he had suspected this all along. Cassia nodded, staring in mute disgust at the drifting, infested carcass of the Cupbearer.

'Yep. Makari who died, halfway through its own life story. But who's still telling it.'

Falx sighed, and wished for a moment she *had* aged comfortably into the kind of inquisitor who took one look at a threat before ordering it virus-bombed from orbit, praising the Emperor, and returning to some finely upholstered manse for a hot meal and a long evening with some dim but pleasant servant girl. Alas, she had not. And for all the enormity of the weirdness unfolding in the cell, it remained her duty, even if self-imposed, to pack it all away again.

'Then I suppose,' she said, feeling the full weight of her one hundred and thirty-six years in her bones, 'we had better find out what happened in the second half.'

CHAPTER SEVEN

GHAZGHKULL GETS SOMETHING BACK

I was a grot, and I was running for my life.

Couldn't tell you what planet I was on, who Ghazghkull Thraka was, or anything like that. I'd come out of a hole, in a tunnel, not long ago, and had lived in that tunnel ever since, scraping fungus from the walls to put in a big metal bucket. I'd bullied the grots who was smaller than me, I'd been bullied by the grots who was bigger than me, and I'd grovelled to the orks who'd occasionally come to collect the buckets. It had been a dark, squalid, terrifying life, just as the gods had intended for my sort. It had been perfect.

This time, though, when the orks had come down to the tunnels, they'd come with shootas, and they hadn't given a squig's cough about the fungus. There hadn't been any explanations, just bullets. And before I'd even figured out what was going on, half the grots in the tunnel had been shot to ragged pieces. As luck would have it, I'd been carrying the big metal bucket when it happened, and that's what saved me. A bullet had pinged off it, right back into the shin of the ork who'd fired it, and I'd legged it while the ork was busy shouting at the bucket.

The orks had set after me right away, with a whole pack of sniffer squigs, and although I'd got a good head start, it wouldn't last forever. I needed to lose 'em, somehow. But how, when I was lost myself? I'd never left my tunnel before, and all the tunnels beyond it looked exactly the same.

Then I smelled it. I didn't know what it was, and it was so faint that it must've been coming from miles away. But somehow I *knew* it meant safety, and as mad as that was, it wasn't like I had options. So I ran towards it. It led me upwards, gradually, and after a while the tunnels started looking a bit different. The walls weren't fully grown over with fungus yet, and I saw they were made out of machines. Not proper, orky machines either, but fussy ones with too many right angles. These had been someone else's tunnels, not long ago.

The further up I went, the more bare the walls got, and the less places there were to hide. Which was bad news, 'cos I badly needed a breather. In the end, I had to settle for collapsing behind a hump of shot-up machinery in a wide chamber where it looked like there had been a big fight. I could already hear the squigs snarling in the tunnels behind me, but all the fear-juice in the universe couldn't have squeezed another step out of me without a few gasps of air first.

I was so puffed out, actually, that it took a moment for me to clock the other thing hiding behind the machine. It was like a grot, but... infinitely worse? Its face was all flat and boring, like its ears and nose had been chopped off, and *it wasn't even green*. It was a human, of course – one of your larvae,

I reckon – but I didn't know that then. I just thought it was some kind of rubbish animal.

Its face was filthy, with streaks through the grime where water was coming out of its eyes, and it wouldn't stop whimpering and putting its finger over its mouth while it stared at me, as if that was meant to mean something. I didn't care. The squigs had reached the chamber now, and I could hear the orks too, barking orders as they fanned out to find me.

'Why does it have to be this one anyway?' growled one resentfully.

"Cos he wants a lucky one brought to him, remember?' boomed another, which sounded like it was bigger. 'And this one dodged all the bullets *and* managed to break Bin-feaster's leg with a zogging bucket. Sounds lucky to me.'

I was just trying to figure out how much worse my situation had got with the news that the orks wanted me alive – there were grots in my warren who'd been taken away and come back with their limbs sewn on wrong, or extra bumholes – when I spotted the manacles on the other creature's wrists. There had been chains on 'em, by the looks of it, but they'd been filed off. *This thing was on the run, too.*

Grots can think quick, you know. Especially when their lives are on the line. Before that wretched creature could even wonder why I was suddenly grinning, I'd grabbed its arm, bit down hard on it so it screamed, and then kicked it out into the open.

The orks roared with laughter as they saw the thing, and the whole pack of squigs shot towards it with tongues lolling. Knowing what I do now about how fragile humans are, I'm amazed it screamed for as long as it did. But I didn't stick around to watch – as soon as it had stumbled out into the view of the orks, I'd sprinted off in the other direction, ducked into a side tunnel, and started heading towards the source of that weird smell again.

The distraction had finally got the orks off my trail, but I didn't stop running. And as I carried on up through the maze of alien machines, I started coming across more and more orks, so I kept to the shadows and the quiet places where I could.

There had definitely been a big fight here, not long ago, going by all the smashed-up barricades and stuff. But as I watched the orks, I saw they were making it theirs, just as surely as the fungus was growing over the deep tunnels. They were setting up barracks, brew-huts and fight-sheds, while grots welded together squig pens and drilled drop-holes in the floor. And for every mob of orks headed into one of the new brew-huts, another was on its way out, tooled up for a fight elsewhere. An ork could be born into a place like this and just… be *part of something*, straight away.

At one point, my path took me sneaking across a gantry over a big pit full of vats, which I figured was some sort of place for making food. Working the vats, all chained together by the hundred, were more of those weak, colourless creatures. They were being watched over by orks with lashes and clubs, 'cos they weren't even worth wasting bullets on, and as I snuck overhead, I saw what it was they were cooking up. Corpses, of their own kind.

I cackled so hard then that one of the guards looked up, and I had to run again. But I couldn't help it. Now that I'd spent a while not running for my life, I was coming to realise that whatever this place was, it was *brilliant*. Even the 'being hunted down' part would've been perfect, if it'd been happening to some other git.

It was just something I'd come out of the ground knowing.

An instinct, I suppose. That this, all of this, was what the world was meant to be like. Orks, doing exactly what they wanted, and grots, coping with it. And other creatures too, like those wretches at the vats. 'Cos orks might have been made to rule everything there is, but they wasn't made to be alone in the universe. You ain't really won something unless there's someone alive who knows they've been beaten, and you ain't going to have many more fights if you don't leave anyone wanting revenge.

Eventually, after another few hours of skulking upwards past ever more orks, I got to a place where the smell I'd been chasing was thick in the air, and I reckoned that I'd nearly escaped. And when the smell led me into a hall tall enough for a hundred grots to stand on each other's heads, held up by giant stone pillars, and with a humongous pair of doors at the far end, I was certain. Through that door was freedom. And as luck would have it, it was open just wide enough for a runt like me to squeeze through.

The problem was, after everything I'd seen, I wasn't so sure I wanted to escape any more.

I stood in front of that door, trying to work it out, for ages. And in the end, my mind got made up for me.

'There's the little git!' bellowed a voice at the end of the hall, shocking me out of my daze, and I knew that voice just as well as I knew the baying of the sniffer squigs that'd started up along with it. I'd dithered so long that they'd caught my scent again, and followed me all the way up.

That was that. Without a second thought, I started ramming myself through the crack between the huge doors, and it was only once I'd wriggled nearly all the way to the other side that I wondered why the orks behind me were roaring with laughter.

'I ain't so sure he's that lucky after all,' said one of 'em. 'Run all this zogging way, ain't he, just to end up right where we was trying to take him in the first place.'

He was so big, by then, I didn't even notice him at first. I skulked into the big room beyond the doors already cringing, 'cos I expected it to be full of massive, angry orks. But it looked completely empty. Almost… peaceful, as weird as that sounds.

There was a giant round window, all fancy and… *gothick*, like the windows on this spaceship of yours, and there was dim, orange sunlight glowing through it. I dunno what *exactly* was happening on the other side, but it involved a lot of booms, rattles and rocket-whooshes. I'd been born knowing what war sounded like, like it was in my blood, and there was no mistaking it here.

Across the room from the window, hung up on ropes so they was facing it, was a row of dead humans. They were all dressed in uniforms with loads of buttons and gold string and stuff, like they'd thought they were special. But now they were just swinging slowly in the orange light, with bin-gits wandering all over their faces, just as dead as the corpses in the vats below.

There were statues, too, of humans in yet more fancy uniforms. They'd had their faces bashed off and glyphs scrawled all over 'em. But among them, untouched, was one giant statue of an ork in armour, stood facing the window with its brow crunched up in deep thought. I was getting dead confused as to why the humans would've wanted a statue of something like that, when it breathed.

The giant turned from the view of the war, and walked across the room to a huge table made from polished wood and gold, but covered in stripped meat-bones. A hand as big as I was swiped away a heap of detritus to reveal an ork-drawn map beneath, and the giant frowned down at it with one meat eye and one metal one.

A wave of big cannon-shots sounded on the horizon, and as I looked at that huge face staring down at the war-map, it was like the gun-thunder was the sound of its brain thinking. I still had no clue who this was, remember, but somehow I still expected it to look... happier than it did. Instead, it looked like it had a head full of problems, all wrestling with each other and smashing into the walls of its skull. That wasn't how an ork should look.

The giant grunted in frustration, and scratched a glyph on the map with a lump of charcoal, before sticking a knife in it as a placeholder. Then it reached for something else on the table, and picked it up for a closer look. It was a banner. Barely one, mind – just a hammered-flat bit of sheet metal on a stick, with something daubed on it in faded, red-black paint. Looking at it only deepened the valleys creased into the leathery green of the giant's face.

It winced, like a knife'd been shoved into its skull through one of the scar-ridges where metal met bone, and dropped the banner, moving its hand to clutch the side of its head instead. The lips of its great maw drew back from cracked fangs, and from between those tight-clenched teeth came a long, shuddering growl. It weren't so much a growl of pain, 'cos though orks feel pain sure enough, they experience it in the same way as light or sound, or any of the other ways their bodies tell 'em stuff. Nah, this was *frustration*. Like its head suddenly weighed ten times as much as it had done, and wouldn't think right.

'**Ain't the same,**' said the ork, maybe to itself, and maybe to the dead humans. It weren't talking to me, though. Just as I'd not noticed the ork because it was so big, it hadn't noticed me because I was so small.

'**Ain't... the same,**' it repeated, angrier now, and talking round another big wince from its head. **'We're fighting. We're winning. There's slaves, and loot. More, every day. *But why don't it feel right?*'** As the ork's space-deep voice got more and more contorted, I heard metal creak and saw the tiny banner bend under the force of those arm-thick talons. Was this warlord... talking to a sign?

'Curse yourselves,' the ork hissed, glaring up at the ceiling, before letting loose a roar that made bits shake free from it. **'WHY WON'T YOU TALK TO ME? Ain't I done well enough for you? Ain't I *taken* enough?'** The rage seemed to ebb a bit, and the giant looked back at the banner in its claws. **'I done what you told me, last time you spoke in the green. I sent for a grot. A lucky one. So if that's your problem, zoggin' well solve it for yourselves. Send him back, if that's what you want. If that means so much to you.**

'Stupid gods,' cursed the warlord, and held the banner in front of its face, glaring sullenly at that little scrap of sheet metal. Then there was a little *clicky-whir*, and the lens of the ork's metal eye spun. Changing focus, to look past the banner at the snivelling little speck of green it'd noticed at the far end of the hall. The meat eye shifted slightly to follow it, and slowly, like a mountain rearranging itself, the ork lowered the banner, and tilted its head down to look right at me.

'You hear any of that?' asked the giant, lower and more threatening than the artillery in the distance, and I shook my head as much as I could, with every muscle clenched in terror. Then I cringed as hard as I could, as if it could make me disappear, while the ork strode across the hall towards me, faster'n anything that big should be able to move. There'd be no point in running, even if my legs hadn't been locked rigid with fear, so I pissed on the gold-and-red carpet, and waited to die. The great-boss reached down with a hand as big as

I was. *This is it*, I figured, *I'm gonna be eaten*. But instead, it extended its thumb and first finger like the pincer off of a sea-git, and grabbed my shoulder.

'**Might as well give this a go,**' it muttered, and even talking under its breath, the sound was like thunder, coming on a wave of hot breath that made my ears flap. '*You,*' it said, stabbing a finger like a tree trunk towards my face. '*You're Makari, you are.*'

There was a searing heat in my skin where the two great fingers were touching me, and a flash of green light so fierce it wiped away my sight. But when I could see again, I weren't looking up at some nameless giant. I was looking at Ghazghkull, the Prophet of Gork and Mork. And looking at him, 'cos he was me now, and I was him, with a handprint on my shoulder to show it, was Makari the grot, his banner-waver.

INTERROGATION VIII

'Armageddon. Did Ghazghkull ever tell you why it was so important to him?'

'I tell you this, question-git, if there's one thing I wish, it's that he had. I have no idea why he was so Mork-snikked obsessed with the place. I actually dared ask where we were going once, way back on Urk. And 'cos the boss was in a good mood that day, he answered. Sort of. All he'd say was that it was an important place. He was drawn to it, like he was one of them sticky rocks... what are they? Magnets. Like he was a magnet, and it was an anvil. When *Wurld Killa* left Urk, I reckon the whole thing got drawn along with him.

'Why was it important? Dunno. Not sure Ghazghkull knew, really. The way he talked about Armygeddon, when we were there... it was like it was a holy place. Like there was some score to settle. I guess he knew the gods had their own reasons why it should belong to orks, even more'n everything else does, and that was good enough.'

Cassia was leaning forward on her chair, looking genuinely fascinated. 'Was it the gods that sent you back, Makari? Or did Ghazghkull do it?'

'Do not talk of them as if they are real,' said Hendriksen, face etched with unease that was driven by far more than a base aversion to heresy. The idea that talking about something made it true was so natural to the orkoids in the room, it was starting to rub off. 'In fact, do not talk of them at all,' he continued. 'Let us hear of the war instead.'

'No, brother – we have all heard the story of the Second War for Armaggedon. Let us hear the answer to Cassia's question. So who put you back in the world, Makari?'

'No idea. Maybe I never left it. Maybe the Great Green was just the inside of all of our heads, and I was an idea for a bit. Maybe it was all inside a magic boot. Why do you keep expecting me to know how the universe works? When your grunts get chucked into one of your big wars, do the commissars take the time to explain the general's reasoning? Nah, they tell 'em to get stuck in and do the job. Same for me.'

'So, what was your job?'

'Have you even been listening? I'm a banner-waver. I was there to wave a banner.'

Ghazghkull gave me the banner, and told me it was waving time. Somehow, it looked more impressive now it was in my hands. Perhaps it'd had a bit of a paint job since Urk. Seeing it stirred Ghazghkull, and he shook off that strange unease he'd seemed to have been stuck in when I found him.

It was like he'd reminded himself, in a way. Felt like he'd been in that fancy human room too long, thinking about tactics. Trying to work out *what to do*, when he should've just been *doing*. He'd given Bullets and all the other clan-bosses missions, and they were all at the front being orks. But he'd been so caught up in all that, that he'd forgotten to go out and fight, himself.

And Grotsnik, I was about to learn, had seen his isolation, and hemmed him in like a legs-git pouncing on something new in its web. I'd managed to find my way to Ghazghkull through grot-sized vents and tunnels. But as Ghazghkull led the way out of his new boss-hall, I discovered that if *he* wanted to get outside, the only way out was through a big room that Grotsnik had filled with all his experimental medical gubbins.

I'll say this for the doc – he'd upped his game since Urk. That room was crammed with rows of operating tables, and while some were for orks, most had humans nailed to 'em. Some were missing bits, some had had bits added to 'em, and some had been stapled together. Most of 'em were alive, and screaming. In one case, a human had a grot's terrified head sewn into its chest, shouting right back at it.

And clanking around the room, swapping syringes and refilling blood buckets, were a small army of Grotsnik's successes. Or his failures. It was hard to tell. Either way, they were orks who'd had some, most or all of their body parts swapped out with bits of machinery, and more guns than you'd reckon would be essential for the practise of medicine.

That made sense, I figured. Setting up here didn't just mean that Ghazghkull had to go through Grotsnik to get to the rest of the world – it meant the rest of the world had to go through Grotsnik to get to Ghazghkull. And with his collection of cyb-orks to hand, the doc now had more than enough muscle behind him to decide whether they got through or not. The whole business stank.

And there, now, was Grotsnik himself, with his gnarly old hands in a half-conscious human's ribcage. Think he was replacing its heart with a squig's, or something. When he heard Ghazghkull coming he turned, and his eyes went wide with surprise.

'Mighty warlord,' he said, trying to sound happy that Ghazghkull was out and about. 'Going to take in the air?'

'Nah,' rumbled Ghazghkull. **'Going to war.'**

'But we have surgery scheduled,' he blustered, removing the goggles. 'The new implants! Of course, the great warboss does as he wishes, but without these new... improvements I've planned, the headaches may get so much more *nasty*. It would be terrible to get one in front of the troops...'

The git. I wouldn't have bet half a bad tin of squig guts that his so-called 'improvements' were doing anything to help the Prophet's headaches. Quite the opposite, I reckoned. The nerve of him! Keeping the boss thinking he was sick, stopping him from being with his troops... it was like he was trying to make him his *pet*. Looking at him smirk, I couldn't help it. Gork bless me, I lost my temper.

'Boss said he wants to fight, *git*,' I snapped, gnashing my teeth. 'Or do you need to work on yer own ears?'

When he saw me, Grotsnik's face went blank, and then reset into a look of proper hate. It was like he knew who I was, straight away. But before he could say anything, Ghazghkull curled up his finger'n thumb, and flicked me flat on my face.

'Oi,' he said, as I spat out a smashed fang. **'Less of that. It's ungodsly. He's an ork, you're a grot. Right?'**

I snivelled, as was right, and retreated behind the boss again.

'He ain't wrong though,' said Ghazghkull. **'Surgery's off. And if I get a headache in front of the troops, then I get a headache.'**

And that was that. We left the laboratory, and although I couldn't resist turning round and smirking at Grotsnik before the door shut, that was the last we saw of him for a good while.

We went out onto a wide steel parapet then, and it was so bright I had to close my eyes for a good few seconds. But when I opened 'em again, I saw something magic.

The fortification we were standing on was right at the top of a hump of metal as big as a mountain. A *city*, somehow, like a nest built by stinging-gits, only big enough to punch up into the guts of the sky. And all around it, in every direction, was a massive, beautiful war.

Tiny dots moved in swarms, which I thought were orks and humans at first, until I made out the little exhaust plumes rising from them. They were only zogging *war machines*, moving in squadrons too big to bother counting, through a sea of rubble and smoke and bodies. Orks, gathered together into a tide that couldn't be stopped, and all the humans they could ever want to kill. They were fighting, and winning, and growing stronger with every moment. It was a war. But more'n that, it was *holy*.

As I gawped, the boss was talking about fronts and sieges and encirclements and that. Blood Axe stuff. I had barely any idea what he was on about, but the gist was that we were thrashing your lot. Still, it sounded like Ghazghkull wasn't quite satisfied with it all. He didn't have that *certainty* he'd had on Urk – that faith, which had kept him still as a statue through those days in the icy dark. It was almost like he didn't know what to do.

The boss stopped talking altogether, after a while. I got the sense that he was... leaving the air clear. So that if, by any chance, Gork and Mork had happened to give me a big list of their plans for Ghazghkull while I'd been dead, I could reveal it now. I knew then, that that was why I was back. 'Cos Ghazghkull just wasn't sure any more.

But he was out of luck. 'Cos it's not like I'd been in the brew-hut with the gods all the time I'd not been alive, having chats and stuff. I'd just been dead, you know? Well, I suppose you don't. Anyway, I had nothing useful to say, so I just stood by Ghazghkull and kept looking out at the war.

The sun was setting by then, blazing red like Ghazghkull's eye through big clouds of volcano smoke, and out of that smoke came the best things I'd ever seen. They was gargants: a whole big herd of 'em coming out of the dust, with their huge angry faces making 'em look like gods themselves. But as big as they were, they seemed tiny for being so far away.

And that was what made me realise what the problem was, here – that even the biggest things look little when they're miles away. It was like that for Ghazghkull. He might've had more power than ever, but it was being conducted through a much longer reach. And it made him smaller, if you like. It's one reason why your lot are so rubbish at fighting, I reckon. Your Emperor's just some git on a chair who might be dead, half the galaxy away, and he doesn't even shout at you through a box or anything.

+Are we going to let that stand?+ asked Hendriksen wearily, in Falx's mind. Even his zeal was fatigued from the onslaught of blasphemy that the interrogation had produced by now.

We've had enough disruptions already, replied Falx non-committally, doing her best to conceal the fact that Makari had accidentally struck upon one of her deepest anxieties about the state of mankind. *Let it pass.*

'Back on Urk,' Biter went on, unaware of the minor theological crisis going on in her head, 'Ghazghkull only had to walk out on his balcony to be with his troops. But penned in the middle of that human city by Grotsnik, he might as well've been on another planet. It was hurting him. Ghazghkull needed to go where he'd be *seen*. Where he could remind the mobs, personally, what they were about. And where, if I'm going to flatter myself, they could see my banner. He needed to do something properly orky. So I thought about different tactics I'd heard of, and how I could suggest 'em without it seeming like I was telling him what to do. And in the end, as the gargants waddled across the red-lit waste before us, I said it.'

Biter lit up then, like they were really relishing the words they were about to translate. They even raised a finger to accent their performance, medals gleaming greasily on their puffed-up chest as they gave a crafty look up to an imagined Ghazghkull of their own.

'Have you considered a full charge at the enemy, with everything we've got?'

Ghazghkull wasn't taken with it. Said he'd spent the whole of the war so far trying to get the clan-bosses – all of 'em except Straturgum, admittedly – to realise there was such a thing as other tactics beside just chucking everything at your enemy. But then sitting and thinking about it all was just giving him headaches, and I think he suspected the gods was getting bored. So I told him he should just do what he wanted to do, 'cos he was an ork after all. And that's what orks should do.

He was quiet for a little bit. Then he twitched his head to the side, like he'd just spotted something.

'I've had an idea,' he said. **'What did I say, back in the hall? About thinking, when I should be doing?'** Nobody had said that. It was something I'd *thought*. I ain't said it out loud, though, so that was weird. But would you have wanted to correct Ghazghkull on that? Yeah, thought not. So I nodded.

'I should be just… getting stuck in. The gods won't tell me how, because it's so obvious I should have seen it by myself . I should just do what I want. They'll make themselves heard through that. And what do I want? A big charge, I reckon. With everything. South. Volcanoes are goin' off, so it'll be dead hard. And there's that jungle…' Ghazghkull nodded, mind made up. **'Yeah. It'll be good. Really good. I'm going to take one of those gargants and head south. Bring the banner.'**

I felt relief like you feel when you make it over a mek's fence just before the guard squig gets you. The Prophet was alright. Letting me give advice was one thing, but if he'd gone with it, I don't think I could've believed in him quite like I had done. And yeah, I realise he *did* sort of go with my advice. But it'd gone through his brain and come out again as his, so it wasn't like I'd told him what to do.

We went south. And it was really good. It might've been the best thing ever.

Falx listened, with a mounting sense of despondency, as Makari described one of the most perilous conflicts in mankind's history as if it were a Militarum conscript remembering a grand old night of shore leave.

Armageddon's nightmarish equatorial jungle, which the incompetent Governor von Strab – a believer in the Imperial Truth if ever there was one – had thought impassable, had proved a playground for the swarm of orks that had gathered around Ghazghkull. Makari hooted with glee at how Grudbolg's Snakebites had stabbed their way through a whole ecosystem somehow comprised of apex predators. It talked about volcanic hyperstorms as if they had been light shows put on purely to celebrate its master, and described clashes with Imperial armoured columns as if they had been amusing mishaps taking place after one too many drinks. The nadir of the account was undoubtedly when Makari got to the battle of the Mannheim Gap, where the godlike might of the Legio Metalica had been squandered by von Strab in a doomed counter-attack on Ghazghkull's offensive.

Hearing the near annihilation of a Titan Legio reduced to 'a load of massive metal lads having a fist fight' was depressing to say the least, but it also gave Falx the most bizarre sting of envy. Mannheim Gap was a source of genuine grief for humanity. The fallen Titans had been irreplaceable, not just materially, but spiritually: walking bastions of hope, in a sprawling dark where such a thing was more precious and finite than any material wealth.

And while the orks had lost twice as many of their dreadful Gargants, the atomic rupturing of their own war machines had been just as thrilling to them as that of the Titans. *It was all just fireworks to them*, she thought bitterly. Broken toys, to be replaced with new ones. *Even when they lose,* she realised, with a coldness settling on her gut, *they're winning*.

And as Ghazghkull pushed forward the front of his invasion, the orks were winning anyway. It seemed the warlord was at last fulfilling the desires that had consumed him on Urk, and it was clear from Makari's animated state, even with its smashed nose, its shattered arm, and the ragged wound on its shoulder, that it was in a state of perfect contentment just recalling it.

'It was the best time we ever had together,' Biter said. 'And I do mean together, sort of. I mean, I was still scum to him, as it should be. But he was proud, in his way. It was then that he made me this.' Biter gestured at Makari with their chin, and Falx saw the gretchin was proudly rattling its necklace of relic shrapnel.

'He made a necklace for you,' deadpanned Cassia. 'How lovely.'

Makari paid no heed to the jibe, though.

'I stood just behind him in every battle,' it gushed, rambling so fast that Biter struggled to keep up. 'I taunted his enemies when he came for them, and then I kicked their bodies after he'd downed 'em. It was just us, doing what we did best.'

'Just you, apart from a hundred million orks,' corrected Hendriksen, and this at least earned some scorn.

'I meant there was no Grotsnik,' said Makari, through the translator, "cos he was still stuck up in Hive Volcanus. There was nothing to meddle with what the gods wanted, and I felt like maybe Armygeddon *was* a holy place, that we was building the Great Green there, one fight at a time.

'I dodged every shot that came at me, somehow. Or maybe the bullets swerved round me, like when that ork tried to shoot the grot I'd been, back in the warren under the city, and hit the bucket and shot himself instead. And even more'n on Urk, I started being known as a sort of good luck charm. Orks who'd usually not think twice before kicking me out of the way treated me with… respect. They even *asked my permission* sometimes, before touching the banner.' Makari's face turned sour, then.

'Makari didn't like that at all,' noted Biter helpfully, while the grot had paused to think.

'I suppose what sorted that out was the tank,' the Blood Axe said pensively, in his Makari voice. 'Sometimes, when there's scrap going spare, grots build tanks. They're awful. And with all the excitement of the war, and all the scrap the mek-wagons had been grabbing as we moved south, a load of the horde's grots had made a tank. A *huge* one. Still rubbish, but as big as one of your *bin-blades*. And… well. They'd called it *Big Makari*, in my honour.' Makari was cringing now, as it heard Biter say the name, and looked profoundly uncomfortable. 'It had… my face done on the front, with spaceship guns for eyes.'

'Which he must have hated,' Falx inferred. 'Since you don't honour a grot, and so on and so forth.'

'Yes, at first,' said the ork, after conferring with Makari. 'But he came around to it. They said it was alright in the end. Partly because the tank caught fire the first time it fired its main cannons, and every grot aboard it burned to death. But also because the tank didn't honour a grot – it honoured *Makari*. Do we have to have a debate about that?'

The ork asked the question innocently enough, but Falx was beginning to notice just how often the Blood Axe probed the edges of her tolerance under the guise of frank talk, and it turned her already dark mood pitch-black.

'No, xenos. In fact, I think we have heard more than enough of glorious victories altogether. As I said, we've all heard the story of this war – there's little to learn from hearing it retold through gloating. Tell Makari to move ahead in the story. Ask it about Hive Hades. And about Yarrick.'

Falx looked right at the prisoner as she spoke, and just as she suspected, the malevolent joy fell right off its face as it heard the legendary commissar's name. Seeing that grotesque little face twist in sudden misery was a tonic, and Falx treated herself to the smallest gloat of her own.

'We have talismans of our own, after all. And few are more potent than Yarrick. I want to hear all about how he beat Ghazghkull.'

CHAPTER EIGHT

GHAZGHKULL'S DILEMMA

We were still winning when the siege of Hades began. And we kept winning. But there came a moment, like that moment where you smell that a storm is gonna break, where every ork on Armygeddon realised that *we should've won by now*.

If von Strab had stayed in charge, we would've done. He was like Dregmek – a braggart, but the bad kind – and the boss had picked apart his defences just as mercilessly as he'd picked apart the Deathskull warboss' body in Rustspike.

Yarrick, though… When that old bastard took over, things were different. He didn't have enough of any of the things he needed to keep us out of Hades, but still he managed it. 'Cos he knew he *had* to hold out. That was his reality, and he was too stubborn to let anything change that – even Ghazghkull. He had a will that seemed almost like an ork's, when you were up against it, and the boss couldn't believe his luck in having come up against such an unlikely specimen of humanity.

I remember when the first big push on Hades failed. It'd been an airborne assault, using Evil Sunz bommerz, packed with battalions of Genrul Straturgum's best shock troops instead of bombs. They had Deathskull guns, Goff-forged armour and explosive bullets from the Bad Moon powder mills – plus packs of feral Snakebite squigs, just so all the clans could get in on it. The hive had nowhere near enough anti-air guns to see off even a tiny bit of that attack. But do you know what Yarrick did? He took every artillery piece that'd been bombarding our lines from the hive's walls… and he turned 'em so they pointed straight up. Just like that, he had so many guns that he didn't need to aim, and not one bommer made it back.

When the boss heard, it took him a while just to accept it'd happened at all. He kept just shaking his big head, and insisting that Yarrick hadn't done such a thing at all. 'Cos only he himself could've done something so cunning. But then Ghazghkull stepped outside his boss-wagon, and saw the bits of smoking red metal strewn over the landscape, and he went berserk. He kicked the ork who'd given him the news to death, and then another three who just happened to be nearby, just to calm down enough to talk. And when he could speak, he actually *cursed* Yarrick. It was the first and last time I ever heard him angry at an enemy, and it could only mean one thing – he had a *grod*.

Yeah, I know. 'What's a grod,' right? I'll bet there's no human word for it, just like there's no ork word for that thing where a human really, really likes another human, and it causes loads of problems. Actually, I suppose the concepts ain't that different, now I think about it. A grod's a favourite enemy, if you like.

Now, for an ork to have a grod who ain't an ork is rare.

But for an ork like *Ghazghkull* to have a human grod? That was mental. I suppose it helped that Yarrick was a bit like an ork, although I doubt he ever thought of it like that. He even had a klaw just like Ghazghkull's. And it was so big on that puny body of his that it should've toppled him right over. But it didn't, 'cos he didn't want it to. And that was more orky than the klaw itself.

Anyway, Ghazghkull kept smashing his head against the problem of Hades and Yarrick, but no matter what he tried, it wouldn't give. It was the old thing about an irresistible fist and an immovable face. Y'know, *could Mork make a box so proper that Gork couldn't kick it open*, and such. And eventually, after months of this, it got to Ghazghkull. For the first time in his whole life to date, he questioned whether he really was an irresistible fist after all.

But orks always think they'll win, right? Yeah, I thought the same. But Ghazghkull's mind had become something very different from the mind of any other ork who'd lived in a long, long time. He could imagine being beaten. And more than his size, his strength and his cunning, that was the thing that made him unique. I like to think it became his greatest strength, eventually. But back then, when he was feeling it for the first time, it was a weakness. And it nearly did for all of us.

I had a hammock, tucked away in the rafters of the throne room of Ghazghkull's boss-wagon, which I'd climb up to for a few hours' kip, whenever there wasn't a night fight on that I needed to wave the banner for. Usually, I had the place to myself, 'cos Ghazghkull was way too hard to need to sleep, and tended to spend the night outside, roaring with the clan-bosses who'd followed him from Urk as they gambled and feasted and fought. And if Ghazghkull weren't in the throne room, it was just a room, weren't it? So I got probably the only peace and quiet in the whole of the ork siege lines.

But one night, I got woken up by what I thought was thunder or artillery, until I realised it was words. Ghazghkull's words.

'I ain't sure the gods believe in me anymore.'

I peered down over the edge of the hammock, looking to see who he was talking to. But there was just him, sitting dead still on his throne, with all the lamps unlit so you could only see his metal eye glowing red in the dark. He had the same air to him that he'd had when I found him at the start of this round of being Makari, only about six times worse. And he reeked of fungus brew. It weren't right.

'We're only gonna keep winning if the boys believe we are.'

I thought about answering, then, but something told me I shouldn't. So I kept listening.

'The boys'll only believe that,' he continued, staring ahead into the dark, **'if the bosses believe it. And the bosses'll only believe that… if I believe it.'** He took a huge breath in, and gave an even huger breath out, and then spoke so low it could've been the wind outside. **'But I ain't sure I believe it. And I ain't sure, *because I ain't sure the gods believe in me.'***

I carried on saying nothing. But make no mistake, I weren't hiding. I was certain the boss knew I was there, even though I was out of sight up in the roof. But if I spoke back, then that'd mean the boss was talking *to* me. And if it's hard to imagine the most powerful ork in the galaxy admitting weakness, then imagine him admitting it to a grot. If I stayed quiet, on the other hand, then we could both of us pretend I was eavesdropping, and it wouldn't technically be any different to Ghazghkull talking to himself.

By the sounds of it, the boss had some things he needed

to say. So I lurked, just like I used to do back on Urk during the boss' plotting sessions, and I gave him someone to be overheard by.

'They've stopped talking to me. I still get the headaches. But there's no green in 'em. Just darkness. And I don't know if it's because I should know how to win without them telling me. Or if it's because they've found some other ork who's more worth talking to, somewhere else. Either way, I've let them down.'

Now, orks might not be able to feel fear, but I will remind you that grots very much can. And I was more scared then than I'd been in my lives. Ghazghkull not feeling up to it was like... well, I was gonna say it was like the sun going out. But Ghazghkull had seen that happen once, and beaten it through sheer confidence. This was worse than that. Ghazghkull's horde was unstoppable, but even the biggest machine's got one cog that'll grind the whole thing to a halt if it jams. And here, the cog was Ghazghkull.

'I don't feel like the rest of them. Like the bosses. It started on Urk. But it's worse, now. That lot... they live to fight. It gives them everything they need. Like it should be. And I act like I'm the same. I beat them at arm wrestling. I bet on squig fights. I drink until *they* are sick. But I'm pretending. I've lost my rukkh-razzha, my battle-bliss. I need... more.'

The boss said nothing, for so long that I wondered if he was done. And when he did speak, he sounded so lost that I could hardly believe this was the same ork I'd watched beat a giant warp-fing into pulp aboard the *Wurld Killa*.

'I need something else,' said Ghazghkull, **'but I don't know what it is.'**

* * *

The next day, Ghazghkull tipped me out of my hammock for another day's banner-waving. It was just him and me again, but neither of us let on that the night before had even happened. As long as we did that, I figured, it *wouldn't* have happened.

That was the theory, anyway. But it didn't work. That evening, as the day's attack plan failed – it was a gargant with a big drill on it, but Yarrick dug a tunnel right under its arse and blew it up – Ghazghkull celebrated along with the other clan-bosses. But now I knew what was going on under that metal plate of his, I could see he was just pretending.

And as the days went on, I felt it spread. Wasn't like anyone had actually figured it out, mind. They didn't know the Prophet had lost his faith. But they *knew*. The war-shouts got weedier. Trukks went slower. Guns seemed to run out of ammo quicker, and cannons blew 'emselves up more often. The whole war got a tiny bit less holy every day. And it got worse by such tiny steps that nobody would've noticed. Unless they was looking, which of course Ghazghkull was. And I knew that the worse it got, the more he'd be sinking into that head of his.

This might surprise the big hairy human, but I was actually relieved, the day his lot finally showed up to save the day for Yarrick. By which I mean the *Space Marines*. Not the grey ones like him, though – it was the red ones, and the blue ones, and the green ones, all dropping down at once across the whole of the planet.

And yeah, I'll say it. Then, we weren't winning any more. We were getting battered.

Ghazghkull stuck at it for a while, smashing away at the walls of Hades as if nothing had changed. I think he knew the war was doomed, but he'd spent so long trying to beat his way into that Mork-snikked city, that he simply couldn't leave it unbroken.

And in the end, to be fair, he did get inside. But there weren't much point in it by then. The horde from the *Wurld Killa*, which had once seemed like it could never run out, had been dwindling for a good while. And when the fighting finally stopped in the twistiest, turniest little corridors under the hive, Ghazghkull had lost nearly half what he had left. Worse yet, 'cos he'd been so focused on that one city, every other front had fallen to bits. At least Yarrick got away, so Ghazghkull still had his grod. But it weren't much consolation.

I thought the boss was gonna give up, after that. And he could've done, easy. If he'd chosen to run headlong at the nearest lot of beakies, the clan-bosses would've followed him happily to death, knowing that they'd had a decent run at conquering the universe. Certainly a better go than most orks ever got to have.

Ghazghkull didn't give up though, thank Gork. 'Cos *decent* wasn't good enough for him. What he'd managed on Urk, and what he'd nearly managed here, had been special. It'd been something new – which ain't something you can say of many ork wars – and even if he'd mislaid his faith, he couldn't give up on the whole thing.

In the brew-huts, they call it a Blood Axe Goodbye. It's when you tell your mob you'll get a round in after you've been to the drops, but then you leave without paying, and never come back. That's what Ghazghkull did. He made a big speech, announcing that they'd nearly conquered the planet, and ordered a big, final assault on Hive Tartarus, which he said was the last human-held city in the world.

It was all a load of rubbish, of course, and he'd chosen Tartarus by dropping a knife into his throne room map. But as far as any ork knew, he was still speaking the will of the gods, so they charged off happily to their deaths. Then, quietly, he gathered up the clan-bosses – as well as Grotsnik, I was miserable to learn – and we all sodded off in a spaceship, while Yarrick and the beakies were distracted at Tartarus.

I'd hoped that wiping the slate clean at Hades and leaving would bring Ghazghkull back to his old self. But you know what I said about Gork, and what he likes to do with a grot's hope.

He did put on a good show. Any other warlord would've been asking for a shanking from his cronies after a defeat like Armygeddon. But the boss still knew how to do a speech, and the beating-of-the-mind he gave the clan-bosses as their ship left the system was a proper walloping. He said that this war hadn't been the end of their great rampage, but the very start – a sort of test run, if you like, for learning how humans worked, and how best to defeat 'em in future. He taught 'em about the importance of *knowing yer enemy*, like I reckon the sour-looking human over there fails to teach her bosses all the time. Heh.

Like I say, it was a good speech. It certainly won the bosses over, and Bullets even made a little speech of his own, about how they'd find another world like Urk, build up a giant horde all over again, and head back to Armygeddon to finish the job. They all cheered then, and had a big fight to celebrate while Ghazghkull watched, and Grotsnik took measurements to see how much his head had grown. I don't know what the doc thought of Ghazghkull's speech. But I know he had his planning-something-face on as he fussed over the boss with his measuring stick, and if there was one ork who knew what was going on in Ghazghkull's brain... well, it'd be the one who'd stapled it together in the first place.

Anyway. That's one truth about Armygeddon. That the defeat

was deliberate, and just the opening bit of a big master plan concocted by Gork and Mork. But there's a second truth too, that only Ghazghkull, and me, and maybe Grotsnik knew: that we got the snot kicked out of us, fair and square, 'cos Ghazghkull lost heart.

And there it is. Your real, proper truth about Ghazghkull Mag Uruk Thraka... Can I go now?

Hendriksen actually laughed. Not a bitter cough of scorn, or a mocking cackle, but a genuine, raucous, ale-hall bellow that boomed through the whole of the brig. It was as if the whole of the interrogation had been nothing but the set-up to this punchline, and he had appreciated the effort enough to briefly put his anger aside for mirth.

'So you expect us to believe,' he said, after steadying his breath, 'that Ghazghkull Mag Uruk Thraka, the mightiest, most ambitious, most toweringly brutal monster in all the foul green host of orkdom, became... depressed?' Just saying it again made him laugh, but as Biter explained the concept of depression to Makari, taking quite some time over it, his amusement faded.

As the Blood Axe spoke, the prisoner seemed confused at first. But then its murderous little eyes widened in astonishment, as if it had just found the answer to a riddle it had gnawed on for years, and it yipped a single phoneme at the translator.

'Absolutely, yes,' reported Biter, and Hendriksen's face fell, unsure of what this meant.

'That's certainly a piece of information,' said Cassia, looking just as bewildered. Falx, however, felt something like triumph for the first time since she had entered the cell. She had acquired Makari hoping to get inside the mind of the creature's master, and learn its weaknesses. And now that hope had been achieved. Whatever else transpired, the operation had paid for itself in knowledge.

But Falx's mind was not one to sit for long in contentment, and it was maybe three seconds before it had managed to hitch a worry to her sense of achievement.

'It certainly is,' she said, following on from Cassia, and then she spoke her mind aloud. 'But it does beg a fairly significant question. If this is Ghazghkull's great vulnerability, then why have you just divulged it to his enemies? The warlord's retreat from Armageddon already has a watertight rationale – so why did you expose the truth of it? You seem unusually coopera- tive, all of a sudden.'

'Well,' said Biter, not even needing to consult the captive. 'Perhaps you are aware that Makari disappeared for a number of years, following the retreat from Armageddon? There is a reason for that.'

We were headed to some dump of a world called Golgotha, since some coggy-tater in Hive Volcanus had listed it as being full of orks, and we didn't have any other ideas.

And by we, I mean Ghazghkull. He didn't have much of anything, in that strange epilogue to the war. He played along with the raucous shipboard life of the clan-bosses, just as well as he'd played along before. But now they was all packed in together on that poky spaceship, it was dead clear just how different from them he'd become. Just as Ghazghkull's body had grown to dwarf those of lesser orks, so too had his mind, and as the voyage went on, he spent more and more time holed up on his own, away from them all.

Grotsnik, of course, jumped on the boss' solitude like a bin- git on fresh sick. He made up for all the time he'd lost while

Ghazghkull had been away from Volcanus, spending more time tinkering with the boss' bonce than not, it felt like, and I was certain he was doing everything he could to agitate the Prophet's crisis.

The headaches, which hadn't been that bad during the stalemate at Hades, came back bigger than before, with seizures as nasty as any the Prophet had been gripped by on Urk. And while Grotsnik's constant presence stopped me being able to ask, even if I'd been bold enough to, I was sure that Ghazghkull saw 'em as further proof that he'd been dropped by the gods. More than that, I became certain that the doc knew what was going on with Ghazghkull. The way I saw it, Grotsnik saw Ghazghkull as his creation, and wanted to keep him bogged down in doubt and madness until he finally cracked, and became the doc's personal monster.

Bullets' declaration of a return to Armygeddon had only been a suggestion, really. But Grotsnik reinforced it constantly during the boss' long bouts of surgery, repeating the idea that it had been Ghazghkull's own plan over and over until the boss seemed to think so himself. Personally, I couldn't have hated the idea more, and Grotsnik rooting for it only entrenched me further in hating it.

It was true that Armygeddon had a certain pull to it. That strange, godsly feeling we had all felt during the war was something that stuck with you, even as a grot, and it was easy to see why the Deathskull boss had been so quick to suggest it for the next scrap. But to me, and especially to the bit of me that was Makari, it was a huge waste of potential.

The Great Green was about unity. About finally connecting every one of the teeming, scattered pockets of orkdom in the galaxy, and getting them all together for the war to end all wars. I even wondered, sometimes, if Ghazghkull should've dropped his mobs on Armygeddon early on in the fight, and headed straight off to keep recruiting. I definitely thought that was the case now. With the war left behind, it was the perfect time to learn a lesson about getting bogged down, and begin mustering a force so big it could swamp planets without even slowing.

But instead, Ghazghkull was all but ready to scrape up a repeat version of the force he'd left Urk with, and head right back to the place that had beaten it. The place which Commissar Yarrick would be working night and day to turn into the very zoggin' definition of a box so proper that Gork himself couldn't kick it open.

Another Armygeddon war was the simplest option open to us. It was what any other warlord would've done. But Ghazghkull weren't just any old warlord. Part of his genius had always been in getting past the idea that the simplest, quickest, fightiest option was always the best one. So why, I thought to myself, was he settling for this rubbish? Everything that had come to pass before now – the unification of Urk, the exodus on the *Wurld Killa*, and the second chance Ghazghkull had won himself by scarpering from Armygeddon – it was all gonna go to waste, purely 'cos the boss was sulking too hard to come up with a better plan than someone called zoggin' *Bullets*.

When we got near Golgotha, I decided to do something really reckless. The sort of thing that should've been unthinkable for a grot. But I was starting to feel like the only thing on that ship that gave two teeth about the gods anymore, so I resolved to do it for their sake. I was gonna tell Ghazghkull he was making a mistake.

Believe me, I wanted to leave it. To let him come to his senses on Golgotha, and realise in his own time that he was on course for a repeat of the disaster we'd just left behind.

But I couldn't be sure that'd happen. And if I didn't speak my mind now, I wasn't sure I'd get another chance.

'Cos remember, I was stuck in a metal box with Grotsnik, who's probably the most devious sod I've ever had the bad luck to meet, and who not only held a massive grudge against me, but had already managed to kill me once. Already, I'd clocked his cyb-orks loitering about with knives down dark corridors on the ship, and it was only a matter of time before one of 'em found a corner I didn't think to check for murderers.

In the end though, it weren't Grotsnik I should've worried about.

When I plucked up the nerve to confront the boss, we was on the ship's bridge, in one of the rare moments where none of the clan-bosses were around, and Grotsnik was getting some shut-eye. Ghazghkull was staring moodily out into space, and it seemed like a bad time to interrupt him. But then, when was it ever not?

Now or never, I thought, and opened my gob.

'Smekhn-unh-snikhek-nukh,' I said to him, my voice coming out even higher pitched than usual 'cos of the fear in me.

'You what?' said Ghazghkull, taken aback, as if a spanner had just asked him a question.

'S'what you told 'em back on Urk, after the unification. Grot phrase. Hide now, stab 'em later.'

'Yeah, I know,' said the boss, more confused than angry so far. **'Why are you on about that?'**

''Cos of this idea about going back to Armygeddon,' I said, gulping.

'What about it?' said Ghazghkull, and looked right at me. I realised then that I'd never actually made eye contact with him before that moment, and I never wanted it to happen again. Even though he only had one eye, there was enough threat in it to melt clean through steel, let alone a grot's courage. But I whispered a panicky plea to Mork in my head, and carried on.

'You might win it,' I squeaked, and then thought better of it. 'You will win it,' I corrected myself, even though we both knew I'd been right the first time. 'And when you do, you'll have a planet. But if you don't go back there, you could have a million planets.'

Ghazghkull just stared at me, not moving a muscle, and I figured at this point he'd either started changing his mind, or was just waiting to see how much I'd dare say before he killed me. I'd crossed the line either way, so just like I was in a spaceship right on the edge of a black hole, I stuck the engines on full blast and hoped for the best.

'When you showed me the Great Green, back when I made the banner, every star in the sky was green. It was the whole galaxy, ruled by orks – not just Hades Hive.' I was *hypy-ventilising* now, and my heart felt like it was about to shake itself apart, but I felt green fire in me, and it was like it burned away the fear.

'Boss, you managed to get the six most stubborn gits on Urk working together with just your brain and your fists. There's a whole galaxy of gits just as stubborn, all scrapping with each other when they could be turning the whole thing green – and you're the only one who can bring 'em together. The gods *do* believe in you, boss. Bullets, and Ugrak, and all of them lot believe in you, too. *I* believe in you, and I'm a bleedin' grot. The only person who don't believe in Ghazghkull right now, is Ghazghkull.'

It was only when I heard the echo of my voice that I realised I'd been shouting. But somehow, I still didn't feel scared. And against everything I expected, Ghazghkull was thinking it over. Rolling his jaw about, he was, like he was chewing the thought of it. Then his head settled, and he looked at me again. His eye looked less killy now, which I thought had to be a good sign.

'Yeah,' he said. 'You're right.'

'Really?' I said, 'cos I hadn't expected it to be that easy.

'Oh yeah. It's clear, isn't it. I must've stopped believing in myself... or you started believing a bit too much in yourself, *Makari*.' Ghazghkull stood to his full height then, head scraping the bridge ceiling, and he was the spitting image of the figure from the end of that vision I'd just reminded him of. Only this time, he didn't look half as friendly. The fear was back, all at once. 'Either way, as you like to say, if a lowly, stick-thin little streak of offal like you reckons it can tell me what to do, something has gone wrong.'

He took a step forward then, and stooped down slowly, his head coming closer like a green mountain until it was only a couple of tusklengths from mine.

'*Hasn't it?*' he said, soft as ash, and the force of his breath still nearly knocked me over.

'Yeah,' I said, 'cos contradicting him now didn't seem the smart choice.

'It's useful, though, you talking to me like this.'

'Is it?'

'It is. You've reminded me that a real ork doesn't take counsel from grots. A real ork, Makari – and I'm as real as it gets – doesn't even take counsel from the gods. Or from anyone, but himself.

'You,' he said, and extended a single talon till it touched my shaking chest. 'You were a mistake. A weakness, that I thought was a strength. But from now on, there will be no more mistakes. *There will only be strength.*

   'You tell Gork and Mork I'll be alright without them,' said Ghazghkull, with the bleakest smile I ever saw, and he put his thumb and forefinger to the sides of my head. Then he squeezed. And with a wet pop like a grot's head getting burst, my second life was over.

INTERROGATION IX

'So that was it?' said Falx after a while, not quite sure what else to say.

'For a long time at least, yes,' said Biter gravely. 'Makari has told me that if you want to know about what went down on Golgotha, you'll have to go and ask Yarrick.'

'I'd rather not,' said Falx. 'The man deserves every bit of his status as a hero of the Imperium, but he's possibly the most uptight, self-righteous bore I've ever had the displeasure of being seated next to at dinner.'

Falx could see Cassia's mouth hanging open in her peripheral vision. Raised in a Militarum penal regiment, Yarrick would have loomed nearly as large in her spiritual world as the Emperor Himself did. But the girl was in Falx's world now. And the lord inquisitor believed that if you made it your business to understand aliens, it was a good first step to be realistic about humans.

'You have met him, then?' enquired Biter, doing a bad job of pretending not to be interested.

'Yes, twice.'

'And did he… talk about Ghazghkull much?'

Falx snorted with faint amusement as she considered her reply. 'If you mean to ask, did Yarrick consider Ghazghkull to be his *grod*? Well. I can certainly confirm he hated him with every fibre of his being.'

That seemed to satisfy Makari, at least, when Biter passed it on to the grot.

'Enough of Yarrick,' Hendriksen said irritably – for he too had met the legendary commissar, and held an opinion even more pronounced than Falx's. *'Did you come back again?'*

Falx was amazed, frankly. During the prisoner's relating of Ghazghkull's squabbles on Urk, Brother Hendriksen couldn't have shown more contempt for the story and its narrator. Now that Makari's story had taken on the air of a reincarnation saga, however, not unlike some of the more outlandish tales told around braziers of psychotropic herbs in the shamans' caves of Fenris, the Rune Priest had become noticeably more gripped.

'Well, they are here in the room,' needled Biter, not missing the opportunity to provoke the wolf. 'So I think yes, they must have done at some point.'

'You know exactly what I'm asking,' warned the Astartes, and Biter stopped pushing their luck.

Ghazghkull came round eventually. I knew he would. But I don't mean that in a… *reckon-siliatory* way. He decided he wanted to bring me back, I mean. But it weren't anything to do with faith, or the Great Green. He just thought I'd be a useful tool – or even just something to shut the mobs up, 'cos they kept asking where that good old banner-waver of his had gone.

It was in the middle of a fight, the first time. And you'll find this easier to get through your too-thin skull than the last time I came back, 'cos there was none of that business of being a normal grot first. One moment I was just an idea in a load of fungus, or whatever, minding my own business, and then I was in a trench, pointing a rusty blast-gun over a parapet with shaking hands.

I stumbled and fell down off the firing step, 'cos it turned out this Makari had a leg binned at some point and replaced with a bit of wood, and I hadn't been ready for that. But as I got back to my feet and tried to climb back up the step so I could see over the trench lip, a hand came down out of the red-black sky and yanked the blast-gun off me.

'**…then I'll get *him*, if it'll stop you going on about it!**' thundered Ghazghkull from somewhere above me. For the hand was his, and a second later it plunged back down and shoved that battered old banner into my hand.

Well, I say it was the old banner, but that's an interestin' one. Throughout the last war, the banner had taken a lot of bullets that should've hit me, and one of my few official duties had been to patch it up with scrap and repaint it each time. By the time we'd left Armygeddon, the banner was more'n half patches, and I'd redone the picture on it so many times that I think I'd accidentally become a good painter. Though I never did get the expression on his face right.

Now, though, by the looks of it, the banner'd been shot up so much that not only was there none of the original metal left, but there weren't even any of my patches left. In fact, it was three times the size now, and the painting on it was a *disgrace*. Ghazghkull looked like some kind of… *rubbish gargant*, and whoever'd drawn him couldn't do hands at all. Clearly, a long, long time had gone by. But I was more bothered by the fact *someone else'd been using my banner*.

Probably the ork lying face down on the trench floor with a fresh hole through its head, I reckoned, as the giant hand clamped around my shoulder, and turned me round to face the body, and the crowd of orks around it. The dead ork had been wearing a ridiculous hat, a bit like some of the human *preatures* we'd seen on Armygeddon, which now lay in the rubble next to its burst bonce. I wondered if this'd been Ghazghkull's attempt to invent an ork version of a *preature*, and felt embarrassed for the corpse.

'**There. Makari,**' said Ghazghkull, sounding annoyed, and there was a quick fizzle of pain where his hand lay on my shoulder, as it gave me the hand mark. It felt… insincere. Barely even hurt. '**Happy now?**' growled the boss. '**You've got your "proper banner-waver" again. Count yourself lucky I didn't just kill you for asking for the millionth time. *Now shut up about it, and take that wreck.***'

'Alright, Makari,' said Bullets, nodding at me, 'cos it was him Ghazghkull had been talking to. The Deathskull, who'd been young when he'd been promoted to clan-boss over Dregmek's carcass, looked *well old* now. He'd always been big, but he must've been half as tall again now, and while he'd once been skinny as a whip, his gut had finally got jealous of his shoulders. Bullets had always been good to me. Treated me like dirt, obviously. But in the right way. 'Missed yer,' he said, which made me scowl, so he added 'you little turd' for good measure.

Next to Bullets were some orks I recognised, and some I didn't. There was Ugrak, who was wearing a suit of giga-armour so big that I thought he was a dread, until I saw those wonky eyes leering at me from two different storeys of its bucket-shaped helmet. Then there was Shazfrag, who looked like he'd been blown up and rebuilt a few times, and Grudbolg, who'd already been ancient on Urk, and now looked like something that'd been under a bog for a million years, and was pissed off about it. I didn't see Snazdakka there, and Genrul Straturgum weren't in the trench either, but there was a much younger ork who looked to be wearing his uniform.

'The general had had an unfortunate accident,' said Biter regretfully, placing their mildewed cap on their chest in a ludicrous gesture of remembrance. 'But fortunately, he'd been replaced by an ambitious young officer with an even greater grasp of the art of fights. This was none other than *Colonel Taktikus*,' they revealed, saying the name as if anyone in the room might have had reason to care, 'freshly returned from a long and devious struggle against a brilliant adversary, wherein he learned...'

The Blood Axe rambled on, but Makari had long since stopped talking, and looked confused, annoyed and slightly alarmed all at once.

'Biter,' said Falx patiently.

'Hmm?'

'Nobody asked,' she told them, at the same moment as Makari snapped at the ork with what she was prepared to bet were the same words in its tongue. Biter cleared their throat awkwardly.

'Sorry,' they said, forcing the distinctly unorkish word between their tusks. 'I just had a lot of respect for him, is all. It's a Blood Axe thing.'

Anyway, there was no more time for lookin' about. Ghazghkull had given an order, and he didn't do that for fun. Soon as he'd spoken to me, Bullets raised his head and bellowed the order to charge down the trench, then leapt up to the parapet with an agility that all those years and extra tins of grub had clearly done little to diminish. He grabbed me as he jumped, plopping me in the rubble on the other side of the trench, and I looked out, with the oversized banner in hand, at the biggest war I'd ever seen.

There was a city in front of us so big I thought it was a mountain. I thought it was *loads* of mountains, to be honest. And in front of it, on a wide plain of scrubby green weeds, war machines were knocking each other to bits on a scale that made the best laughs of Ghazghkull's southward push look boring. It was all so big that it took me a couple of seconds to realise the plain weren't covered in weeds at all. That was *orks*, that was. More'n I'd ever seen in any life.

It was so vast, so... *fighty*, that I didn't even glance away from it when I saw Ghazghkull's enormous boots plod forward to the left of me, in the corner of my vision. He'd not even spoken to me after bringing me back, and seemed to have forgotten me already, so I didn't see why I should bother paying attention to him. And he had murdered me, after all.

But then, it wasn't like he'd not been *entitled* to kill me. And it would've been worth it, if he'd eventually looked back on that chat we'd had and come to his senses about Armageddon. Looking out at that big fight, I gave into one of my most ungrotly habits, and hoped. Maybe this was it. Maybe this was the start of the Big One I'd tried to inspire him to: the first, mighty step in a rampage that would drown the galaxy in green. It certainly looked big.

But then I smelled sulphur. Not just sulphur, neither. Fuel, and sewage, and ash and rot and hot rock... this nose weren't put there by Mork for decoration, you know? Smell's the best of a grot's senses, and it never forgets the smell of a place. The nose knows. And the nose knew, then, that I'd been here before. That city in front of us was Volcanus, the place where I'd begun my second life, only with a load of new fortifications. And this was Gork-smacked Armygeddon. Again.

The big idiot had gone back after all. And if he wanted me to wave his stick for him as he squandered his destiny here, he could forget about it.

In fact, it wasn't even like he properly wanted that. He'd only summoned me to stop Bullets' gob. And as I thought it through, I realised that he'd probably been being... is *sarcastic* the word? *Fine*, he'd been saying to Bullets. *You want Makari back? You care that much about a grot holding a stick? Well here's one for yer.* Only thing was, Ghazghkull's will was so powerful, he could make a whole person exist just by saying something he didn't mean.

I looked out at that big, pointless fight, and at Ghazghkull's back as he ploughed into it, and realised I was an accident. Nothing more'n a throwaway point, in a conversation the boss'd already forgotten. And I know it ain't right for a grot to think highly of itself, but I knew I was more'n that.

You remember they always said I was lucky? Well, I still was. But that didn't mean bullets couldn't hit me. Just meant I didn't *want* 'em to, and they tended to oblige. That sense of... *preservashun* weren't such a concern to me now. Quite the opposite. And given the proper hurricane of bullets that was headed towards the ork line, now that the charge had started, the sort of luck I was after weren't hard at all to manufacture.

In fact, there was a nice little stream of rounds smacking into a dead ork just a few steps away – some gunner whose aim was off, probably. I decided to help him out. The last thing I heard was the ringing thuds of the banner gaining a load of new holes, and the little wet rips as my body did too. I was dead before I hit the ground.

'Do you think Ghazghkull realised it was actually you?' asked Falx.

'Makari thinks *Bullets* realised,' Biter clarified. 'And that he must've told Ghazghkull, given what happened after.'

'So it happened again?' she suggested, raising an eyebrow.

'Oh *yes*,' said Biter, as Makari held out its unbroken arm, plus both legs, and began counting off fingers and toes, muttering under its breath all the while. After losing count and starting again twice, the grot abandoned the effort with a shrug, and Biter passed the gesture on to Falx. 'Many times,' they summarised.

'But if Ghazghkull had a purpose for you, and summoned you to do it,' asked Cassia, gnawing on her lip as she tried to reason her way through Makari's sordid moral universe, 'weren't you dishonouring Gork and Mork by giving him the slip every time?'

'Nah,' came the translated reply. 'Just Ghazghkull. I don't think he knew what the gods wanted, in them days. Don't think he cared.'

'But still,' Cassia continued, with something of her old penal legion hardness creeping into her tone, 'he gave you an order.'

That made Makari laugh, when Biter told it.

'You really don't get grots, do you, big human? Remember what I told you earlier – 'bout how it ain't ungodly for a grot to try escaping its master, since it means the ork has to prove their right to power by stopping 'em? Well, this was just that, but more.'

Makari went on to narrate a seemingly endless, increasingly creative series of summonings from Ghazghkull, followed almost immediately by equally inventive deaths on Makari's part. And from the way the gretchin told it, it seemed that each time the two met – however briefly – the ork warlord had become ever more despondent. It was becoming clear that the malaise which had consumed the ork during the siege of Hades Hive had never truly gone away. The gods (*or whatever aspect of madness he interpreted as their voices*, she corrected herself, piously), had maintained their silence inside his ravaged skull. And as the war for Armageddon had escalated into the apocalyptic, perpetual stalemate of its peak, it seemed Ghazghkull's weakness had taken hold of him again.

Falx felt this was a line of enquiry that could stand a little further pressure.

'If the progression of battles I'm inferring from these… morbid vignettes is correct,' she said, stopping Biter mid-flow as they described Makari beating itself to death with a wrench, 'then we must be nearing the point at which Ghazghkull was last sighted on Armageddon. And I'm guessing that Makari may know something about why he left.'

When the interpreter put this to her captive, Makari stayed tight-lipped at first. In the slowly swaying light of the cell's bulb, its eyes slid in and out of shadow, seeming bright with fury during one illumination, and then gloomy with remorse in the next. Once again, Falx was exasperated by the futility of trying to deduce the grot's feelings, from a face only capable of variations on the theme of malice. Eventually, however, Makari broke out into a wicked grin.

'Yes,' said Biter, 'they say they do.'

CHAPTER NINE

GHAZGHKULL'S EPIPHANY

'**I ain't gonna say sorry,**' said Ghazghkull, glowering down at me from the reddest sky I ever saw.

'**I ain't gonna say sorry,**' he repeated, as his hand left my shoulder, and he straightened up to his full height, "**cos I'll never say that to anyone. Not to any other ork. Not to the gods themselves. And definitely not to a grot – no matter what a devious, infuriating little piece of work he is.**'

A thick bank of smoke blew across the boss, obscuring him, then flashed from the inside with vicious light, as the cannon strapped to his klaw opened up against some target hidden deeper in the murk. I didn't hear it though, or at least I didn't notice the noise, 'cos every nerve in my body was screaming green bloody murder at the pain of the burn where he'd touched me. Felt like it'd seared through to bone this time, and it was all I could do not to drop the banner that I now realised was clenched in the claws of my left hand.

But as the pain started fading into a raw, sullen throb, I thought about what he'd just said to me. For a start, it was the first time since he'd killed me – the first time during this whole ridiculous campaign – that he'd actually spoken directly to me. *Devious, infuriating little piece of work*, he'd said. And I ain't vain, 'cos a grot shouldn't be. But nobody minds being flattered all the same, and that had been some high praise indeed. My impulse on waking up had been to find a bullet to get in the way of, but if he was gonna talk to me like that, I figured, maybe I'd hear him out. And besides, there was something different to him this time that I couldn't quite put a claw on. He just seemed more… *him*.

'Gork thrash your hide, Makari,' Ghazghkull cursed, growling the words like gravel as the smoke cleared, and he reloaded the cannon. **'You've given me some headaches, you have. But headaches are where I do my best thinking. And so, Makari, I've been thinking. Follow.'**

With the hiss and clank of pistons, Ghazghkull turned, and began to stomp ponderously up a steep slope of broken rock, in the direction he'd fired his gun. Only it weren't rock, I noticed, when I looked down to start scrambling after him – it was little fragments of armour that'd been blown up so many times they was almost like gravel. As my mind got settled in its new hidey-hole, I became aware of a lot of shouting, every-where. And a *lot* of explosions.

'And like I ain't saying sorry,' the boss explained, as his feet shifted whole dunes of smashed-up metal and ceramite in his climb up the ridge, **'I ain't saying I was wrong either. I wasn't wrong to kill you. And I wasn't wrong in coming back to this world.'**

I hopped between the little platforms of flattened scree his feet'd left, using the banner-pole to steady me, until I arrived, wheezing myself ragged, at the top beside him. The smoke was back, and obscured everything above Ghazghkull's waist. But I could hear him breathe in deep somewhere up above it, like he was savouring something. Like he could see something I couldn't. He breathed out, long and steady.

'**Do you smell it, Makari?**' he asked.

I did. Smelled like bleedin' Armygeddon. But this weren't the time for smart answers, so I lurked, sitting myself on a cracked-open beakie helmet near his right boot.

'**Do you see it, Makari. What I've made here?**'

Of course I didn't, 'cos of the smoke. But then the wind snatched it back again, and from the top of that ridge, I saw the most beautiful, terrible thing.

War, it was. But written in the biggest letters you could find. Mega War. *Holy War* – an echo of that perfect, ancient violence that every ork knew, deep down, they'd been designed for. Machines so big they moved like clouds, carving each other up in great slews of sparks. A sea of bodies – ork and human, living and dead – flowing over a perfect wilderness of trenches and craters and pounded rubble.

As I looked up from that divine catastrophe at its towering *arkytekt*, my vision passed over swarms of aircraft – ours and theirs, it didn't matter – wheeling in flocks so dense they might've been smoke themselves, and bursting in sudden, bright clusters of death. My eyes moved up and up through that blizzard of fire and steel, until they settled on it. Solid and deep green and immovable, at the heart and crown of it all: the head of the Prophet.

He had his head tipped back, with one eye closed in rapture and leathery nostrils spread wide, like he was letting each sense have its turn to revel in what he'd done. But then I clocked it; that hadn't been the wind, whipping the smoke away. That'd been Ghazghkull, breathing it all in, so that I could see. He'd taken all that annihilation and fury and mayhem, the entire will and fury of two interstellar empires, and he'd only gone and bleedin' *smoked it*.

His chest swelled with enough war-smoke to choke a whole mob of grots, and as he held it in, the clouds above him began to flash with light. There were shapes moving in that glow: huge shadows, drifting into each other and smashing together in sprays of darkness. Spaceships, I realised. Massive things savaging each other to scrap, in a fight that made what was going on down here look rubbish. A fight so big, we could only see it as shadows *projekted* by the light of its own fury.

Ghazghkull was still breathing in, like he'd never run out of space inside himself. And as he did, one patch of light right over his head was getting brighter and brighter. Like something was coming.

This is holy, Makari, said Ghazghkull, as that light got too bright to look at. And I swear to Mork his lips didn't move, even though I heard the words clear as anything in my head.

When the light faded, his eye was open, looking right at me. And next to it, plunging down where it had punched through the sky, was a zogging great rock. A rock with guns all over it, that fired in all directions as it came down, just for the joy of shooting. When the rock got halfway down the sky, a cluster of rockets – they must've been big as a city – lit up on its arse end, and it started coming down even harder towards the ground. I held the banner up as high as it would go, and I couldn't help but shout at the top of my weedy lungs, for the *beauty* of it all.

But I never saw the rock hit. 'Cos Ghazghkull grinned a grin as wide as Gork's, and out from between his tusks came all of that smoke, thicker and angrier than it'd been before, and covering everything I could see.

'**Really does smell good, don't it?**' said Ghazghkull, and I had to agree. 'Cos it did. And yeah, it was still the smell of Armygeddon, like I'd already known – the smell that'd made me decide to piss off, at the start of the war. But now it was different. Richer. There was a whole cluster of new scents layered in it – all the oils and potions that a hundred different beakie-mobs used to anoint their armour, and all the blood and guts left behind when that armour cracked. The sweat and terror of human soldiers from all across the galaxy, and the weird elements cooked up in the hearts of mek giga-weapons. It was a grand old smell.

'**Come on then,**' said Ghazghkull, and against the light of what must've been the rock smacking down into the ground, I saw his *silloowet* trudging off down the other side of the ridge.

'What're we attacking?' I asked, reckoning it'd be alright to ask a question.

'**Nothing,**' said the boss simply. '**We're leaving.**'

Well, I hadn't expected that.

'Doesn't look like we won yet though?' I said, surprised that I felt so disappointed at the idea of leaving, all of a sudden.

'**Not yet,**' agreed Ghazghkull. '**We will, mind. But me, and you? We're done here.**'

As we walked across the battlefield in the smoke, Ghazghkull explained. And it was weird, 'cos although I'd seen millions fighting from the top of that ridge, we only seemed to come across corpses, like everyone'd gotten out of our way so we could talk.

He'd made the war so big, he said, that the humans had been forced to ship in troops from a slice of space so big, it took even starlight a thousand years to get across it. Whole *worlds* worth of the puny gits had been fed into the grinder Ghazghkull had made of this planet, as well as enough steel to empty the mines of whole star systems. There were many-many-and-five different beakie mobs here, six great-mobs of human gargants, and no less than many-and-seven fleets of the humans' big pointy spaceships.

And that wasn't even starting on the orks. The boss had come here with a horde, sure enough. But unlike the first invasion, where that'd been chipped away by the war, this time round his forces had doubled every year. Orks were flooding here from distant worlds, just like they'd flooded to Urk from the outer planets, he said, 'cos they'd *felt it*. They knew something was happening here. Something special. And they didn't know exactly what it was, but in the same way a magnet wants to smash itself on steel, they wanted a part of it.

It wasn't like the fight was just here, either. Seeing as so many humans had been funnelled into this big scrap, there were loads of planets nearby just waiting for a good kicking, and Ghazghkull had already heard reports of massive invasions splitting off from his own, led by orks he'd never even met, to go off and boot 'em to bits in his name.

'**You wanted me to unite the orks, Makari. Do you see, now? That's exactly what I've done. And I've done it just by fighting, every step of the way. Fighting here, just like I said I would.**'

He paused for a moment, so I nearly scampered into the back of his shins, and turned back to point a talon at me. I couldn't see his face then, just the glow of his metal eye in the smoke, and when he spoke again, it was in a cold, hard voice that made the rest of the world seem to fall silent.

'**So don't ever doubt me again. Not ever. I took my time, yes. We both know I had… moments. But I found the best**

way – the way of the gods – and it led me here. That was always the plan. And that's the truth, 'cos I said so.' Then he carried on walking.

Now, I remembered things *slightly* different from that. But then, as I think you know better than you say you do, there's room in the idea of truth for more'n one thing. And when Ghazghkull reckons something, other truths just have to get out of the way and make room for it, yeah? Just like the Prophet had walked to Rustspike holding in his brain, and fighting all those animals along the way, so too had he planned for this all along. That's just what happened.

After a while walking without saying anything, we stopped, in the place Ghazghkull said we was meant to wait. The rock, he'd told me, had been a bit of fun to cover our escape – a *distraction*, so that Yarrick, who'd not be keen to be given the slip a second time, would be too busy to spot a single ork ship peel away from the fight in orbit. The clan-bosses were already gone, he said, sent off on wars of their own at last, and I could only hope Grotsnik had been forced to take the same privilege. It was just us now on Armygeddon, at least of all the orks I'd ever known, and in a little while, the meks' machines would whisk us away into space.

Ghazghkull stood and brooded about holy stuff, like he tends to when he has to wait, and I made myself comfortable on a dead human without too many wet bits on it. It was eerily quiet here now, since the fight had moved off to the brutal new fronts left behind after the rock's impact. Every few seconds, some dying human screamed somewhere in the gloom, but that was quite relaxing to be honest. It was one of them… *companionary* silences.

But thinking back, I could've sworn Ghazghkull had been gearing up to say something else to me, and decided against it. And since I'd been born a cheeky git, and died as one many times, I couldn't help myself.

'Boss?' I asked.

'Yeah?' he answered, in a tone that said I'd better choose my words dead carefully.

'You were saying that you wasn't sorry, and that you wasn't wrong about killing me, or coming here, but that you'd been thinking about it all...'

'I was saying that.'

'Well, it sounded like... Um... It sounded like there might've been a bit more in that train of thought, that you ain't said yet.'

Ghazghkull stared at me for ages, but he looked curious more than he looked angry.

'I have no idea what Mork was thinking when he made you, grot,' he said at last, rubbing his skullplate with the heel of his hand. **'But it was a one-off job.'** He sighed, then marched right up to me, and spoke.

'It was the headaches, alright. They got worse, and for all the work Grotsnik did, it barely seemed to slow 'em down.'

Funny that, I thought.

'I thought they'd maybe get better when we landed here. And they did, for a bit. But then they started getting worse again. You remember a few months back, when you beat yourself to death with that wrench?'

'Yeah,' I said, scratching my face so he wouldn't see me grin.

'Made me angry, Makari. Really angry. A fit came on me, right in front of all the bosses, and I had to start fighting one of them to cover it. I won, of course. And there was no hard feelings. But it was close. And it made me think about why I was getting the headaches.'

'Was it the gods, boss?'

'**Yeah, Makari. It was the gods. They'd been speaking to me this whole time I thought they'd gone quiet. They'd been speaking to me by kicking me in the head. What does it mean when I kick someone in the head?**'

'That you want 'em to listen.'

'**Right. So in the end, I listened. And at last, it all made sense.**' Ghazghkull looked up into the swirling, silent smoke, and sighed again. '**The gods saw what I did here the last time. They saw Golgotha, and they've seen all this. They looked on it, and saw it was good. But they've grown impatient, Makari. Like I was, looking down at that brawl from the balcony on Urk. When I realised how much... more it could be.**'

He swept his klaw all around him then, leaving little eddies in the smog where it caught on the pointy bits.

'**Turns out there is too much of a good thing. And you saw, just now, how good this is. But it's as good as it'll get. That lightning's all bottled up, and it can't get any bigger. What's happening here... needs to happen *everywhere*. And that's what we're off to do now.**' I nodded, 'cos he still hadn't said the thing I knew he'd been doing everything to avoid saying, but he was nearly there.

'**And... well. I suppose what I'm saying, Makari, is not that I'm sorry,**' he said for the fifth time, '**or that I was wrong,**' he said for the fifth time, too, and then growled in frustration. '**And by Gork and Mork and the Great Green itself, I swear you really *are* the luckiest grot who ever crawled out of a hole, that I'm even considering saying this to you, but...**'

He grimaced, like a normal ork might at the prospect of a session under Grotsnik's knife, coming to the edge of it, but shuffling slower and slower with every step.

'**You—**'

But he didn't get any further'n that. 'Cos there was a squeaky, rumbly clanking noise, and we both looked round to see a big shadow limping through the smoke. A human tank it was, absolutely knackered, with a load of shell-holes in it, and half the tracks hanging off on one side. That was a surprise, as I'd thought all the armies had moved on by now. But then I suppose Gork and Mork can be quite creative sometimes, when they really need to make a point. The tank's turret swivelled round with a sound like a snotling getting poked with a drill, there was a hollow thud from somewhere inside it, and it fired.

Ghazghkull made a confused face, and looked down at the hole in the armour, right over where his guts were.

'**They shot me,**' he observed, like it didn't make sense.

'You alright, boss?' I asked, as the tank just sat there like it didn't know what to do.

'**Oh yeah,**' he said. '**Armour'll need patching up. But I don't think it went in. Always said I had the hardest gut around.**' He poked a klaw-tip into the hole, and peered down his chest at it. '**Huh. Warhead didn't even go off.**'

Then the warhead went off. A fountain of blood and shrapnel shot from the hole in Ghazghkull's armour, and the Prophet of Gork and Mork keeled over backwards. The only sound then was the squeak of the hatch on the tank's turret, as a human face peered out with a look of such shock that I thought its eyes'd fall out. It started screaming down into the tank, presumably for someone to get another shell loaded, and I could hear the frantic shouts from inside, even when the hatch slammed shut again.

I scampered over to where Ghazghkull's head lay, on the smashed-up armour that covered the plain, and I realised I had no idea what to do. He weren't dead – it was just a tank shell, after all, and he was Ghazghkull – but he'd be out of it for a few minutes, and hurt enough that it'd take him a few hours to recover. Problem was, we didn't even have a few minutes before that tank was gonna fire again. I almost wished Grotsnik'd been there. He at least would've known how to sort this out. But then my nasty little head got to work, and I had my own answer.

'Dealt with it, boss,' I said, a minute or so later, as I picked a lump of gore that I'd missed off my hand, and picked up the banner from where I'd left it leaning on Ghazghkull's chest.

'What?' said Ghazghkull, his eye narrowing groggily as he came to.

'It was easy. I'd heard the humans in the tank, even when the hatch was closed, and I knew there had to be a reason. Then I remembered all the holes in it, and I figured one of 'em at least had to be grot-sized. It was.'

I grinned, and in the reflection on the lens of the Prophet's metal eye, I saw all the bits of flesh still stuck between my sharp little teeth.

'Didn't take long after that, boss. Wish you could've seen their faces, though.'

'Alright,' said Ghazghkull, and took a deep, shuddering breath, before clenching his jaw and sitting up. *'Alright,'* he said again, and I saw that he was looking up at the sky, where the gods probably were. **'You've made your point. I'll say it. Makari?'**

'Yes, boss?'

'You were right. The gods want me to unite the orks. There. Now, let's go and turn the stars green.'

ACT FOUR

INTERROGATION X

Makari had tried, unconvincingly, to act like Ghazghkull's second exit from Armageddon had been the end of the story it had to tell. But everyone in the room, and Brother Hendriksen in particular, had been adamant that it was not.

And so they had continued for a while, dealing with Yarrick's pursuit, the battle of the haunted gulf, and Ghazghkull's purloining of an entire space armada from the warlord Urgok. It was just fight, after fight, after fight, told with tireless relish by that cackling wretch and its Throne-forsaken interpreter.

By the time they had endured six hours of the Octarian War, however, in which Ghazghkull had defeated a seemingly never-ending sequence of ever-larger tyranid beasts in single combat, Falx had been flagging. The interrogation had been going on for its twenty-second straight hour without a break by then, as they hadn't paused the questioning since Xotal's death, and in the end it had taken a stern mental prod from Cassia for Falx to even admit to herself that she was fatigued. She'd tried to point out to the ogryn that Hendriksen had been on his feet just as long as she had, but that had only earned her a tight-lipped look of scepticism in reply. Cassia had not needed the nuance of psychic communication to point out how ridiculous a standard that had been to set for herself.

Then the psyker had vacated her head, and abruptly asked for a six-hour adjournment to the session, out loud. Falx had permitted it, and though she had left the cell irritated with the fact she needed rest at all, she had been satisfied at least that she hadn't been the one to call for it.

And now she was here, in the stale-smelling, slightly too-humid space that passed for her quarters. The captain's cabin on the *Exactor* was palatial, but the lord inquisitor had long ago vacated it in favour of this cubbyhole, repurposing her original suite as an armoury. She had tried to convince herself the decision had been made out of spartan humility. And maybe, for her younger self, it might have been. But no matter how many rejuve treatments you had access to, you didn't get to your fourteenth decade without appreciating the worth of a good bed, and Falx missed that gold-braided monstrosity every time she woke up with a new click in her spine.

No, the miserable truth was, Falx had abandoned the captain's cabin as she just couldn't sleep in that big a room, with that many shadows.

Glancing at the servo-skull hovering patiently beyond the bed's drapes, whose ocular read-out she had set to display the shipboard time, Falx groaned in irritation. Four hours had passed, and it barely seemed worth trying to sleep any more. She was just debating whether to call the interrogation back to session early, when there was a thump on the door.

'Come in, Brother Hendriksen,' she sighed, as Cassia slept

like a professional, and nobody else on the crew would know her well enough to be so assured that she had no rest to be disturbed. 'Leave the light off,' she said, waving a hand from the bed as his enormous form lumbered into her peripheral vision. 'You couldn't sleep either? Or didn't you want to?'

'Could have done, actually,' said the Fenrisian dolefully. 'But I wanted to eat more. Skipped a lot of meals, listening to that damned *grønnissen*.' The old psyker sat heavily on the battered armchair across the chamber from the bed, and Falx heard, rather than saw, the cold roast synth-bird he'd brought with him as a palate-cleanser.

'And while you ate,' asked Falx, 'did you wonder the same thing as me? Namely, why Makari would so willingly betray its beloved prophet, now that we know they were so touchingly reunited upon his departure from Armageddon?'

'Don't think it's betraying him at all,' said Hendriksen plainly, as he chewed. 'I think it's a trick. They're trying to play us.'

'That was your reasoning for doubting Makari's identity, too,' she pointed out. 'But that turned out to be real enough.'

Brother Hendriksen shrugged in the dark.

'I still think it's all a deception, lord inquisitor. You're the one with a tendency to change your opinions to suit the facts, after all. You want to watch that.' The Space Marine took another great, cracking chomp, and talked through a mouthful of meat. 'Can be dangerous, you know.'

Falx half-laughed, and let the silence settle on the dingy cabin for a while, like the worn comfort of an old trench-blanket.

'So go on, then,' she said at last. 'What's their scheme, do you think?'

'No idea,' answered Hendriksen, with the casual air of someone who'd long ago grown unconcerned by the scheming of aliens. 'But whatever it is, we'll catch them out before they spring it. Or just after. Either way, this isn't the day the monsters get one over on us, Tytonida. All will be well.'

'All will be well,' sighed Falx, who had lived her entire life convinced of the opposite. 'You say that every damned time – and you really believe it, don't you? Is this… optimism a personal thing, or did the Emperor make your kind with faith built in?'

'*Faith?*' barked Hendriksen, waving a half-stripped bone in mock scorn. '*Faith* is thinking other people will solve your problems. Faith isn't for the likes of you and I, Falx. *Hrm.* We *are* those other people. We solve the problems.' The Fenrisian crunched down on the bone and swallowed the shards, before speaking again. But this time, there was real scorn in his voice. 'And the Emperor might be our father, but He is not our maker. An Astartes makes himself.'

'With a little help from the gene-seed,' added the inquisitor drily, and Hendriksen leaned forward, temper roused.

'The spirit of the wolf is *earned*, Falx. It is not some random boon. It is a curse, as you well know, carried by those of us with the will to surpass our humanity. But it is a blessing, too. It gives me… what you called my optimism. I know all will be well, because whatever ill comes to pass, *I know I will be capable of making it well*. Or I shall die well in the trying. So there is nothing to be concerned about.'

Falx was still combing her mind for the words to express just how spectacularly incomprehensible that sort of confidence was, when the silence was split by the drawn-shriek of a siren in the concourse outside. An instant later, the chamber was plunged into the angry red gloom of the *Exactor*'s emergency lighting system.

Containment breach. The words slunk into Falx's mind like ice water, even before the warnings had appeared on her data-vis.

Hendriksen was already on his feet, knife drawn, with his eyes flicking grimly over the invisible text of his own ocular read-out. Moments ago, a maintenance servitor had found the brig door open, with the full squad of Falx's private guard dead around it. And now, even as Falx scrambled into her ship-coat and snatched up her pistol belt, a new alert was pulsing in the ship's dorsal barrack deck. A cabin had been breached.

'Cassia,' gasped Hendriksen, just as Falx pinpointed the source of the second alert herself, and he sprinted for the door.

Falx followed. And while she thought about reminding Hendriksen of his assertion that all would be well, she soon decided it would be better to save her breath for running.

Cassia had not had a clean death.

Just as was the case with an ork, you just *couldn't* kill an ogryn cleanly, at least if all you had was a knife. And going by the awful landscape of gouges, slashes and punctures that had been carved into her mountain of a body, it had certainly been a knife. By the looks of it, the struggle had started at her desk, while she had been at work on her journal. The Imperial Truth held that ogryns could not write, of course. But over the last two years, through repeated study of old Ordo Biologos texts borrowed from Falx's personal library, she had been teaching herself. Cassia had developed a fine hand for calligraphy, of late. But now her journal, like everything else in the room, was coated in thick, congealing blood. The Truth, Falx supposed, had been restored.

'Biter,' growled Hendriksen, from where he squatted on his haunches beside the psyker's body.

'The servitor,' replied Falx.

'Bjorn's claws, woman, what do you speak of?'

'The servitor that brought Xotal's tank in. After Biter went to help it clamp the wheels, they put their hands on it. They must've snatched the clearance stud from it, and kept hold of it 'til we were gone.'

'Impossible,' growled Hendriksen. 'Those things are bolted on. No ork is that fast.'

'This one was,' retorted Falx, and looked back at the wreckage surrounding the body of the woman who might one day have become her acolyte.

Cassia had fallen in a tangle of smashed furniture, and from the patches of dark ork blood mixed in with the lake of her own, and the stink of ozone in the air, it seems she had put up a good fight on all fronts. But looking at the deep puncture wound in the side of her neck – the first inflicted, Falx presumed, and deep enough to open her cable-thick carotid artery – she had not stood a chance.

'Well fought, girl,' whispered Hendriksen, as his eyes, widening with wrath, flicked to the trail of black blood leading to the cabin's secondary entrance. It led to the barracks' mess area, and beyond that lay the *Exactor*'s dorsal transitway.

'They'll be headed to the aft escape pod cluster,' said Falx, as she registered the slashed canvas where the access device had been cut from the wrist of Cassia's ship-coat. Hendriksen was already gone when she turned, pounding across the barracks with the scent of ork-blood in his augmented nostrils.

But even the old wolf was not a fast enough hunter for this quarry. As he saw the same new data-vis alert as Falx – of an unplanned pod jettison from the aft cluster – he stopped in his tracks, muttering a Fenrisian curse. As they were still making transit through the warp, there was no point trying to shoot the pod down; it would have tumbled back into realspace the moment it left the *Exactor*'s Geller field.

The ork had escaped.

Brother Hendriksen should have howled in frustration, or torn a steel table from its mountings, or manifested his fury as a storm of unfocused psychic energy. But he did none of those things. Instead, the shaman took a long, steadying breath, shook his head as if to clear it, and pulled out the last of the synth-bird. It was Falx, then, who lost her temper.

'Pox you rotten, Rune Priest! How can you be so callous as to *eat*, at a time like this? She's dead, Hendriksen. *Dead*. Does that mean nothing to you beside your damned appetite?'

Hendriksen swallowed, wiped his hands on his thighs, and then began to walk slowly towards her. After the messy confrontation that had forged their bond, all those years ago, Falx had always thought twice before speaking to the wolf in anger. And now, as his eyes locked on hers, shining with a deathly, cold stillness, she remembered why.

'Never presume what I do, or do not feel,' he warned, in a voice soft as a predator's steps in snow. 'I will mourn. But before that, there will likely be violence. My body is large, it must be fuelled. This is not some merry feast, *Lord Falx*. This is me maintaining my capacity to kill.'

Falx swallowed hard, and pressed her heels against the steel of the deck to will herself against stepping backwards from the psyker.

'Of course, Brother Hendriksen,' she said, nailing down her temper. 'I misspoke.'

'Forgiven,' said the Space Marine, but the ice did not leave his eyes. 'Now, the grot. Unless our escapee has also found time to tinker with our monitoring systems, the creature remains in its cell.'

'You intend to kill it?' asked Falx, wanting nothing more now.

'No. I intend for us to finish interrogating it. This is a vessel of the Ordo Xenos, inquisitor. Let us do what we do best.'

Although the cell had been left open, and the prisoner's restraints had been cut, they arrived to find the grot sitting cross-legged at the foot of the interrogation chair. And despite its shattered arm, its smashed nose, and the great gouge where its flesh had been cut away for the Cupbearer, it was grinning. It did not look afraid to die. If anything, Falx thought, it seemed faintly crestfallen as Hendriksen did not move to strike it, but entered the room with no regard to the creature, and set down the heavy roll of fur he had fetched from his quarters.

'I hate to ask the obvious,' ventured Falx, as Hendriksen untied the thongs securing the bundle, and unrolled it on the cell's floor. 'But how are we going to interrogate the thing, if it doesn't know a word of Gothic?'

'There are older ways,' said the Rune Priest simply, and began to strip out of his shipboard overalls. Seeing the collection of items laid out on the unrolled fur, Falx began to realise what the shaman had in mind. There were bundled herbs, pitch-blackened animal skulls, and horn vessels stoppered with plugs of crude wax. There were runes formed from the twine-fastened bones of infants, and strips of desiccated, evil-looking meat. And at the centre of it all glistened the long, cruel sharpness of a kraken's tooth.

He really does mean old ways, she thought. And despite herself, the fascination for all things alien which had led her into this disaster of a life flared anew.

The paraphernalia on the pelt had nothing to do with the Emperor's light. These were things from the long darkness of the Fenrisian winter; unguents that had glistened in firelit caves long before the Master of Mankind had ever come to bring His hunters back to heel. But they had never been forgotten. And for all that Hendriksen had espoused the discipline and doctrine of sanctioned Imperial psykers – *he had been trying to set a good example for Cassia*, she only realised now – he had always kept these eerie relics to hand.

The Space Marine was fully naked now, and his body was terrible to look upon. Falx had never been particularly interested in male bodies, but even if she had been, she would have found little to relish in Hendriksen's. It was masculinity amplified into nothing but a weapon: something *constructed*, with all the accidental grace of nature stripped away, and replaced with the monolithic brutalism of an armoured vehicle. As Hendriksen grabbed a pot of some reeking oil, and began smearing it over a torso pocked with scars, scalpel-seams, stretch marks and the angry welts of embedded socket ports, Falx found sudden insight into why the Astra Militarum's main battle tank had been dubbed the Leman Russ.

Hendriksen's tattoos, she saw now, had been inked when he had still been human. They were warped now, stretched over the places where bones had been rebuilt, and where hillocks of muscle had been forced to grow. In their contortion, you could almost see the ghost of the boy he had once been, stretched out over the frame of a monster, and Falx felt a moment of pity for Hendriksen as he traced over their lines with a fingertip dripping with rancid tallow.

When his body was prepared, Hendriksen took up the kraken's tooth, whispered what was either a prayer or a curse, and began dragging its point across his chest, thighs, forehead and shoulders with nothing but coldness in his eyes. The wicked fang was guided by ancient ridges of scar tissue, where it had bitten the Rune Priest in years long past, and blood sprang hungrily from the reopened wounds. Repulsed by the grease the shaman had applied to his runic markings, the flow parted around the tattoos, so they continued to shine as blue as his eyes did, through the dark red sheen of gore.

Clothed now in nothing but his own blood and his ancestors' words of power, Hendriksen walked forwards in a trail of sopping red footprints, beard dripping as he approached the prisoner. Makari was not grinning any more.

'Ghazghkull left Armageddon,' he stated, as he crouched down and squatted until his eyes were level with the creature's. 'He built up his forces, in preparation for a broader war, and for a long time, he evaded pursuit. But not forever. He was hunted down, grot, wasn't he? By *Ragnar*.'

As the bloodied apparition said the name of his former Wolf Lord, Makari's eyes widened in recognition – and in hatred. The creature hissed between wet, blackened teeth.

'You saw the fight, didn't you?' continued Hendriksen. 'I know you did. I see it in your xenos eyes. *I smell it on you.*'

Those last words emerged as a growl that made Falx's scalp pucker around the skullplate at the nape of her neck, and while she opened her mouth to speak, she could not find the words to express her unease. Hendriksen's head snapped round anyway, fixing her with those horrible, expressionless eyes in their mask of cruor.

'Cassia always held that a picture spoke a thousand words, did she not?' said the shaman. 'So I shall do this thing to honour her. We have heard enough of this wretch's words. Let us see what is in its mind directly, at last.'

Turning the blood-matted, shaggy immensity of his head back to Makari, the Rune Priest reached forward with a dripping arm, and in a motion too fast for the gretchin to react to, clamped his hand around the beast's skull.

'Vihss-megh Krongar,' he commanded, in some archaic version of his native tongue. His voice was wind whipping through bare black branches. It was the creaking grind of sea-ice, tightening around the timbers of a ship. It was a blizzard, and Falx became lost in it.

CHAPTER TEN

GHAZGHKULL'S EVEN BIGGER FIGHT

Masonry shatters with the impact of bolt-shells; the air is thick with smoke.

Above, the shell of a great cathedral has been cracked, beneath a sky ripped through with war. It is either night, or day made dark by fire, and the bruise-black storm clouds are raked by the bright talons of fire. You do not know if they are the wreckage of the mighty ships which trade blows beyond the veil, or more drop pods, marked with the head of the wolf.

Below, there are bodies. You crawl among them. As your taloned hands scrabble over the flagstones, groping a way forward through the black breath of war, they encounter flesh and sundered armour. There are the bodies of my brothers, with limbs sheared cruelly, cleaved by wicked blades. There are the bodies of your masters, riven by chain and shell.

Here, now, is the slack jaw of a great ork warrior; you use his tusks as footholds as you scramble over his legless torso, and then dive back among the dead, as gunfire rattles and shells sing above your head. Quivering in terror, you reach desperately over the corpse, and pull your bullet-riddled banner over to join you.

There is a deep rumble, and the floor shakes; ahead of you, a column of stone sags and begins to fall slowly sideways. It falls like the fist of one of your brutish gods, raising plumes of fire and dust. It is only an aftershock, you know, of the blast which felled the ribs of the roof. Beset from all sides, your Prophet detonated a great store of munitions hidden in the walls, so as to cut both himself and his opponent off from the support of their warriors.

He knows he must fight this combat alone. Because he has had a vision. You were there. It was his greatest vision yet, and his most violent, seizing his body as if the gods themselves had him in their jaws. He came round from it knowing that this fight was destined; that it was the narrowing he had to pass through, in order to bring about the flourishing of your Great Green.

But the falling roof has cut you off from your master just as thoroughly. You had been following close behind him, when an explosion sent you sprawling. A grenade, you realised, as shrapnel lanced into your flesh. And behind its shockwave came my brothers, throats alight with the war cries of the ancient mountains.

You ran from their advance, scurrying back to cower in the smoke. Ever since, you have been crawling among the bodies, trying to find a route back to your Prophet through the labyrinth of carnage. Until now, every wretched advance has met a dead end, forcing you to backtrack, and you have grown ever-more anxious at the bellows of the Prophet, as they have rolled out from the duel at the centre of the great structure.

But now, you have a way to rejoin him. The falling column has crushed orks and the sons of Russ alike, and for now at least, the way ahead of you is clear. Shrieking the blasphemy you might call a prayer, you raise the banner in your spindly limbs, and you charge across the waste of smashed stone. Slap-click-slap-click; your unshod, taloned feet smack against the masonry as you sprint through the ruins towards the dirge of the Prophet's roars.

You do not know what aid you plan to offer him, only that you must be by his side, by the will of your gods. So you push through the smoke that hovers like the terror in your head, and you run on. You hop over the limbs that poke from the rubble; you cringe-crouch as more debris smashes down to either side of your path.

But neither stone nor bullet finds your flesh, and soon you reach the wall of rubble that has made an arena of the shattered cathedral's heart. Greenness sings in your veins, as you notice a gap in the wall. The hand of a saint is propping up a stone the size of a mastodon – or a squiggoth, you think – leaving a gap too narrow for either ork or man, but wide enough for one such as you.

The banner will not fit, so you leave it behind, and scramble into the crack on your elbows. Your master's rage booms from up ahead, near deafening you in the confines of the crevice, and shards of stone carve deep gashes in your limbs in your haste to reach him. The walls crush ever closer, but all their weight seems as nothing beside the narrowing window of your destiny.

You reach the end of the passage, and your chest clenches around a breath: framed by the jagged outline of the stone blocks at the barrier's edge is the beast that intends to turn the stars themselves green.

Ghazghkull Mag Uruk Thraka stands on the raised dais of the cathedral's altar, towering above those statues which still stand in the desolation around him. And as a voidship's death high above casts a mantle of green plasma-light over his colossal form, he throws his head back and roars in holy triumph.

But there is a second giant, pacing in a wide circle beyond the reach of your lord and master. It is Ragnar Blackmane, and he wields the relic Frostfang with the skill of centuries – although you do not know that. You merely note that he is waving a chainsaw of unparalleled size.

As the Wolf Lord stalks his quarry, so you see ripples spread from his boots, and you fear it to be your master's blood. But then you see: the hydraulic feeds of his armour have been slashed, one by one, and have made a foul lake of the dais.

This is scant comfort to you, however. You are reminded of the Prophet's slaying of the warlord Dregmek, long ago, in which the larger ork had been made vulnerable by the slow crippling of his armour. The towering battle-harness worn by your lord is more like a building than it is like armour. It is of a mass beyond your imagining, and now you dread that Dregmek's fate will be returned upon his executioner.

But Ghazghkull is not Dregmek. The Prophet curls his lips back from fangs as long as your arms, and in a voice as thick and black as the spilled hydraulic fluid at his feet, he taunts Blackmane in the tongue of men.

'Finish this.'

It is a command for an ending, but the ork who speaks for the gods sounds more as if he is impatient for something to begin. Either way, the Wolf Lord obliges. Thinking his foe hobbled, he sprints up the steps at the dais' edge, boosts himself from the shorn stone of a martyr's statue, and leaps in a soaring arc towards his foe.

Ghazghkull lunges. That he moves at all, under such a weight of steel, is unfathomable. But that he moves with such speed, is unthinkable. It is a miracle to you. As the tower of his body surges forward, he plants one mighty iron boot up on the altar of the Emperor Himself, and he too propels himself into a leap.

'Get him, boss,' you screech, despicably, from your hole.

Ragnar's bolter erupts in a storm of point-blank fire, spraying explosive bolts into the Prophet's face as they sail towards each other. But so thick is his skin, and so dense is the bone beneath, it may as well be a handful of sand.

The two giants collide, and crash to the nave with a thunderous clashing of plate. There is a brief, savage struggle, and then they rise, locked in a mortal embrace. Ghazghkull's great jagged cage of a claw is clamped fully around Ragnar's torso, and as you hear ceramite splinter beneath its closing, you shriek in exaltation. But then you see it: Frostfang has been driven, point first, into the Prophet's neck. The relic's vicious teeth have been jammed by the thickness of his hide, but already they are juddering as the motor whines to free them, and scraps of rubbery skin are beginning to be thrown free of the wound.

As your cry of triumph descends into a moan of horror, you scramble to extricate yourself from the stone and run to your master's side. But the gap is too narrow. Maybe three Makaris ago, when you had been a runt of incredible feebleness, you might have made it through. But in this form you are stuck fast, with just your head free, and one arm reaching out in futile desperation.

There is a tremendous, wet crack, as the thumb-blade of the Prophet's claw punches through Ragnar's breastplate, spilling a thick curtain of the Wolf Lord's heart's-blood. It is a mortal wound.

But in the same instant, a great rope of snarled, twisted skin is torn free from Ghazghkull's wound, and Frostfang's teeth leap into a furious blur of motion. Even as you struggle in vain, the blade chews through the leg-thick tendons of your master's neck. And then, in a great spray of chipped bone and pulverised flesh, his spine is severed.

With his last gasp of breath, the Prophet speaks a single phrase into the dying Ragnar's face, but you do not hear it over your own wails of despair.

The head of Ghazghkull Thraka falls to the floor. It lands on the adamantium plate that seals his holy wound, and the shock of the impact reverberates around the whole of the cathedral. It is enough, in fact, to jog the statue's hand that props up the tunnel you are trapped in. With a heavy, muted thud, the huge stone block above you falls flat.

The cathedral's nave begins to spin wildly, and you spend a few moments wondering why this is, until you realise you cannot feel your body any more. As your head comes to rest, after rolling a short way across the nave, you blink the masonry dust from your eyes.

Your vision is fading fast. But before it goes entirely, you see one last vision as you gaze involuntarily up the steps of the dais. Ragnar is standing shakily on the ruin of the Prophet, with a ghastly rent in his chest. He is swaying, barely keeping his feet beneath him. In one hand, he holds aloft the head of Ghazghkull Thraka. And before the green rises up from the black to take you, you see that your master's tusks are set in a great, triumphant grin, and you know that all will be well.

INTERROGATION XI

Lord Inquisitor Tytonida Falx became aware that she was not a gretchin at roughly the same moment she became aware that she was vomiting. Or at least, that she was trying to vomit. She had no idea when she'd last eaten – it was usually a question of days, rather than hours – but her stomach was doing its best to empty itself, regardless. It felt like a fist, clenching in time with the hammering inside her skull, and bringing up a thin, searing mouthful of bile with each squeeze.

For a time, the nausea was her universe. It was all she could do to keep herself propped up on shaking arms and keep retching, in the futile hope it would eject the memory of being Makari. When the sickness began to fade slightly, she tried opening her eyes. But the grating of the cell floor appeared to be expanding and contracting as if it were *breathing*. And she had the horrible sense that what she could feel through the leather of her gloves was not a grid of metal, but the horrible, spongiform rigidity of fungus. Falx began to vomit again, and continued for a long time.

'By Mars and Terra, Hendriksen,' she croaked at last, when a half-opened eye revealed a normal-seeming floor. 'I had no idea the shamanistic traditions of Fenris were so... visceral.'

'Believe me when I say, inquisitor,' replied the Rune Priest, as she rose shakily to her feet, 'you got off lightly.'

One look at the Deathwatch veteran told her he meant it. Hendriksen looked ghastly. She had worked with psykers long enough to know the effects of overexertion, but the extent to which projecting Makari's memories had depleted him was like nothing she'd seen before. He was... withered, almost, in as much as the word could ever apply to a Space Marine, and especially one so robustly built as Brother Hendriksen. The thin layer of fat sheathing the musculature of his torso had been burned away entirely, leaving skin hanging loose from slabs of wood-dense brawn.

But his face was the worst part of it. His eyes bulged from sockets blackened with the crusted blood of the ritual, while his cheeks had drawn in to reveal the subtly inhuman construction of his skull. Usually, you only saw a glimpse of it – a flash of sharpness when he threw his head back to laugh, or when he snarled in irritation. But now, there was no hiding it. Above a beard newly shot through with brittle whiteness, his lip was ridged with the roots of *fangs*. Falx stared at the face of her oldest ally and felt only a deep, atavistic fear.

'I am sorry for the... discomfort,' he said, tilting his shaggy head towards the floor to spare her the primal unease of meeting his gaze. 'It has been many years since I took recourse to the old methods. I forget what they are like, to the uninitiated.'

'It is of no consequence,' said Falx, fighting off another wave of spasms from beneath her ribs. 'We witnessed something truly unique there. There was no other way we could have reached the end of the creature's tale, and–'

'You could've just asked,' said Makari, in accentless Low Gothic.

'*I beg your pardon?*' snapped Falx, tensing every muscle in her body to keep from screaming in shock.

'Pardon for what?' asked the creature, as that awful, mocking grin widened beneath its shattered nose.

Falx just stared, and so did Hendriksen. She had no idea whether the question was sincere, or whether the gretchin was playing games. And that, more than anything else, frightened her. Between her eye for detail, and Hendriksen's psychic gift, they had developed an indomitable intuition for xenos thought, over the years. They had learned to read the body language of sapient fractals; called the bluff of beasts which could only be seen beneath the lethal sunrise of a dying pulsar. And now, they had been outwitted by… by *this*.

Makari hopped up into the interrogation chair, lithe in spite of its shattered arm, and sat cross-legged on it like some horror from the *faery-tales* of ancient Terra.

'I'll even sit in the chair,' it crooned, in the words it *just should not have known*, and then slapped the metal in exasperation. 'All these questions, for Mork-snikked *days*, and now you've got nothing to say! I can see why you're not a very popular inquisitor, *Tytonida.*'

'There is nothing left to ask,' intoned Hendriksen, like a snow-flurry licking the last embers of a fire into stillness, and began advancing on Makari with his knife drawn.

Falx wanted nothing more than to be rid of the beast. But still, she could not help but disagree with the Rune Priest. There was the matter of Biter, for one thing, and of Makari's so-called 'capture'. And something else, perhaps?

Of course!

'There is one thing,' blurted Falx, getting the words out just as Makari drew breath to mock them further, and Hendriksen's gaunt, sorrowful face swung round to look at her as if she were insane.

'Ghazghkull did not die,' she stated.

'Nah, he did,' argued Makari, grin broadening as it tapped its clammy brow with one talon. 'You just saw his head come off, remember?'

'But it did not last,' snarled Falx, too fatigued now to marshal her rage. 'Know this, xenos. There is nothing – nothing – I would rather than there be no reason for us to speak further. But the matter of Ghazghkull's return was the impetus for this whole misadventure. I have, I will admit even to you, ventured beyond the bounds of reason in pursuit of an understanding of him, *and I will be damned if I do not hear the truth of it now.*'

'Reckon you're damned either way,' cackled Makari. 'But I've truth if you want it. For whatever good it'll do you.'

The question loitered in the gloom of the cell, in silence broken only by the furtive rushing of Makari's breath through needle teeth. The brig was never truly silent. Whether it was the morose rattling of horns and claws along cage bars, or the susurration of prayers to incomprehensible gods, there was always something stirring in the dark. But now, it was as if a chasm had opened up between Falx and Makari, and the whole of the stygian menagerie had stopped to see whether she would step over its edge.

An alert appeared on Falx's data-vis. There had been many alerts, dealing largely with the fallout from Biter's escape, but Falx had dismissed them all. By now, the bridge staff were well acquainted with her style of captaincy, and had relied on their own intuition to restore the *Exactor*'s security. But this missive was from the attendants of the ship's Navigator, and one did not ignore their words lightly. Apparently, a rare clemency in the currents of the empyrean had given them an opportunity to cut hours from the end of their voyage to the Naval base at Mulciber, making transit to the system's Mandeville point within the hour. Even as she took in the report, Hendriksen's voice seeped into her skull, although it was a haggard echo of its usual self.

+Do you see, inquisitor? The ending of our journey beckons, like the great aurora. Even I will concede that, for all it has cost us, this venture has offered knowledge in excess of any expectation. But let it end now.+

The story is not over, Brother Hendriksen.

+And neither, I would wager, is this creature's trickery. Look how it grins, how eager it is for you to venture further into its grasp. Come, Tytonida – let us make haste to Mulciber. Let this cursed thing be the problem of the admiralty's intelligence officers.+

Falx sent a simple affirmation back to the Navigator's suite, and she saw Hendriksen's shoulders sag with relief, even as the emotion leaked into her own mind. But it slid off her anger like water from wax as she stared into Makari's lustreless red eyes.

'Now then, Makari, will you tell me the end of Ghazghkull's story?' she asked, folding her arms and setting her jaw in a steely smile.

'Oh, it's not the end, human. Not by a long way. It's just all there is for now. Still… clever of you to guess I've got something special to show you.'

'It's that relic, isn't it,' said Falx, nodding at the string of holy shrapnel the grot was fidgeting with. 'It's connected to him, somehow.'

'*Very* clever!' hissed Makari, narrowing its eyes and shifting forwards in the steel chair. 'And it can show you something far more impressive than the Space Marine's trick just now. You said you wanted to know Ghazghkull Mag Uruk Thraka... Well. That can happen. What is it to be then, Falx?'

+Lord inquisitor!+ barked Hendriksen, in sudden alarm. +You go too far!+

Yes? replied Falx, choosing not to deny the statement.

+You know full well the agreement we have brokered – the prisoner is to be given over to Naval intelligence the moment we enter realspace! The cruiser *Hammer of Eustathios* is moving to the Mandeville point as we speak, with a boarding shuttle ready. The prisoner must be secured for transfer now – or would you squander what goodwill you have managed to claw back with the Imperium of Man before it is even bestowed you?+

Falx thought for a long moment, as both Makari and Hendriksen looked at her. She tried to tell herself she was weighing things up. But in truth, her mind had been made up the instant Hendriksen had protested. She could not help it; once she was told she was going too far into the dark, Falx's only instinct was ever to go further.

Orm Hendriksen, you know me too well to think I can turn my back on an opportunity like this.

+Yes. And that is why I am trying to save you from it, as I have done countless times before when your curiosity has near doomed you.+

Do you remember the first time you saved me?

+Better than you do, I imagine.+

And how did you find me to be, then?

+Blind drunk and belligerent, as you well know. Slurring something about 'the worst bastard xenos of all being the ones we heap with laurels', wasn't it? And then swinging a punch. At a sergeant of the Adeptus Astartes.+

Quite. So why didn't I die?

+It would have given you the easy way out you were after, for one.+

But what else, Hendriksen?

Hendriksen projected the sensation she had come to recognise as the psyker's interpretation of a sigh – in particular, the sigh he used when he realised that Falx's mind could not be changed.

+I said I respected your audacity, Tytonida. I said that showing such boldness – such recklessness – in the face of certain death… reminded me of what it was to be human.+

So, then, she concluded, as she peeled off one glove, and walked briskly to the interrogation chair with her arm outstretched, *I hope you will be similarly reminded now. And I hope you will trust my good intentions when I confess I have no plans to surrender the prisoner to the admiralty.*

+I suspect I have little choice in the matter, at this point.+

Falx leaned in close enough to Makari to feel the creature's hot mildew-breath on her face; close enough that it could have had its jaws round her neck in a heartbeat, had it wanted her dead. Then she looked it right in the eye, smiled, and grabbed the shards of the round that had created Ghazghkull Thraka.

CHAPTER ELEVEN

GHAZGHKULL DIES, FOR A WHILE... AGAIN

So this is death, is it? I've had worse.

I need not die. Not if I do not will it. My enemies did not die when I took their heads. Nor when I took them again. Not because they were tough. Because *you* did not will it. Because *I* did not will it.

Now, I wish for death. If I did not, I would not bear this wound.

But what comes next; this thing you have shown me... it is vast. It is great and violent and sacred. I will have it for myself. You showed me where to carve the path, and here, in this place, is where it narrows. This thin curtain, this *death*, is all that stands in my way.

How frail it is. I will tear it down. I will breach its gates, as I have breached every gate before me. I will tear down its walls, as I have torn down all walls.

But conquest has made my body strong. Too strong now,

I see. The blood clings to my veins, and will not cool fast enough. It defies me. So I snarl, and my anger finds voice where I should have none. If my blood will not cool, then it will *burn*, and I will go to you in flames.

I am moved, now. My head, held up by the hand of my enemy. It regards me, as it lifts my remains, and I regard it in turn. There is triumph on its face. This thing thinks it knows victory, in defeating me! It thinks it knows *power*. But for all the plate it wears, for all that has been done to make it into a thing of war, it is vermin. I study the bones beneath its skin. I see how its body is gnarled and swollen. How its whole self has been *made*, in the hope it might hold on to the stars in the name of a dead god. It is a vain hope. Those stars will burn green, in the end.

The vermin is dying, I see, even with such mild wounds. It is like a joke, I think, as it bares its feeble tusks. Like a poor copy of an ork, twisted together from the parts of a weaker beast. But you made us right the first time. Not even the *primarchs*, the peak of their dead god's work, could be as perfect as the lowest part of the Great Green.

The anger swells, now, as the vermin holds my head up in the broken temple. And I think. That I had to die today... annoys me. *But why could it not have been a primarch?* That fight, I would have relished. I crave that fight. But I cannot have it, and it makes the embers of my anger glow white with rage. In time, it brings the thunder beneath the plating of my skull. I howl as it pounds down on me from my centre, and the world begins to come apart.

This is not death. Not yet. This is worse.

Lightning flashes where there is none. Shadows split into colours I have never seen before. I see corpses twist into the shape of fungus, and I see the stone walls breathe. I taste acid brightness, and hear the running of wild beasts in the dark. Suddenly there is bellowing and shouting, in voices I cannot understand. It comes from everywhere, and drowns everything. I do not know if they speak to me, or if they are me speaking to someone else.

I am lost in the desert, with a shattered skull, and I do not know who, or what, I am.

I am afraid.

But then the voices speak at once, and I make sense of them at last. They are your voices. And when I know this, I can make words of them, as I have long learned to do. I seize your mighty voices in the storm, and I listen.

YOU ARE THE WARLORD OF WARLORDS.

YOU ARE OUR PROPHET.

WE SPEAK THROUGH YOUR TUSKS

AND YOUR FISTS

AND YOUR HEAD.

YOU ARE GHAZGHKULL MAG URUK THRAKA,

AND WORLDS BURN IN YOUR BOOT PRINTS.

I hear you, now, and my self returns to me. The end is near. But I do not feel weak. I feel stronger than I have ever felt. Because beyond this, there is something new. Something terrible. Something perfect.

My rage does not fade. But it has become bliss now. The

bliss an ork should always feel. It is a shame that I did not get to fight a primarch. But I will, in time.

Darkness spreads on the smashed stone below. I know it is death coming. It feels like I look down on it from up in space. From the grin of Gork itself, with your eyes. I look down on my enemies, rushing to the side of their boss, but they are not worthy of your gaze. So I look past them. And through the smoke and the ruin, I see a great mass of green.

Orks upon orks upon orks, all looking at my head held high. They fall still. They think this is the end. But I have learned this is not true, and now I must teach them. Just as you arrive with the thunder, to remind me who I am when I am lost in the desert, I will remind them who they are.

It is why you put me on Urk, and why you led me here. The orks had forgotten who they were. They had forgotten what they were made for. For so long, they were only… existing. But orks were made to fight, and to win, and to make slaves of all they do not kill. Under my hand, they have remembered. Under me, they are *living*. I look out over the orks, and with the last of my strength, I break into a grin. A great snarl of triumph, like the gash you've carved across the sky. So that they know they are winning.

That is all they need. If the horde believes we're winning, we will keep winning. They will believe it, because I believe it. And I believe it, because you believe in me.

Green fades to black, and I can barely see the orks now. But I can hear the shout that rises from their throats, as they see my victory. I will see them again soon. But then, a thought comes to me.

How am I to come back to the world?

I remember how it was, when I was lying there with my

skull smashed. How I knew you would not help me, until I helped myself. That is how it has always been. I carry myself, and you make me stronger. But I cannot carry myself back from death. If your will is for me to return, but I am the instrument of your will, how will it be carried out? And what will happen while I am gone? Doubts gather. They are like storm clouds in the fading light; the thunder comes again. But this time you are clear in it.

THERE ARE OTHERS.

YOU MUST TRUST TO THEM.

I squint at what I can still see of the world. There is Finds-Bullets-He-Has-Not-Lost, still with me after all this time. They are sawing an enemy apart with their great chain-choppa. They are roaring my name. As is proper. But there, nearby, is Snazdakka, once warlord of the Bad Moons on Urk. They are eyeing up the Deathskull, already calculating their odds of seizing power, now I am gone.

I have spent this whole existence beating the heads of orks together, so that they fight in one direction. Without my will to enforce that, surely they will set on each other. Everything I have made will fall apart. *Maybe*, I wonder, *I have not done enough.*

Again, I feel the edges of the thing I have come to know as *fear*. Ghazghkull, the most powerful ork there is, is going to die afraid.

NO, HE IS NOT.

WE SAID, THERE ARE OTHERS.

THINK HARDER.

LOOK CLOSER.

I do as you ask. And in the last circle of the world that has not turned black, I see something I did not see before. It is something small and green. It is Makari, my pathetic banner-waver. Or, it is their head. That is surprising.

Makari is dying. But Makari always comes back. And although I would never speak this to an ork, Makari always knows the right thing to do.

Vision is gone now. My thoughts grow slower. Even the anger fades. But I will die fighting. Because you have asked me to put my trust in someone who is not myself. You have asked me to trust a creature you made to be unworthy of trust. And which, at this moment, is dead. It is the hardest battle I have ever fought.

It is a battle I win. Because I am Ghazghkull, and I never lose. But as the black begins to sink away into a much deeper green, a final doubt occurs to me.

Makari always comes back. But it is me who brings them back, by the granting of their name.

If I am not there, who will find Makari?

INTERROGATION XII

Falx vomited far less, this time. There was a thin trickle of blood dripping down her upper lip, and the air was rich with the stink of fungal decay, but she could convince herself the latter was mostly just Makari's odour. As much as she hated to admit it, whatever the grot had just done (or whatever had been done through the grot; she had long since become unmoored from comprehension on that front) had been a much cleaner experience than the psychic projection cast by Brother Hendriksen.

The instant she thought of him, there was an almighty thump of flesh on metal, and she turned round to see the Deathwatch veteran face down on the floor. Cold dread clenched her gut for a moment, until she noticed he was still breathing. But in some ways, his death would have been easier to swallow. The idea of a Space Marine *incapacitated* just did not sit well in the human mind. Even to a human mind as jaded as hers, the idea of Astartes invincibility was as dependable as gravity: an article of faith strong enough to masquerade as objective truth. But there he was, a transhuman psyker the size of a bear, unconscious on the deck.

Leaving Falx alone with the monster. Just as it had been at the start.

She returned her gaze to Makari, determined not to let her terror make itself known on her face. *I am still in control*, she told herself, even as her data-vis swarmed with alerts. Half were from the *Exactor*'s bridge crew, who had sent the frigate's entire guard complement scrambling for the brig the second they had become aware of Hendriksen's status. The other half were from Lieutenant Garamond, the Naval intelligence officer seconded to the *Hammer of Eustathios*. These alternated between demands for 'the asset', and demands for an explanation of the massive psychic discharge his astropath had detected aboard the *Exactor* as it had exited the warp.

Falx's every instinct screamed for her to flee towards the safety of the onrushing Militarum squads, and to offer the lieutenant custody of the prisoner at his earliest convenience. But she forced herself to belay every single Militarum deployment order, and did not even bother speaking to Garamond. Whatever happened next, she suspected, would put an end to his complaints one way or another, and the bridge crew could keep him occupied until then.

Sighing, Falx shut down her data-vis altogether, rose on creaking knees, and folded her arms as she locked eyes with Makari. The grot was still and silent on the interrogation chair, and it was not grinning for once. That battered, knobbly face radiated as much malevolence as always, but it seemed more sober now, somehow. The mask of the capering, spiteful trickster had been discarded, and beneath it sat the malign emissary of an ancient and fundamentally hostile power. That interrogation chair, now, held a faint suggestion of a throne's aspect.

And yet, I am still in control, Falx thought again, as if repetition might conjure belief. And to her astonishment, it worked. Falx *was* in control. She was not dead, the *Exactor* remained in her hands, and Makari was still confined to its brig. What's more, she had just been inside the mind of one of mankind's greatest enemies, and come out with nothing worse than a nosebleed. For once, Falx spared herself the usual fixation on everything she had not yet achieved and saw, for the very first time, just what a formidable creature she had made of herself.

She had always wrestled with her purpose as an inquisitor of the Ordo Xenos. With her purpose as a human, really, in a universe where such a condition offered so little cause for hope. It was a struggle that had dragged her younger self into the depths of despair. And after meeting Hendriksen at the very bottom, she had spent the rest of her life trying to find the surface again.

But now, eye to eye with this virulent little node of hostility, she'd found her duty at last. Whether she did it for the carcass on the Throne, or just for herself, she would stand in the face of whatever darkness was to come with eyes wide open. The truth would either kill her or it would leave her stronger, but either way, she would no longer let herself be burdened by fear.

Falx snorted with a mix of relief and amusement at the thought. *Perhaps I left a little of myself in Ghazghkull's mind,* she wondered. *Or perhaps I took a little of Ghazghkull with me.* Kryptman had always warned her that if she gazed too long into the abyss, it would gaze back. Maybe he'd been right all along, and Falx had just been wrong to interpret his words as a warning.

It was time, she felt, for another look into the abyss.

'Come on then, Makari,' she cajoled, with a loose smile that her face had almost forgotten how to shape. 'That was interesting enough, but you're holding out on the really interesting stuff. You're going to tell me how Ghazghkull came back from death.'

'Or what?' hissed the grot, leaning forwards until its broken nose was just a hand's breadth from her face.

'Try me,' replied Falx with acid-sharp sweetness, narrowing the gap to a finger's width.

'Fine,' said Makari at last. And with a slump of its shoulders *almost* too small for Falx to notice, it began.

CHAPTER TWELVE

GHAZGHKULL'S BIRTH

Something touched my shoulder. Might have been a hand?

But since I was surrounded by orks, all shoving each other and shouting, that weren't a surprise. It was weird how it stung where it touched me, and I had a strange feeling that meant something, but I was jostled away from it before I could work out what.

I was trying to remember what errand I'd been sent here on, and who was gonna kill me if I didn't do it, when there was a big meaty cracking sound from somewhere in the crowd, and an ork started hollering.

'It ain't working! It ain't doing anything at all! I'm saying the name, but they're just looking at me like normal zogging grots!'

'Keep trying,' shouted another ork. I couldn't see more than a dozen tusklengths in any direction through all the jostling bodies. But I knew from the smell alone there must've been a dozen or more orks here, in not too big a space. There was another big cracking noise, and I heard what I was dead sure was my name, even though I'd never heard it before.

'Makari?' asked the ork, through frustration-gritted tusks. The crowd shifted, and I saw it was Bullets. I don't know how I knew that was his name, but I did. He sounded furious, and desperate, and in front of him was a grot, looking down in baffled terror at the crude banner that had just been shoved into its hands. Bullets hefted a huge, gore-slick chunk of stone into the air, stared at the grot expectantly, and then brought it down again with a snarl of exasperation when nothing happened. *Crack!*

'Next!' snapped Bullets, as the freshly brained grot was tossed on the pile behind him, and the banner was snatched from its hands to give to the next grot in line.

'Makari?' asked Bullets, and once more nothing happened. *Crack!* 'Next!'

Makari? Crack! Next!

This went on for some time. It occurred to me, after a bit, that I'd been sent down here to fetch fresh ammo – and to zoggin' hurry, if I didn't want my head eaten. But then the ork next to me got battered out of the way by another ork with a big metal arm, and that weird burny-stingy thing was on my shoulder again. It was definitely a hand, I reckoned now, and a big one too, clamping down proper hard.

'Makari!' roared Bullets, into the face of the next doomed grot. And before I knew it, I'd answered him.

'Here, boss!' I shouted, loud as I could, and the big Death-skull's head shot round in surprise. He was so taken aback that he dropped the rock, so the grot died anyway. But nobody was looking at that. They was all looking at me. And that scared the guts out of me, 'cos I was still trying to work out what *me* was. So I did what came naturally, and cowered.

'Loot my zogging trukk,' said Bullets, in an awed whisper. 'It is him, isn't it? That's just how he cowers.' Then he clocked the hand on my shoulder, and as his gaze worked its way up to whoever it was attached to, rage bloomed in his eyes.

'Hold up,' he said, in a deep, deep growl. 'Is that... the hand of the *boss* you've got there?'

'Yes,' replied Grotsnik coldly, at the exact moment I remembered the concept of Grotsnik, and looked up over my shoulder at him. It certainly *was* the boss' hand. It was Ghazghkull's! But for some reason, it wasn't attached to Ghazghkull. It was stuck on a sort of frame, attached to a harness worn by the doc, with levers he could pull to make the fingers move.

'I thought,' said the doc, 'that since he was out, I might as well make some... improvements. And since the hand was going spare, I figured this was worth a try. You're welcome, by the way.'

'Ain't thankin' *you* for nothin',' barked Bullets, and I got the feeling he'd be going for the doc's throat, if it weren't for the big cyb-orks standing to either side of him.

'You will, soon,' said Grotsnik quietly, but Bullets ignored him and spoke to me.

'It's... it's good to see yer, runt. But things ain't good. You saw what happened, up in the ruins. Things are... touch and go. The boss has lost a lot of blood, and–'

'He's dead, Bullets,' interrupted Grotsnik, and as he said it, the memory of the last thing I'd seen hit me like a headbutt from the boss himself.

'He can't be,' hissed the lanky, blue-tattooed warboss. 'He'll pull through. We all know it. Now zog off back to your cave. The boys are fighting hard up there, and we need Makari with 'em. They need to see the banner, to know the boss is alright.'

'No, Bullets,' said Grotsnik, still all quiet and cold. 'He is *not* alright. We're beyond that. We *do* need Makari, however. But down here with me, not dodging bullets upstairs. Must we... fight over it?' Next to the doc, a cyb-ork spun its massive drill arm, menacingly.

Bullets looked like it was taking every drop of his faith in the Prophet to hold back from the obvious answer. But in the end, just like the boss himself had taught us all back on Urk, he managed put the urge aside.

'Fine, Grotsnik. You've got 'til sunrise. And Makari? If he tries anything dodgy, just... well, he'll probably kill you first. But try to shout, yeah?'

'I know what you're thinking', said Grotsnik, as the door closed behind us.

'I'm thinking you've been busy,' I muttered, as I craned my neck to look around. Just as the doc's set-up on Armageddon had been a step up from his digs in Rustpike, this was a step up from that. There was machines in there I'd never seen the likes of – huge great whirling things crackling with black light, shapes made out of lasers floating about in mid-air... I ain't a mek, so I'm missing the words, but you get the picture, yeah? There was some familiar stuff, too, but on a whole new scale. Wall-high banks of transfusion squigs, tubed up to vats of machine-stirred blood. A tank of what I thought was eel-squigs, lit by the crackles of blue lightning down their spines. And was that...? Yep. It was only a bloody *squiggoth*, with its head removed so it wouldn't go berserk, but its chest still rising and falling as a pair of forge bellows clanked away to keep it alive. But even the trukk-sized beast was just a minor detail, really, compared with the structure in the middle of the dome.

It was Ghazghkull. Or most of him, anyway. The doc hadn't just taken his hand off – it looked as if he'd decided to give the Prophet a complete refit, taking him apart into more bits than I could count, and mounting them on a giant, roughly ork-shaped scaffold. All of it was strung together with tubes and bunches of sparking cable, and as two of Grotsnik's cyb-orks started trudging round a capstan down on the work-floor, all the pieces started coming together at once.

At the same time, what looked like the bits of a battlewagon started sinking from the ceiling on thick, clanking chains, and my eyes nearly fell out of my head, I was staring so hard. It was *armour*. The biggest set of armour I'd ever seen, with a klaw on one side that looked like it could chop a dread in half like a squig-liver sausage, and a gun on the other that made Dregmek's shoota back on Urk look like a snotling's slingshot.

Down it all came, and as each bit settled into place, a whole squad of grots clambered up to start welding, nailing and strapping it in place. And then, last of all, coming down from the very apex of the dome so that it blocked out the lights behind it, was a great horned silhouette. The Prophet's severed head. As it settled into place in the socket between those huge armoured shoulders, a whole row of floodlights slammed on around the scaffold, and Ghazghkull's face grimaced down at us, without so much as a spark of life in its eyes.

'Changed my mind,' I said to Grotsnik as I gawped, when I could find it in me to speak at all. 'I'm thinking you're a complete zogging maniac.'

'The word is genius, Makari,' sneered the doc, as he stalked over to the godlike corpse beneath the centre of the dome.

'I'm also wondering,' I said, once there was enough room in my head for suspicion, 'how it was that you just happened to have all this kit set up and ready, just in time for the boss to die. I know you're a vile git, Grotsnik, but–'

'Ah!' cried the doc, turning round with a cruel grin and

raising a finger. '*That's* what I knew you were thinking. That all of this must have been my plan, somehow? Is that right? That I set all of this up, and lured Ghazghkull into his death, so I could resurrect him as my personal puppet?'

'Yeah,' I said. Because in fairness, that's exactly what I'd just thought.

'Well, forget it,' said Grotsnik. 'I might have found out about Ghazghkull's plans by sneaky means – I do spend a lot of time in his brain, after all. And I might have set up certain… *contingencies* down here, in case the duel with Ragnar went poorly for the Prophet. But was this all a scheme? No, Makari. I'm just an opportunist, is all.'

'Don't trust you,' I snarled.

'I'd hope you wouldn't,' said Grotsnik, grinning even wider. 'But don't you think, if this had all been my doing, I'd at least be gloating about it?'

'Fair,' I said, as he paced over to what looked like the generator out of a stompa covered in fungal growth, and started flicking primer switches.

'Look, Makari,' said Grotsnik, as he frowned in concentration at a spinning dial. 'If you're still convinced I'm up to no good here, consider this. You probably hate me more than any ork alive, correct?'

'Yeah!' I hissed, with some enthusiasm.

'Good,' said the doc. 'It would be odd if you didn't. But now consider this. If that is the case, then why – *why, Makari* – would I have interrupted the work of a lifetime, to go and correct those morons outside in their boneheaded attempt to bring you back? Even if I had, do you really think I'd be so stupid as to then order you into my lab where – runty and pathetic as you are – you'd have at least a fighting chance of doing me in?'

'Well, you did do that,' I said, cackling at the thought.

'I did do that,' he admitted. 'But because I had a zogging good reason. I needed you here, Makari. Or I suppose… the gods needed you here. The *boss* needed you.'

'You've got plenty of grots to fetch and carry for you,' I said, gesturing at the creatures working away on the scaffold. 'Why go to the bother of getting your least favourite grot sicked out of the Great Green for the job?'

Grotsnik growled then, but it was the sort of growl an ork makes when he's knackered from thinking too much, rather'n a threat.

'Because as mad as it sounds, Makari, I think you were the only creature who really knew Ghazghkull. I've spent years trying to get closer than you, and yet I never managed.'

'It's 'cos you've spent all that time causing him pain,' I hissed, bunching my fists into pathetic little nodules of meat. 'I always served the boss, and the gods. You just wanted to drive him mental, and make him into some giant freak to do your bidding. Or just… amuse you.'

'Mmmh,' said Grotsnik calmly, picking a bit of rotten meat from between his tusks as he nodded.

'You don't deny it, then?' I said, not sure what to make of that.

'Nah,' said Grotsnik. 'I thought it was obvious, really. I just like experimenting on things. And hurting them.' He stretched then, and his shoulder, which'd grown hunched from all the time he'd spent bent over Ghazghkull's skull, made a sick-sounding cracking noise. 'But I was serving the gods, in my own way.'

'What, by driving the greatest ork alive mad, for a laugh? Come off it, Grotsnik.'

'All that time with Ghazghkull,' he scorned, shaking his

long, cruel face in disapproval, 'and you never worked out that his strength sprang entirely from his madness. Did you not see how, as I worked deeper and deeper into his skull, the gods spoke ever louder? And how, the louder they spoke, the greater Ghazghkull's feats became? Makari – Ghazghkull's pain was his power.'

I hated how much that made sense, and as I looked up at that great, dead mountainside of a face above us, I realised it was as true as anything can be.

'*If* that's true,' I said, as Grotsnik hauled down a big lever, and the generator came to life with a shriek of captured lightning, 'then what d'you need me for?'

'Because I think you helped him live with the pain,' said Grotsnik. It was almost a whisper, like he suspected the bosses outside might overhear him, somehow. 'I hate you, grot. You hate me. But why do you think we, as a *spee-shees*, paint black and white check marks over everything we can get our hands on?'

"Cos they look really killy?' I ventured, knowing it was the right answer.

'For the same reason we've got two gods, wretch,' spat Grotsnik. 'Contrast. The Great Green is one thing, but to make the whole... I suppose you could say it takes all sorts. And Ghazghkull is what Ghazghkull is today – hmm, or rather what he was until fighting Ragnar, anyway – because of the *both* of us.'

'Yeah?' I said, unbunching my fists but crossing my arms, so he still knew I didn't trust him.

'Yeah. Who d'you think installed the bionic eye on Dregmek, that meant he missed every shot he fired at Ghazghkull back in Rustspike, just for example? Like it or not, grot – and you won't like it – I've been just as much a part of the gods' plan as you have, all these years. And it's just as painful for me to swallow, but you're still just as much a part as I am, in whatever they've got planned next.'

'What's that, then?' I asked.

'No idea,' said Grotsnik, with a grunt, as he dragged an enormous cable from the generator to the scaffold where the Prophet had been reassembled, and heaved it into a socket as thick as his whole body. 'At least in the long run. But I know right now, it involves you coming over here, and helping me pull this really, really big lever, so the boss can come back and figure out the rest.'

If only it'd just been the lever. But Grotsnik never, ever sets anything out straight. That lever – that whole massive generator, in fact – weren't for bringing Ghazghkull back to life at all. That was just what the doc needed to make a zap big enough to jump start the *real* machinery he'd set up for the job.

'Course, he only told me this once it was already switched on, and couldn't be stopped. Which was when he also told me that there was a four in five chance the process would fail, blowing us, the Prophet, and half the planet into bits that'd make dust look big. So that was relaxing.

The main generator, the doc said, was in space. But it was also sort of in another dimension, because of how unstable it was. Like I said before, I ain't a mek, so you'll have to figure it out for yourself. The main thing was, it was gonna shoot loads and loads of electricity down from a hole in the sky, right into the Prophet's bonce, and we had just a few minutes – Grotsnik didn't know how long exactly, of course – to get him ready.

Climbing up onto the boss' shoulder plates, I bullied the doc's grots into winching a great big hose into Ghazghkull's mouth, then cranking open his jaw with a trukk-jack so I could get it by his tusks. I nodded down at Grotsnik, who stood by the headless squig, and with an expression that was pure, nasty glee, he switched on the hydraulic press above it. Dunno how to describe the sound of all the air in a squiggoth's lungs being forced through a hose by an industrial crusher, along with most of the lungs as well, but I'm sure you can imagine.

Grotsnik started shouting then, about 'critical alignment' or something, and a big siren started going off, nearly deafening us both. Apparently there'd been a plan for that tank of squig-eels I'd seen earlier, but since the generator was about to fire, there wasn't time for nothing clever any more. So Grotsnik bust open a hatch in the side of the boss' armour, right over his guts, and just upended the whole tank into it, water and all. I'll tell you now: I'd bet every tooth I have that he did that for no reason but his own amusement.

But with that done, and with the last rivets clamped into place, sealing the armour that would hold the boss together until his own body could finish the job, there was nothing left to do but wait to see if we'd be blown into the Great Green ourselves. The siren was getting really annoying by then, so Grotsnik shot it. And in the silence after, I looked at him, and he looked at me.

I wondered if maybe we'd have found some common ground, after the rush to get the Prophet's body ready for his return, but no: that one shared look told us that we both hated each other's guts as much as ever. We was grods, I suppose.

Anyway, that was when a beam of light like the searing hot piss of Gork himself came smashing through the roof, with a noise so loud it wasn't a noise, and everything went green. There was no way of telling whether the machine had worked, or whether we'd blown up the world and ended up in the Great Green.

Well, no way of telling until this next bit happened, anyway.

CHAPTER THIRTEEN

THE PROPHET LIVES

It begins in white.

I am cold. The wind howls. I am beneath the ground.

I wonder, did I fail you?

Have you sent me back, to have another go, and get it right this time? Will I rip the tongue from the beast you send, and walk through the storm again? Will I have my brains torn out again, so all that remains is the sound of your voices? Must I do it all again, I wonder?

I will, if I need to.

But then, I smell hot metal, and burned flesh. I did not smell this, the first time. I feel my skin. It is burning, sloughing from my flesh, inside a shell of forge-hot iron. This is good.

I feel the ground quake, and I think it is the impact of your mighty green foot, until the boom comes again, and again. It is the beat of my heart. And as it thunders, blood surges through into my limbs, carrying with it the ecstasy of your violence. It spills from gashes and rivet-holes, and quenches my seared flesh in clouds of steam.

I feel life in my bones again, deep and green and wrathful, as your divine spores spread their tendrils. Your voices deafen me, beneath the metal that binds my skull. But where it was once agony, now there is only bliss. It is more than my head can hold, though. And so with my first breath, I throw my head back, and I roar your war cry for all the galaxy to hear.

I feel cool air on my face, and immensity above me. I stand, with a grinding of fresh-joined bones, and I hear steel scream and bolts crack as I free myself.

Finally, the sight of my one eye begins to return. And I bare my fangs in joy, because I realise now, why you have chosen vision as the last of these gifts.

The sun is beginning to rise over the shattered city of my enemies, and I stand in a crater at its heart. Dawn is coming, but above me, the night is still wild and black and infinite. The stars shine fierce, laid out for me to plunder. And every one of them shines green.

It is the first thing I have ever found to be funny. And so, with my second breath, *I laugh*.

INTERROGATION XIII

Falx didn't know when Makari's tale-telling had segued into a full-fledged psychic projection. But as the reality of the cell surfaced again through the violent immensity of Ghazghkull's rebirth, she found herself reflecting on something the grot had said earlier. *Speech is just another way of hitting people with your brain*. She had not realised just how literally Makari had been speaking.

But to her horror, it soon became clear that the vision had not entirely ended. She was back in the cell, certainly. But the light was flickering now, strobing over the needle-toothed creature that watched her. And in the guttering dimness between each burst of light, she swore she saw that the walls were coated in thick, glistening fungus.

But worse than that, Ghazghkull was still laughing.

Falx had heard a lot of things, over the years, that would have reduced stern men and women to madness. But this was the worst sound she had ever endured. And now it was no longer inside her head, but crashing through the steel of the brig, it was clear just how inhuman it was. It was absurd, indeed, even to call it a laugh, so profoundly alien was the joy it embodied.

'You wanted to get to know Ghazghkull, didn't you, Lord Falx?' said Makari, in a whisper that dripped with venomous relish. 'Well, now's yer chance. 'Cos he's coming.'

The floor shook, as something far too large to be human stepped forward in the darkness behind her. Deep, cold terror lanced from the plate on the back of Falx's skull, and as another great footstep fell, she steeled herself to turn, one last time, and face the dark. But there was no need. Because this was *her* monster.

Brother Hendriksen stalked past her in the guttering light, vast, gnarled, and wearing only the clots of his own gore. He was something that belonged more in a tale told to frighten children on some frigid feral world than in the confines of a voidship, and if it weren't for the relief Falx felt at his appearance, she would have been terrified of him. His bolt pistol remained in its holster; the old wolf was beyond such things now, in a place of fangs and claws.

Makari, meanwhile, seemed unconcerned as its death approached. The xenos seemed radiant with anticipation if anything, basking in the brutal laughter that still shook the cell as if it offered the protection of a Titan's void shield. It offered far greater succour, Falx supposed. For what even was death to Makari, when it stood in Ghazghkull's psychic shadow? When that febrile green body was torn apart, whatever was inside it would simply sink back into that laugh, and find its way back to its master.

Falx blazed, at once, with the certainty that she could not allow that to happen.

'No, brother,' she said, as the beast that had been Hendriksen towered over Makari. It was not the command of a lord of the inquisition, but the quiet appeal of a damaged old woman, to her only friend. She just prayed to the Throne, with all the faith left in her, that Hendriksen was still there to hear her.

The Fenrisian turned his head, and Falx found herself looking into the eyes of an animal. There was a reason beyond loyalty, of course, that the ancient Rune Priest had stayed with her through all these years, even as the orbit of her ambitions had swung ever further into the gloom of heresy. Hendriksen's pride had never allowed them to speak openly about it. But he, too, had been drifting further from the Emperor's light over those long years of duty. And as those wild eyes flicked over her, with thick drool looping from the yellowed fangs below them, it was clear how far into the dark he had sailed.

Each son of Fenris must fight a battle, Hendriksen had told her once, *from the day they take the Wulfen cup, and are reborn as a son of Russ*. It was a curse of sorts, written, with cruel elegance, in the very same genetic script as their primarch's blessing. Once Falx had come to know Brother Hendriksen, she had understood at last why the Space Wolves lived with such bombastic, rambunctious vigour: they hoped that if the fires of their feast-halls burned bright enough, the night might be warded off.

But Hendriksen's fire had been burning low for a long time, and the wolf had been waiting at his door. Now it stood inside the threshold, looking out at her.

Falx swallowed hard, trying to focus past the thunderous malice of Ghazghkull's laughter, and the wicked glee on Makari's face, as the gretchin watched them fall apart. She had never had much of a facility for basic conversation, let alone speeches.

But it was time for her to attempt a beating-of-the-mind of her own.

This is what he expects, brother, she spoke aloud in her mind, as she looked at those predator's eyes and hoped someone was still listening behind them. *You were right, of course – this was all a ploy. In giving us Makari, Ghazghkull meant only to spread his own legend, while that bastard Blood Axe helped himself to whatever information he plundered before running. Ghazghkull was counting on us to act to type – small-minded, frightened, and incapable of conceiving of any solution but extermination to xenos problems. He was certain we'd be good Imperial citizens, and send his damned familiar back to him in a fit of zealous butchery.*

+So?+ barked Hendriksen at last, from somewhere in the depths of his winter, and Falx fought to hold back the surge of hope that threatened to spring from the fact he had responded at all. The fact that Makari's grin was now wavering, as the silent communication stretched between his captors, didn't make it any easier.

So, she said, *will you prove Ghazghkull right, brother? If there's something to be learned from this rotten imp's tale, it's just how much Ghazghkull gained by acting against type. He has redefined our understanding of the orkish mind, and what it is capable of.*

+And we shall slaughter him, just the same.+

Ragnar tried that, brother. Hendriksen snarled, mentally and in the confines of the cell, but Falx continued undaunted. *In Ghazghkull's defiance of his instinct, he learned what orks were always meant to be. And if we defy ours? Perhaps, old friend, we'll learn to be human again.*

For just the briefest instant, the wolf in Hendriksen's eyes was gone, and that bright young boy from before the Wulfen cup, to whom the Adeptus Astartes were just the bright, distant servants of an unknowable god, looked out. Falx had never seen Hendriksen look so fragile. She had never seen him look so strong.

'Let us put an end to this problem,' said Hendriksen out loud, and Makari virtually wriggled with glee as his blood-black timber of an arm swung out to grab it by the throat. But Makari could not see the faint, weary smile that had found the corner of Hendriksen's mouth when he glanced back at Falx. Rather than crushing Makari's neck, the Rune Priest dragged it by it, walking briskly out of the cell, and down the adjoining corridor of containment units. Falx worked a crick from her neck, and followed him.

As they proceeded into the brig's depths, she risked a glance at her data-vis. The demands from Lieutenant Garamond had come to an abrupt halt, she noted. But then a flood of back-logged alerts began pouring across her vision, and she saw why. The *Hammer of Eustathios*, along with every single Naval vessel in dock at Mulciber, had been called to the system's edge.

Where an armada of catastrophic size had just emerged from the warp.

Fleet command was in uproar. The ships now arriving had somehow shrouded their numbers as they had encroached through the warp, and had transmitted the Mulciber yard's up-to-date passcodes ahead of them. It had been assumed they'd been a casualty of the Munitorum's record-keeping, some undocumented fragment of a battle group inbound for resupply.

But of course, they were ork vessels. Falx's heart jumped as she realised where they had almost certainly acquired the passcodes. Throne knew how they'd retrieved Biter from an escape pod adrift in the warp, but it barely mattered, in the end. There were thousands of ships in-system already, with a second wave of emergences already beginning, and Mulciber would have struggled to repel them even with a year to prepare, let alone a few hours.

And at the armada's heart, Falx saw now, as she scrolled through frantic picts taken by outer system sentries, was a behemoth of a vessel. It was easily three times the mass of the largest ship in the defence, and it was purpose-built, rather than coaxed into function from the wreckage of a non-ork voidcraft. But what really gave it away was the banner, three miles high, that projected from its dorsal ridge like a sail-rigged mast. It bore the image of an ork with many arms, stood atop carnage. The image of Ghazghkull Thraka, whose laughter still boomed through the brig.

But as Hendriksen came to a halt at one of the corridor's empty cells, and yanked open its foot-thick door, that laughter began to falter. The lights strung along the ceiling stopped flickering, clearing the shadows of any illusion. And as he held Makari up to behold its new home – padded, and fitted with a partial stasis field to make absolutely certain its occupant could come to no accidental harm – the laughter stopped entirely.

'No!' wailed Makari, all composure falling from its face abruptly as it realised what was happening. 'No!' The gristly little monster bit and clawed at Hendriksen's forearm, but might as well have been fighting against gravity. With a contemptuous snarl, the old wolf hurled the grot into the cell, and slammed the door with a leaden thud.

'Ghazghkull has come,' he remarked, after a moment spent reviewing his own data-vis.

'Good,' said Falx. 'He shall be just in time to see us leave, bearing his most valuable possession. I have already instructed the ship's Navigator to execute our departure.'

'Where shall we go?'

'We'll have time to figure that out en route,' said Falx, and Hendriksen grunted his assent.

'Fine. But first, we eat.'

Falx would have smiled, relieved to see such firm proof that her companion had held on to himself. But something was wrong.

Makari had been shrieking in rage all the while they had been talking, though the sound had been almost comical, muffled by the cell's door so it sounded like the whining of an insect. Now, however, while the grot's high-pitched screeches continued, they were underscored by something deeper.

It was a roar. And as the lights began to flicker once more, it grew louder and louder, until it began to shake the deck itself. Falx felt as if some vast carnivore was thundering towards her, jaws splayed, and one glance at Hendriksen told her that he felt it too.

The bellow rose to a crescendo of abject fury, until the air itself began to shimmer with its force. The lights along the corridor sparked and then burst, one by one, plunging the corridor into darkness.

And the darkness was green.

ACKNOWLEDGEMENTS

I have less people to thank than usual for this one, as 2020 was not exactly a social bonanza, and I worked on this book in almost total isolation. But thanks nonetheless to Ashleigh, my wife, who saw me through the whole thing, and helped me find exactly the voice for Makari that the little sod needed. Thanks to Andy Chambers, the man behind the Big Man himself, who gave us Ghazghkull in the first place, and who gave my imagination so much delicious fodder back in the good old days. Thanks as ever to my agent, Jamie Cowen, who ends up stopping me going mad at least once per novel, and who ensures I actually do the paperwork that gets me paid for the things, despite my disinclination. Finally, and overwhelmingly, thanks to Kate Hamer, for the most rewarding experience I've ever had working with an editor. Working out the nuts and bolts of this story with her was a joy from start to finish, and she was a brilliant support when I found myself in a tight spot. Oh, and of course – cheers to all of you reading this. The only thing cooler than being able to write these stories, is knowing people read them and enjoy them. It means a lot to me. See you next time!

ABOUT THE AUTHOR

Nate Crowley is an SFF author and games journalist who lives in Walsall with his wife, daughter, and a cat he insists on calling Turkey Boy. He loves going to the zoo, playing needlessly complicated strategy games, and cooking incredible stews. His work for Black Library includes the Twice-Dead King duology, the novel *Ghazghkull Thraka: Prophet of the Waaagh!*, the novella Severed and the short stories 'Empra' and 'The Enemy of My Enemy'.

YOUR
NEXT READ

BRUTAL KUNNIN
by Mike Brooks

When Ufthak and his orks attack the forge world of Hephaesto, the last thing they want is to share the spoils with the notorious Kaptin Badrukk. But with armies to defeat and loot to seize, Ufthak's boyz might just need Badrukk's help – though that doesn't mean they can trust him…